MW00881144

It's Complicated

Natalia Uva

Copyright © 2012 Natalia Uva

All rights reserved.

ISBN: 1515012786
ISBN-13: 978-1515012788

Please note: This is a work of fiction. Any names, characters, incidents, and places are the product of the author's imagination **or** are used fictitiously. Any resemblance to actual persons, living or dead, business establishments or events is entirely coincidental.

DEDICATION

This is for Patricia Smith. Thank you for being a teacher, a guide, and a friend. Rest in Paradise.

CONTENTS

ACKNOWLEDGMENTS

I would like to take a moment to thank everyone who helped make this novel possible. Thank you to my wonderful editor, Claire, for going over this with me multiple times to make sure it was perfect- you're the best! Thank you to those few who read each chapter again and again to tell me what they thought about it. Amanda, Faye and Vanessa, you rock! Thank you all for lending an ear and being an amazing support system. Also, thank *you* for reading this. This one's for you.

CHAPTER ONE
Alexandra

Love stories are the sweetest tales to tell because they leave an imprint on you, the kind of stamp that forever seals on your heart. They make you want to believe you can find that same kind of love, and that's exciting. I believe that's why everyone loves listening to love stories. One thing people don't realize is that everyone's story is different. You won't always find the same love as Noah and Allie did, or Romeo and Juliet. Not even my story.

It all started when I moved to Union, Kentucky- population 5,379. I mean, here I come with my family, straight from Boston, Massachusetts. You could see the cultural difference immediately.

It was the summer of 2010; I was barely eighteen. The horror of starting twelfth grade at a new high school was unfathomable. Looking in the mirror, I saw... chic. I did not see anything that would fit in, in Union. My hazel eyes were flecked with yellow and my dark brown hair flowed in soft ringlets, framing my freckled face and flowing right down to my back. I dressed in American Eagle to H&M, which I didn't see girls my age wearing around Union much. My nose had a piercing stud on the left side; another trademark of my city life.

We were moving to Union because my mom, who was a flight attendant for a big airplane company, got relocated. My parents had just gotten a divorce in March so she was glad to have the opportunity to get out of the big city. My twin brother Cody was flat out mad that we were moving, but I'm pretty sure that was only because he had to give up hockey. My older sister McKenzie, who was kind of a lush, didn't really care as long as there were "cute country boys!" she was happy- probably because she was going to start college in California in September. Typical.

I just didn't want to leave my friends.

We were set to move in June, with the house already bought in Kentucky. Today was our last day at Quincy Upper School in Boston. Since McKenzie was already out of high school, she got to leave with my mother on Friday morning. Cody and I had to wait until that night because we had to return our books at school.

"I don't want to have to say goodbye to anyone, Cody. I wish we didn't have to move," I said as we walked through the doors of our school. But he could only give me a look as his ex-girlfriend came down the hall, out for blood. Deanna de la Garman was the biggest snob in our school and after splitting up with her after about a year of dating, Cody found he still couldn't quite get rid of her.

"CODY!" she yelled down the hall. "You stop right there. I need a word with you." She glared at me. "What the hell are you looking at, Barnes?"

"Nothing really important Deanna, don't worry. My brother doesn't want to talk to you if you haven't realized. We're moving. He dumped you. Get over it. Go find someone else to annoy the hell out of, because my family is sure done

2

with it," I said back to her levelly. I looked over at my brother who mouthed 'thank you,' before stepping forward to her.

"What do you want, Dee? I have to return my books and Alex and I have to finish packing, so please make it quick." She looked at him, about to go off. She must have thought better of it because she took a breath first.

"Don't date anyone out there, okay? You're still mine," she said, almost in a whisper. "I know we're not together, but you're my first love. Please. Can't we try and make this work?" By now, she was speaking loud enough for people in the hallway to hear. I covered my eyes and sighed. This wasn't going to be pretty.

"Deanna, we've gone over this plenty of times, now! I don't want to make things work. I'm done. All we ever did in the last few months was fight nonstop. I'm not going to have a long distance relationship the same way," he said getting angry. When he spoke again, he mimicked a high-pitched voice. "'Oh, Cody! You can't go out tonight because you promised to Skype me!' 'Oh, Cody! You can't play video games tonight because I'm sick and need you to stay on the phone with me and keep me company.' No, Dee. I'm done with that. You can't control my life anymore. Not here, not in Union. We broke up a month ago. Please leave me and my sister alone and find someone new." He cleared his throat and looked at me.

"Alex, are you ready to go to the guidance office?" I didn't speak, but I nodded at him. He handed me my bag, but as we were about to go, I felt someone pull the back of my hair rather hard.

"What the...?" I looked around in time to see Deanna's fist coming toward me, so I ducked. I sprung up and smashed my left fist right into her nose. I felt it crack, which was sickening. She fell to the floor with a dramatic "OW!" and laid there with blood running down her bronze face.

"What is your problem, Alex? Look what you did to me!" she shrieked in pain. My brother held me back just in case, but I was in too much shock to go anywhere. I'd never gotten in a fight before, especially with someone so close to my family. I heard Cody's voice far away like a dream. It snapped me back into reality as I shook my head.

"Alex, what happened? I turned around to see you knock Deanna right in the face!" Great. I could see Mr. Hogarth, a teacher, coming down the hallway towards us so I quickly explained to Cody what Deanna had done.

"What exactly is going on here, students?" Mr. Hogarth said in a booming voice. He was acting vice principal ever since Mrs. Larson broke her foot. He was tall and gangly, but had the deep, strong voice of an adult black male.

"Mr. Hogarth, she punched me in the face! I was just saying goodbye to her brother when she attacked me!" said Deanna, her face shining red from her bloody nose. She had plugged it with a tampon; the sight of it made me want to crack up.

"Is that true, Alexandra?" Mr. Hogarth said as he looked straight at me.

"Not even close! I was walking away when she pulled my hair and went to punch me, so I ducked and hit her in self-defense. I get good grades and I never get in trouble. Why would I randomly hit Deanna?" I said. I know it wasn't much of a case, but hey- might as well use what I had.

"It's true, Mr. Hogarth," came a new voice from behind. I turned around to see Dean Richmond. My heart dropped to my stomach and Cody protectively stepped in front of me. Why was Dean, of all people, sticking up for me?

"Did you see the fight, Mr. Richmond?" replied Mr. Hogarth. Dean looked back at him and nodded.

"Yes, sir. Deanna instigated it when she was fighting with Cody or whatever. I wasn't paying attention until she grabbed Alex's hair. You know the rest of the story," he said simply. Leave it to Dean to make the whole ordeal sound like it was no big issue.

"Alright, then we have witnesses. Alexandra and Deanna please come to the office with me. Mr. Barnes and Mr. Richmond, you are free to go to class.

"Wait, Mr. Hogarth," said Cody. "We need to return our books. We aren't in regular classes. We're moving to Kentucky and today is the last day we can bring books back." He dug around in his jeans pocket until he found a slip of paper. He unfolded it and handed it to Mr. Hogarth. "See? It states that we're to just return books, then to leave the premises. That's all."

"Yes, well that is all good and said, Mr. Barnes, but I'm afraid I have to follow school code of conduct. Your sister got into a fight and whether or not she was to blame, she needs to be reprimanded appropriately." Mr. Hogarth said with finality. Thankfully, my brother wasn't giving up.

"Call my father, then. He's a lawyer. He'll tell you all about laws, like the one that states you can't reprimand my sister with the school code because, technically, she doesn't even attend this school anymore. She is handing in, three books and then leaving. We are visitors here at Quincy Upper School. Your student attacked a visitor. She is the one who has to be apprehended, not Alex. Go ahead, call my dad. His name is Connor Barnes." Cody spoke defiantly. I swear, if my brother wasn't so into owning his own sports team, he'd make one hell of a lawyer.

"Alright, you've made your point. Now, hurry up and pass the books in and get out. Deanna, come with me." He promptly walked away and with a murderous look from Deanna, they were both gone. Once they were out of sight, my brother and I started laughing, really laughing. Only Deanna would try and make something that had nothing to do with her, completely revolve around her.

"Ahem- can I talk to you, Alex?" Dean spoke so quietly in my ear, I jumped. Once again, my heart started racing. Why did today have to be so dramatic?

"What do you want, Dean?" I tried to sound my bitchiest but instead, it came out more as a whisper.

"You're welcome for saving your ass, Barnes. You'd have been in some deep trouble if not for me," Dean said. That was untrue. He'd told Mr. Hogarth the truth, which was a first for him, so either way I would have been alright. I sensed there was more to this conversation.

Apparently, so did Cody because he interjected in a hostile manner. "Back off my sister, Richmond! You've done enough around here to last a lifetime. Go away before we have a little fight of our own that's been long overdue."

"If you say so, Cody. I'd beat you any time, any day. But that's not why I'm here saving my ex-girlfriend from a fight. I'm here to let you know that I'm just happy your family is moving because everyone is sick and tired of hearing the scandal in the news. No one wants to hear about your dad fooling around with his secretary, or that his oldest daughter is kind of promiscuous. No one cares about what happened four months ago between you and me, Alex. Not even about Cody's breakup. Your family has messed up a bunch of good names in this city." He looked at us with a smirk and walked away.

"Did that make any sense to you at all? What good names did we mess up?" I said to Cody quizzically. He shook his head in confusion and laughed.

"What a prick. He'll get his. Pretty boy's just mad that you confessed and called the cops on him."

"Cody! Don't bring that up... you know what that does to me. I have to go find Kat, Marco, and Dan. They'll be super mad at me if I don't say goodbye to them before we leave."

"Sorry, Al. I didn't mean it like that, I just meant you bruised his big ego. But go, say goodbye to your friends, I'm going to say bye to mine too. Meet me at guidance in a half hour." He waved me goodbye and walked down the hall, probably to catch up with his friend, Mike Thomas. By now, class was out for lunch break so there was a heavy flow of traffic in the halls. Somehow, I managed to find Kat in the slew of people. Katrina Mitrovanof had been my absolute best friend since I was twelve years old. We were in Girl Scouts together when we first met.

She was supposed to be an exchange student, but she decided to move in with her aunt in South Boston so we remained friends ever since. She gave me a big hug.

"Oh, Alex! I was beginning to wonder if you remembered to see me! Is it true you really punched Deanna de la Garman in the nose? Everyone keeps talking about it! I can't believe I wasn't there to see it! Are you..."

I cut her off. "I'm fine, Kat. Yes, I hit her because she tried to hit me first. Guess who came to my aid? Dean Richmond." That got her attention.

"No! Dean? Why? He's such a scum bag, I can't believe it. I heard Dean and Deanna were a thing anyway." Kat's big, blue saucer eyes widened at the very thought. My best friend found gossip like this to be quite scandalous.

"Tell me about it, I couldn't believe it. I can't believe any of this is happening. I don't think they're a thing, at least not anymore. Awkward, much?" I rolled my eyes. I just wanted this day to end. It was weird to think that by tonight, I would be sleeping in another state. My eyes suddenly began to fill with tears.

"I can't believe I'm actually leaving today. I wish this was all a dream, Kat. Why can't I stay with you?" Kat smiled. She shook her head because we both knew it couldn't happen. As it was, she was going to Russia like she did every other summer to see her family.

"If I could bring you to the motherland, I would. We'll just keep video chatting like we do every time we're apart. Am I still coming for your graduation?" I smiled.

"Of course, as long as you're still my prom date!" We made a pact when we were in eighth grade, no matter what we did, or who we dated, we'd go to both junior and senior prom together.

She remembered this as well because as she twirled a strand of blond curl around her finger she said, "Obviously, Alexandra you're funny if you think you'll get rid of me that easily." She gave me another hug, but this one was definitely more heartfelt. Behind her back, I could see our friends, Dan Mitrovanof and Marco Gutierrez. They'd been flamboyantly gay for as long as I'd known them. Dan was Kat's cousin. We were the "whoresome foursome" as Dan liked to joke, even though none of us had willingly had sex with anyone.

"Oh my gosh! Alex is leaving today! I'm already starting to cry," said Marco, who was the more dramatic one of the duo. He ran up to me and grabbed me out of Kat's arms and smothered me with a big hug. I wanted to cry. These were my friends, part of my life for so long. How could I ever replace them out in Kentucky? The answer was simple- I couldn't.

"I know guys. I am going to miss you too. But hey, we'll be able to video chat all the time and text like we usually do. My mom works for the airline; I'll see if she can stretch up some tickets to have you guys visit or something. Either way, it'll happen. I promise," I said to them all. When I gave Dan a hug, he smelled of musk and lilies. He smelled like home...

"Alright, enough sadness. I've got to go pass these books in. I have to finish packing because my flight leaves at six. Text me later guys! I love you all," I said breathing deeply. If I didn't, tears would fall.

I tried to be strong throughout all this, especially for my mother, Connie. She was already frail, thanks to the stunt my dad pulled with his secretary at work. I didn't need her to feel even guiltier about uprooting us.

"Alright, chickita. Te amo mucho, señorita." Marco hugged me once more and we split up. I decided to stop by my favorite teacher's classroom before I met up with Cody. I walked to the English Lab and found Ms. Long sitting at her desk correcting papers. She was only twenty-four, the youngest teacher at Quincy Upper School. That was one of the many reasons we got along so well, because she related to me. When she found out that we were moving she was genuinely upset to see me go. I knew I could go to her about anything and it wouldn't get around. It was like having a psychiatrist for next to nothing.

"Alex, what are you doing here? Aren't you supposed to be leaving today?" Ms. Long said as she looked up from her iPad. She was extremely gorgeous, and sometimes looking at her made me feel pathetic. Janine Long had beautiful long, blonde hair and her tanned skin showed faint amounts of freckles. She had sky-blue eyes that were always rimmed with the right amount of mascara. Talk about a Victoria's Secret Model lookalike.

"I was stopping by to say goodbye because we're leaving tonight. I had to bring my books back in. I figured I'd stop in here before I headed out." I sat down on the edge of a desk.

"That's alright with me," she smiled. "I'm just on my break, correcting papers. I found one of yours. Do you want your score?" I nodded. She reached down into her bag and pulled out a paper I had passed in two weeks ago. I had written an essay about being the anti-view on love. It was easy to do because I did not believe in love. Loving seemed to always mean leaving. I mean, look at my parents, Deanna and Cody, even Dean and I. Love stories are wonderful because they make you feel like anything can happen, but in my life, my story, love meant leaving. I looked at my score. I had gotten one hundred percentile.

"The way you stressed your point of view was wonderful, Alexandra. You really do have a gift with words. I hope you pursue a career as a journalist because you can really go somewhere with this. But do not think that love always has to end in pain. Things may happen, but it's only to allow better people to come into your life."

I looked at her and smiled even though I didn't believe her. She was gorgeous. She was engaged to a minor league baseball player and she just got out of college. She had somewhere to go in life. What could I ever do to compare?

As I left her classroom, I saw Cody walking down the corridor. He waved me over to him so I picked up my bag off of the floor and joined him.

"Are you ready to leave this hell hole behind?" he said jokingly as we walked to the guidance office. I know he said it to try and cheer me up, but I still felt hollow.

"Let's just get this over with. I want to go home and say bye to Dad." I looked up in time to see Deanna coming out of the guidance office. By now, her face had swollen and the bruising had started. I couldn't believe I hit her that hard. I felt almost guilty. Cody, on the other hand, laughed.

"That's a nice look for you, Dee. You should wear it like that more often," he said as he winked at her. All Deanna did was give us a dirty look and march off leaving the doorway to the guidance office open for us to enter. When we went inside, we saw our counselor, Mrs. Walter. She looked at us and smiled.

"Hey, guys we were just waiting for you to come on up. Let's get your books all logged into the system so we can get you both signed out." She took Cody's books first, then mine, and we sat there waiting for her to enter our codes into the system.

About fifteen minutes later, she finally stood up and walked over to us. She handed us a piece of paper each and told us to take that to the main office, where they would scan it to officially sign us out as students of Quincy Upper High. We walked in silence to the main office because we both knew that if either of us said anything, I'd start crying.

The Dean, Mr. McMahon, was there to take our slips. After scanning us out, he wished us farewell and good luck and that was that. We weren't coming back.

It was over. Boston was no longer our home. I'd miss being able to go to Red Sox games right down the road or shop in Government Square. Ice skating on Frog's pond in the winter was something I was really going to miss. Cody squeezed my shoulder and gave me a hug. At least I had one best friend along with me. We climbed into the Prius and drove back to Dad's. I didn't have the heart to call it our home anymore because that would prolong the sadness.

Once we got home, Cody made a beeline for the room that used to be his bedroom. However, I lingered in the doorway, where there were etch marks of our height since we were little. Tears welled up once again, but this time I didn't even bother concealing them. I ran upstairs to my bedroom and fell on my bed, crying my eyes out. This wasn't fair. Why did my father have to cheat on my mother? Wasn't our family good enough for him anymore?

"Hey, are you okay Alex? Dad said he heard you crying," said Cody at my doorway. I looked at him.

"Cody, we're leaving. This is for good, not a vacation. I can't handle the fact Dad doesn't want our family anymore!" I said it. I finally admitted the one thing that was bothering me more than anything. It wasn't just about moving. No, it was more than that.

Cody, to my surprise, welled up with anger. He never shouted, but his words were harsh when he said, "Don't think that way, Alex. Dad would never. Grab your bags, he's taking us now!" With that, he walked away.

Since all that was staying here was my bed and an empty dresser, I grabbed my laptop and my duffel bag. I walked past my dad without saying a word and jumped in the backseat. I promptly put my earphones in and fell deaf to the world for the remainder of the trip to Logan Airport.

CHAPTER TWO
Alexandra

When we got to Logan International Airport, my father tried to break the ice.

"Come on- let me carry those heavy bags for you, Alex. I would like to help you." He opened up the trunk of the Cadillac Escalade he bought as a present to himself, for winning a case last November and leaned in to grab the bags, but I beat him to it.

"Don't worry about it, I'm a big girl. I don't need your help," I said, rather coldly. If having to move because of him wasn't painful enough, it was the fact he had stopped being a father to us and cared only about his secretary whom he was now dating. When he had brought her home, my mother was still living in the guest room of the house. I thought that was inexcusable of him, and couldn't hide my feelings.

My father seemed to register the hostile look on my face because he backed off. He went to go offer a hand to Cody, who declined as well, albeit politely. He walked us to the security door and paused.

"Well, guys," he started uncomfortably. He shuffled his feet as he spoke. "I just want you to know, you're welcome here anytime. If you don't like Union, you can always move back in with Marisol and me. You're still my kids and I love you. I wish your mother didn't have to take you with her. Anyways, ahem.

Go on, now. Please send a text or e-mail me when you land so I know you're safe. You might both hate me, but I'm always here for you." He looked over at me.

"Alex, I understand you have some strong negative feelings for me because of the divorce and I am sorry. I went about things the wrong way, and I apologize. I mean it. You two and McKenzie are my world and I wish I hadn't pushed you out of it," he gave me a hug, which I felt obligated to return, and went over to Cody.

"Cody, my son. Please watch over your sister. She needs a responsible man in her life, and right now, it isn't me. It's you and I know how close you two are. Please be an amazing brother and father figure to her. Keep your mother safe as well, because even though she isn't my wife anymore, I will always be concerned about all of you." He gave Cody one last hug and walked away from the security gate. My brother and I looked at each other with a mix of confusion and sadness. Had I been wrong to prejudge my father based on my mother's angry thoughts?

"Come on; let's get through security so we can board our plane. We need to make sure we're not late," said Cody as he grabbed his bags. I nodded silently and we made our way to the line passing through security. Pretty soon it was our turn. I stepped through the little magnetic door and put my bags on the conveyer belt. After successfully walking through it, I realized I had left my cell phone in my father's car.

"Wait! Cody, I left my phone in dad's car! Can you call him and have him bring it to me?" I pleaded. I couldn't forget my phone. It was my only lifeline back to my friends at this point. Cody pulled his phone out and dialed our father.

"Hey, dad? It's me. Alex left her phone in the back of your car; do you think you can swing it back here? We already passed through security. Uh huh. Right. Alright, thanks anyway." He hung up. "Alex, he says he can't find it. He said he's willing to ship it to you in Kentucky if you want it that badly, otherwise you have to buy a new one," Cody said, walking beside me on the way to the terminal. I was infuriated. It wasn't like he really couldn't find it. He was just too lazy to return it to me.

"Cody, you don't understand! That was my lifeline! My music, everything is on there! Do you know how expensive it is to buy another iPhone? I'll have to save up everything from our birthday. That's way too long to wait," I said in despair. Today just wasn't my day.

As we got to terminal A, we had to stop and ask an airline official where gate A20 to Cincinnati, Ohio was. Logan Airport was pretty crazy today. We got something to eat from one of the vendors and sat down in the waiting area.

"So, I have an idea on getting you a new phone," said Cody. He stuffed his sandwich in his mouth and pulled his phone out. He swallowed and then went to continue his plan. "We'll call mom now before we board the plane, we'll have her run to the store and grab you a new phone and the company will transfer everything over to your new one so when you arrive in Union, you'll have everything on it. I'll even pay for it and you can pay me back when you get the money," Cody smiled. I really did have the best brother.

"I can live with that, I guess. I'll pay you back as soon as I get it," I said to him. So while Cody placed the phone call to my mother, I sat there looking over at the magazine rack, wondering if I should get a book to read for this two-and-a-half hour flight. I made my way over to the book rack, and I started to thumb through the selection. I found a couple favorites that I immediately purchased: *Nights in Rodanthe* by Nicholas Sparks, *Romeo and Juliet* by William Shakespeare, and *The Notebook*, also by Nicholas Sparks. I knew that I wouldn't finish a whole book during the flight but I could always add them to my collection.

I paid for my selections and went back to Cody, who was picking his things up. I heard the announcement over the speaker:

'Everyone boarding the flight 4009 to Cincinnati, Ohio at gate A20 make your way to the jet way. We are now accepting boarding passes. Again, everyone for flight 4009 to Cincinnati to gate A20, please.' The lady's cool voice was resonating off the walls. I took a deep breath and marched forward, next to my twin. Things were changing, faster than I'd have cared to admit. If only I knew what was in store...

When it came time for us to hand in our boarding passes, the lady looked at us like we were mutants. I couldn't understand her confusion as obviously, being different sex, we weren't identical twins but the lady stared. When she spoke to us, I understood why.

"Honey, do your parents know you're going on a flight with your boyfriend?" she asked. I nearly choked on the water I was drinking due to laughter. Boyfriend!

"He's not my boyfriend, ma'am. He's my twin brother..." I trailed off. Why was I explaining my personal life with a complete and total stranger? Who cares what she thought we were?

"Oh, my apologies miss," said the lady, embarrassed. She let us pass, and we made our way down the jet way into our seats. As soon as we settled, Cody put his headphones in and nestled down to sleep. I was wide-awake though. I pulled out *The Notebook* and started to read. I had read this book before. My favorite part of the story was when they finally met up after being apart for seven years. I continued to read as the minutes slowly passed. Finally, I sighed as I put my book down. What good was it? Love like that didn't really exist. It was nice to see someone had the right frame of mind, though.

Beside me, Cody mumbled something in his sleep. He only sleep-talked when he was seriously troubled. When we were younger, Cody and McKenzie would have full conversations with one another in their sleep. It was awful, because it always woke me up. I leaned back, and tried hard to listen to what he was saying.

"... no, not the peas. Anything else, take... Deanna. Horrible girl, keep her away... safe. Union will be... safe." He started snoring. Poor Cody, from what he was saying in his dream, it seemed as if he was really scared of Deanna. I rubbed my eyes and looked out the window. The sight was breathtaking. We've only been in the air for about an hour, but the twilight of the sky made the shadows of the clouds beautifully iridescent. This was nature's way of painting a picture. I wished I were a bird; I could fly up here all the time and always be at peace.

By now, I was getting bored. My brother was still asleep, and we still had an hour and a half to go before touching down in Cincinnati, where we were meeting McKenzie. I hoped she would remember to bring my new iPhone. Thinking about my phone reminded me about my dad. Why did he have to be so different, now? I remembered the older days where the five of us would go up to Lake Ossipee in New Hampshire for the weekend just to relax and get away from the city. We would take a ride out on the lake and go swimming. We'd have bonfires and sing karaoke. I missed those days.

We'd stopped going to New Hampshire when Cody and I were fourteen. My father had started becoming "more serious" about his career as a lawyer. In adult talk, that meant he was beginning the affair with his secretary, Marisol. My poor mother, who was a flight attendant, wasn't home enough for my father's taste, I suppose. But I knew my mother. If Connor Barnes had asked her, she would've quit her job in a heartbeat to stay home and be the domestic housewife type.

I must've dozed off because I awoke to the flight attendant's voice over the loud speaker telling us to buckle our seats because we were beginning our descent. I nudged Cody awake.

"Humph. What happened? What's going on?" he grumbled as he blinked his eyes repeatedly to wake himself up.

"We're landing now, Cody. We're here," I said back to him, grimly. We had a whole summer to prepare ourselves for senior year. It was going to be different without McKenzie here, once she went off to Stanford University in California this fall. She may seem to be a little out there, but she was very book smart. She graduated as Valedictorian of her class and had straight A's throughout middle and high school.

"Are we really? Was I passed out the whole plane ride?" he asked me. I chuckled.

"Pretty much. I wonder what our house is going to look like," I thought out loud. Was it going to be stucco- styled or Victorian? Maybe it was a Tudor house or a cottage. I was excited to find out the architecture of our house. I don't know why, but the surprise of it made me eager to see my new home.

The plane finally landed in Cincinnati's airport. The people around here called it the CVG. We grabbed our bags out of the compartment and waited in the line of bustling people nudging one another, trying to get off of the plane and stretch. I watched a little girl hug her mom and start whining.

"Mommy! I want to get off this plane, now! I need to stretch these legs out." Her southern twang took me by surprise. I forgot we were moving to a place with a different accent. We were going to be so out of place. I grabbed my brother's arm, and guided him in front of me. Getting off the jet way, I looked around. I didn't see any sign of my sister anywhere.

"Cody, I can't find McKenzie at all. She was supposed to be here by now," I said, getting a little worried. We sat at the arrivals' terminal waiting for our sister to show up. Forty-five minutes later, we finally spotted her.

"I can't believe you had to go through such hard trials, Byron. I am so sorry. Is there anything I can do to make you feel better?" I heard my sister's flirty voice wafting through the room like perfume. She made me sick sometimes. She was standing next to a tall, muscular guy who's name was apparently Byron. He was tall and had very tan arms. His sandy-brown hair was sticking in all directions, like he had just woken up. He stood next to her and smiled.

"It's alright, miss. Don't y'all be worryin' about lil' old me. I can handle myself pretty well." He drew himself up. "Now, here's my number. Gimme' a call if you're ever in the area again," he said and winked at her. She gave him a hug, kissed him on the cheek and walked over to us. Her bleach-blonde hair was pulled up into a ponytail. Though you could see her annoyance with us as soon as she spotted us, she attempted a smile.

"Were you guys waiting a long time? There was mad traffic on the way here. I have your new phone, Alex," she said, handing me a bag. I took it from her and opened it up and gasped.

"Thanks, Kenz! Mom got me the new white iPhone! Wicked! Kat's going to be so jealous when she finds out! Did mom transfer all my information to this phone?" I asked her. She looked at me and shrugged.

"I'm not too sure; try turning it on and calling mom. She just told me to bring it for you. But, oh my goodness! You're never going to believe how beautiful our house is! I feel so awesome living in it, already. We each have our own rooms and everything!" my sister gushed. Was she serious? We got to have our own rooms? When we lived in Boston, she and I had to share a bedroom. It wasn't pleasant, so the thought of having my own place made everything a bit easier to handle. I pressed the 'on' switch and waited for the phone to power up. In the meantime, Cody was asking about what the house looked like.

"Well, it's a landominium," said McKenzie as we got to the car. She helped us put our bags in the trunk. "That's kind of like a condo but instead of an apartment, it's a house. We don't have to mow the lawn or anything because the homeowner's association keeps it up. We own the land and the house, though," she said. The thought of having a nice big house on land like that, made me excited.

"I hope they have stables around there," I mused. "I've always wanted to further my horseback riding skills." I had taken lessons when I was six years old, and ended up leaving them when I was fifteen. My father had complained that they were too expensive, so I had to give it up. I regret not going back. It was a warm, June evening in Cincinnati so Cody and I lowered our windows and looked out at the landscape.

"Wow!" I breathed. We had just passed into Kentucky land and it was beautiful. It was nothing like home, but it was pretty nonetheless. I might actually like it out here. I dialed my mother's phone number and sure enough, I heard the dial tone.

"Hello, mom? Can you hear me? It's Alex, I just wanted to thank you for picking up the phone for me. We just passed into Kentucky so we should be home in fifteen minutes." I could hear my mom, Connie Barnes, walking around in the background.

"Sure honey, no problem! Listen, you think you kids could pick up something to eat for dinner? I have a lot of unpacking to do here and so do the rest of you. I have no time for dinner. Maybe swing for a pizza?" she asked. We had pizza last night too.

"That sounds good. I'll tell McKenzie and Cody. Love you, Mom," I said as I hung up the connection. She really wanted us to like it here, I realized. She was trying to make this our home just as much as Boston was. I suddenly felt guilty. I had rebelled against the idea of coming here since my parents split in March. Now, I figured out why she was so happy to be out here. It was a new start, a new home. It was time to bring the family back together, sans father.

"Mom wants us to get some pizza for dinner," I said casually from the backseat. "She doesn't have enough time to get anything cooked tonight." McKenzie looked at me from the rearview mirror.

"Oh! We could stop in Papa Murphy's Take N' Bake Pizza Shop, I heard it was good. It's over on US 42, we'll stop there first because it's about eight minutes from the house," she said. Cody didn't say anything; he was preoccupied with a game on his iPhone. By the time we got there, I was famished. The peanuts on the plane weren't much and I hadn't eaten breakfast this morning. I got out of the car, and looked at the window.

"Now hiring... hey, Cody! You said you wanted a job, right? This place is hiring!" I pointed to the sign. I couldn't work at a food place; I needed to be outdoors with animals, or something. When I was in tenth grade, I helped work at the Frozen Fenway park series in the winter and in the summer time I had my own dog walking business.

"Alright, you go get the pizza and I'll go apply," he said. He jumped out of the car and walked into the place. I followed him in and went up to the counter.

"I'll be with you in one second," said a voice from nowhere. I look up, and see a boy, probably about eighteen, talking to Cody. He handed him a pamphlet and instructed him on how to fill it out. Once he had done that, he walked over to me. He was covered in flour, but he looked like he enjoyed the job.

"Can I help you, miss?" he asked me politely as I was looking at the menu.

"Yeah, um can I have a family sized custom pizza, please? Original crust, too. Thick crust is nasty," I said to him, like he actually cared about my crust preference.

"Sure thing, what would you like on it?" he pointed to the toppings list; there were a lot of selections to choose from.

"Um, can I have the creamy garlic sauce with extra cheese and crispy bacon?" He smiled at me.

"No, you can't." He laughed when he saw my face. "I'm only kidding, miss. Will that be all?" He rang in the pizza price and then went to work making it. The way this boy worked on the pizza made it look like art. Five minutes later, I got my wrapped up pizza, paid, and went back in the car to wait for Cody. When I got in the car, he was already there and he was fighting with McKenzie.

"Shut up, will you? You're so annoying, Kenzie. Why don't you try thinking of someone else other than yourself for once? Just because you dyed your hair blonde, doesn't make you a princess, I hope you know that," Cody said angrily to our other sister who was sitting in the driver's seat, applying mascara.

"I don't care what you have to say, bro. I'm not going to bring you to the mall to get new clothes, new job or not. Wait until dad brings your ugly Prius from Boston and go yourself," she said. They didn't seem to notice I climbed in the car, so I cleared my throat. When that didn't work, I yelled.

"Enough! Deal with this at home, will you? I'm tired and hungry and I just want to go home. Damn, guys," I said. McKenzie gave me a look and backed out of the parking spot. The drive home was quiet and awkward.

I passed the time by looking out the windows. Shortly, we passed Randall K. Cooper High School, the school my brother and I would be attending in the fall. It was very weird seeing a new school and calling it mine. I grew up in Boston and went to schools there my whole life.

"Look, guys. That's our new house," said McKenzie as she turned down a side road. The house was beautiful. It was a cream colored, two-floor house with blue shutters. There were shrubs outlining the walkway from the gate to the door. The grass was a beautiful dark green. My jaw dropped. This was our new house.

"Wow," I breathed. I couldn't believe it. "Cody, can you see this? It's our new house." I opened the door of the car, grabbed the pizza and my bags. The yard lights were illuminating around the house, like a golden lining to the entire property. My mother opened the door and waved at us.

"Like the outside of the house, guys? Wait until you see inside!" It was nice to see my mom finally happy about something in life. I walked up the front stairs and passed through the doorway. Now this was breathtaking. The foyer was a beautiful stained wood finish and the mini chandelier that hung from the ceiling had mock candles flickering through the room. I walked into the kitchen to start my own mini tour. The kitchen had the same stained-wood finish, but with the exception of regular ceiling lights.

By the time I reached up stairs, I ran to what could only be my room.

"Oh my, I can't believe this is my room," I shook my head in disbelief. It was twice the size of the room I shared with McKenzie back in Boston. I was now the proud owner of a king sized bed and a walk in closet. I opened the door to the right of my room to find a connected bathroom between McKenzie's and my room. I stood there and shook my head again. I was at a total loss of words.

"Cody!" I called. "Come look at my room! It's huge!" I walked to the doorway and pulled my twin inside. He looked around at the room.

"You must be happy, huh? Finally got your own room, Al. Put your bags down, mom put the pizza in the oven and its ready now," Cody said. He rubbed his growling stomach as if answering for me, and walked back downstairs. I followed in haste. The pizza smelled wonderful. We all sat down at the wooden table and ate pizza, while catching up about what had happened since we'd last seen each other. It was good to be a family again, even if it wasn't complete. Maybe, just maybe everything was going to be okay after all.

CHAPTER THREE
Alexandra

Summer slowly passed, through Union, like a foggy haze.
Cody got the job at Papa Murphy's and McKenzie was absorbed
in tanning, for college. My mother, who tried so hard for us to
feel at home here, had been overworking herself like usual, so
that we could have extra money to get clothes for school. I was
thinking about starting up horseback riding again; the perfect
stress relief and exercise considering no one was around during
the day anymore.

For the next couple of weeks while no one was home, I
used the computer to research stables close to where we lived.
Finally, I found the Canterville Equestrian Center. This place
had lessons that fit my budget perfectly. I already knew how to
work the three gaits, so I was looking forward to learning how to
jump. I made a plan to go down there and sign up for classes,
but instead, I'd decided to do some joyriding with a beautiful
horse I'd fallen in love with.

On the day before my birthday, about two months after we
had moved to Kentucky, I got my first ever snail mail from my
friends! Sure, we'd text and video chat on the regular, but
getting a package was totally different. I opened the letter first- I
wanted to be able to pretend they were there with me as I was
opening my gift.

Hey, Alex! I cannot believe your eighteenth birthday is
coming up! I don't know when you'll get this, but I hope it's

before the twelfth. Happy birthday! We miss you so much! You'll never believe who got pregnant over the summer- text me later and I will fill you in. Tell Code-ster we said happy birthday as well. We need to have another video date as soon as we can because Marco and Dan have a lot to tell you as well. Dude, they split for a week or two last month! I couldn't believe it. Deanna and Dean had gotten back together right after you left, but split again, which isn't the best news for you... Deanna was crying about Cody at Project Speak. I hope your brother had enough sense to change his number... ah well. We love you! Call me once you open them and we'll talk! Bye, for now! Love you mucho!! – Kat.

I smiled at her letter. That was so thoughtful. I wondered who had possibly gotten pregnant during the summer. I'd have to remember to ask her when we video chatted. Next, I grabbed the big parcel that had come with the letter and opened it. I saw three individually packaged gifts, so I sorted through them to find Kat's.

She had wrapped the gift in silver, foil wrapping paper. Silver was one of my favorite colors. I carefully peeled the tape off of the paper and unwrapped. Inside the box was a beautiful, ornate photo frame of all four of us: Kat standing on the left, with Dan beside her. I was next to Dan, and Marco was beside me. We were holding up the peace sign, and making the "Ducky" face. I instantly felt warm tears spring to my eyes. Beside the photo frame was the scrapbook we had made when we were in ninth grade. It featured all four of us, and we had shared the book over many weeks. I saw a piece of paper tucked inside with a handwritten note: keep it. By now the happy tears kept coming.

I grabbed Marco's package and opened that one next. Inside the wrapping I saw a Pandora bracelet with three charms on it- one was a horseshoe because I loved horses. The other two were a peace sign and a heart. That was so precious! I immediately put the bracelet on. Finally, I saw Dan's package.

Once I had opened it, I could see why they had wanted me to open his last. Dan had given me his mother's diamond earrings- from Russia. He had inherited them when she had died three winters ago. I realized now that they had given me things that they valued and sent them to me so I could have a little piece of them, with me forever. I was truly touched. I smiled through my tears as I quickly sent them the biggest thank you text ever, and told them to meet me online tonight for a video chat.

I put the frame and book on my bureau, and put the earrings and bracelet on. I was so excited about my gifts; I almost forgot to wrap my brother's. I heard the door open, and to my horror, I realized I'd left his gift in the living room. I threw open my door and ran down the big staircase through the hall. I saw that he hadn't yet reached the couch table so I grabbed the gift and threw it into my knapsack.

"Hey, uh... you looking for something?" said a voice from behind me that was not Cody's. I quickly turned around to see... pizza boy! His face registered embarrassment, as did mine; I figured out why I felt breezy- I was only wearing a bra and boxer shorts. Oh. My. God. My eyes widened at his face and I tried to nonchalantly brush off the awkwardness.

"Hey, you're the pizza boy, aren't you? Uh, yeah I'll be right back," I said as I turned around and rushed it to the stairs once again. I slammed my door shut and wildly looked around my room for my favorite shirt. When did pizza boy get so cute? When did I start to care? Sure, I'd seen him one other time while visiting Cody at work, but he was always covered in flour, so I never really noticed him. Without his floury mask, he was actually gorgeous. He was about five foot seven, with athletic, broad shoulders. His greenish-brown eyes sparkled in the daylight. He had perfect white teeth and freckles all over his face. He was nothing short of dreamy.

I pushed all that out of my mind, because I know his type. They sweet talk you; woo you, just to get in your pants. Then, after that's all said and done, they act like you've never existed to them and you're left broken-hearted. Guys seriously sucked.

I finished getting dressed and went back downstairs. Cody and pizza boy were sitting at the table eating sandwiches. Cody waved me over.

"Hey sissy, I want you to meet my boy, Justin. He works at Papa M's and we've actually got a shit load in common. He's really cool, come say hi!" He looked over at Justin, whose eyes were all on me. I shifted uncomfortably in my clothes, thanking the lord all he got to see was my leopard print push-up bra from Victoria's Secret. Now, don't get me wrong, I love my body, but seriously, at times like these I wish I had a nice rack.

"Hey, nice to meet you Justin," I said politely. I walked over to the counter and grabbed some bread to make a sandwich.

Justin got up and grabbed the turkey for me.

"Here, go sit down I'll make it for you!" he quipped. I stared, kind of dumbfounded. What the eff? I looked over at Cody, who smiled and shrugged. Whatever, if he was as good at making sandwiches as he was pizza, I'd deal with it. I smiled at him.

"Thanks, Justin. You really don't have to though," I said even though I took the seat next to my brother. He only nodded in my direction and continued making my sandwich.

"Hey, guys! I'm home," the door slammed shut as my older sister walked in. She took one look at Justin and smiled. "Hey, cutie, you're a new face 'round here. Cody's friend?" she asked, blatantly leaving me out of the equation. McKenzie never could fathom a boy like him being a friend of mine, because in her eyes, I was not pretty enough.

"Yeah, we work together," he said barely giving her a glance. He walked over to me, gave me my sandwich with a big smile, and sat down next to me. That must have made McKenzie angry because she just walked away into the other room. I didn't get why he was being so nice to me. I'd have to talk to Cody later about it. McKenzie walked back into the room and handed us the mail.

"You guys start school on the seventeenth," she said. "You just received the notice in the mail." She looked at Justin one more time, and walked out once again.

"You guys are going to my school, Cooper," said Justin in between bites of his own sandwich. "It's actually a nice place to go. Sports are good too, if you're into that sort of thing," he added. He looked over at me. "You need to meet the rest of the guys; you'll fit in very well with them. We wanted to get a band together. Cody- any good at an instrument?" They started chattering away about band stuff, while I sat there looking at my Cosmo magazine.

"Hey, Alex do you want to come to the mall with us?" Justin's voice interrupted my thoughts. He looked at me. "We're going to go in a few, wanna come with?" The look in his eyes said he wanted me to go more than anything. So, I steeled myself.

"Nah, I'd rather hang by myself, sorry," I said, so clearly not sorry at all. What bewildered me the most was the fact he actually looked hurt when I said it. I instantly felt bad. "Maybe I'll come some other time?" I suggested. That brightened his look a little bit.

"Sure! See you, Alex. It was nice meeting you, finally," he went to give me a hug. I opted for the casual one-handed way, but he grabbed me into a full-on hug. I'll give the boy credit where it's due- he's got some nice arms. Oh, and he smelled delicious. His hugs were amazing too. Wait... no, Alex. Don't go there.

"Yeah, see you..." I slid out of his grasp and grabbed my plate. I hurried upstairs before I changed my mind. I collapsed behind my door on my bed, overwhelmed with thoughts. No. I couldn't go there. I was starting my senior year at a new school. I don't need boy confusion on top of the stress. I logged onto chat to see if my best friends were online. No such luck, I thought to myself.

I decided I was going to wrap Cody's gift instead. I had

given him a mini hockey set, along with drumsticks. I also put the four hundred dollars I owed him from my phone into an envelope. Thank god for my neighbors needing babysitters this summer. I wrapped up the boxes and hid them in my closet. I decided the best place to spend the rest of my minor years was riding. I grabbed my bike and rode down the street to the stable where I'd started to ride.

More than anything, I loved horses. It was my escape from the world. Just climbing on the back of a horse and riding, relieved stress, because up there, you feel like you're flying. I paid the thirty dollars for the day and got to pick my horse. I particularly favored a bay mare named Celtic. She was spirited, like me, but she was understanding. She and I rode as one, more often than not. My favorite place to ride was an open field filled with flowers. I warmed Celtic up and edged her into a trot down the trail to the field. Once I had gotten there, I had Celtic open up to a canter. It was a beautiful, breezy August day. At once, I felt alive.

"Come on, Celtic, my beautiful girl. Let's see how fast we can go!" I kissed at her, and she picked up the pace. Together, we worked as one unit. I loved the feeling I got when I rode. It was like a blissful high, except this high was all natural. I felt like I owned the world. I paced Celtic down to a walk as we edged toward the trail again. She always got an extra treat from me; she was such a wonderful girl. When we reached the stable, I saw my brother, Justin, and my mom. What were they doing here? I came here to get away from them.

"Hey, guys," I said as I hopped down off of Celtic. She

nudged me with her velvet nose, so I patted her in response. "What are you doing here?" Cody came over to me and handed me a piece of paper.

"Just here to give you your birthday gift- we'd have given it to you tomorrow, but we figured right now was the best time, considering where we are," he said and gave me a hug. Bewildered, I opened the paper up to read what it said.

"This slip certifies that Alexandra Barnes, 18, of 1322 Hill Crest Ridge Road is now the owner of the bay mare, Celtic Song.... no way! You guys bought her for me for my birthday?" I said, utterly speechless. This beautiful animal was now mine? I couldn't believe it. I looked over at my mother.

"Sure we did, sweetie. You deserve a gift that makes living here a lot easier for you," she explained to me. "You always seem to be depressed around here, so your brother and I decided we'd do a little snooping and get you something you truly wanted. We'd have waited until tomorrow, but I figured you'd like to spend some extra time on her." She walked over and hugged me as well. "Happy birthday, sweetheart. I will see you later. The boys want to head to the mall, but wanted to be sure they could watch your reaction to your gift. Your father hasn't been able to send out your car so I have to use my mile points I saved up and go get it this weekend. McKenzie is coming with me to drive it back. Do you think you and Cody will be alright by yourselves for the weekend?" She looked at me with such trust and love. I was determined to make living here better for her.

"Absolutely. Don't worry about us, I'll keep two eyes on Cody," I laughed, joking. I smiled over at my twin. "Thanks,

Cody for the gift too. You really are the best, you know." He chuckled and shrugged his shoulders.

"I know, I know. But hey, go enjoy your gift. See you tonight?" he asked. I nodded, and pocketed my paper. I returned to the paddock where I had tied Celtic up while I was talking to my family. I looked over my shoulder to see them walk away. Only Justin had turned around as well and waved goodbye to me. I returned the gesture and got back on the saddle. "Come on, girl," I said to the mare. "Let's go for one more ride."

Two and a half hours later, I finally returned to the stable. It was getting dark out, so I had to turn on the light in the stall. I removed my saddle, and brushed her down. Celtic was looking mighty fine after I got done with her. I kissed her soft nose and hand fed her some apple slices. "I will see you tomorrow, sweet baby," I said to her as I shut the door to the stall. As I was returning the saddle to the racks, I caught sight of something glistening on the ground.

"You found my diamond-encrusted crop!" buzzed someone from the left of me. I turned my head to see a short, blond girl looking completely relieved. You could tell she had money by the way she was dressed: Louis Vuitton riding blazer and matching pants, authentic leather riding boots, and apparently a diamond-encrusted crop.

"Thank you SO much!" she exclaimed as she gave me a big hug, which was pretty awkward. She hugged me like we were the best of friends.

"Uh, no problem. I'm Alex, what's your name?" I asked her politely. The girl looked to be about sixteen or seventeen and her brown eyes had such passion in them- I wondered if she was one of those people who loved life no matter what was going around them.

"I'm Alessandra, but you can call me Lissa. I know what an ugly name I have. My parents thought that if they gave me a beautiful, rich name I'd turn out beautiful and rich. I guess I was short-handed, huh?" I was a little confused. She was actually pretty, and by the way she dressed, I'd assumed she was pretty wealthy too.

"You don't seem to be short-handed ," I said simply. She walked over to the saddle rack and leaned on a white leather saddle.

"I mean, I don't know. I feel like if I looked something different, people would like me. I have no friends, and that kind of sucks," she said in a hollow voice. I instantly empathized, I was about to start a brand new school and couldn't imagine getting to her age and having no friends, I wanted to befriend Lissa. She loved horses and was kind enough, what more could I ask of a friend?

"Well, Lissa," I said slowly. "You have one now- me. I'll be your friend. I'm new. I just moved here in June. I'm going to be a senior at Cooper High next week." I looked at her now beaming face. She smiled widely.

"Really! Oh my gosh! I'm going to be a senior there too! I'll have to show you around. You're new? Well, welcome to Union, Kentucky! Thanks for being my friend, Alex. You won't regret it!" she said excitedly. I handed her a ripped piece of paper off of the envelope of my ownership document.

38

"Here's my number, give me a call or a text soon and we'll ride together or something," I said as I gathered up my stuff. "We can hang out whenever you want. My twin brother works at a pizza place; we could go there and eat if you like." She nodded and scribbled something down on a random piece of paper.

"Here's my number too. I have to go though, my mom is texting me," she grimaced. She pulled out an iPhone encased in- you guessed it, Louis Vuitton. She shook her head and stuffed the phone back into her pocket. "It was nice meeting you, Alex. See you around!" she gave me a quick hug and walked out of the stables. Although I was a little overwhelmed by her personality, I was in no position to pass up friends.

It probably wouldn't be as hard if I didn't feel like I was betraying Kat.

Kat! I totally forgot about our video date! I rushed to my bicycle and pedaled home as quickly as I could. It was about nine thirty when I got home. I rushed upstairs past my family and slammed into my room. I looked at my away message on chat- I had three missed calls, and two messages from Dan and Marco. I felt so bad. I quickly returned from being away and sent a four-way video call.

Alexandra.Barnes to: KatMitrovanof92, MitrovanofX3, and Mr.Fabulous: Hey guys! Sorry for the delay, I have HUGE news for you. Acccpt video call?

Pretty soon, I saw the eager faces of my three best friends on my computer screen.

"Alex! Oh my god, are we glad to see you! How is life in the hick town, sweetie?" said Marco almost immediately. We both put our hands up to the screen for a virtual 'hand hug' like we usually did when we saw each other.

"You guys will never guess what happened to me today!" I went into full detail about what had happened during today's events. I watched Dan and Kat's eyes widen at the thought of their best friend being seen practically naked by a hot guy, even worse- the hot guy is your brother's new best friend! Marco pretended to faint when I told them what Justin looked like- he was so dramatic. Kat especially liked the fact my family had pitched in to buy me the horse; she loved horses as well.

After about an hour on the computer, we all signed off, saying goodbye to one another. I climbed into my bed and stared at the ceiling for a while. Tomorrow was my eighteenth birthday. It was oddly significant that the biggest year of my life, senior year, was the same year I moved. Big things were coming my way, I could tell. I guess the only thing I could do was accept it. But, for the meantime, I'd deal with one nightmare at a time. The first? I'll have to start school with Cody next Wednesday. I drifted into a dreamless sleep and thought nothing of what was to come next week.

CHAPTER FOUR
Justin

My God, was she beautiful. In my whole life, I'd never seen someone as beautiful as Alex. I guess it was luck that her twin brother got a job at Papa Murphy's, the place where I'd worked for the past two months. It was fate, however, that made Cody and I become best friends. I remember the very first time I saw her. She was coming in to order pizza; the same day that Cody had applied to work here.

I thought nothing of it- people applied all the time. But then she came in and stunned me with her natural beauty. I almost couldn't speak; I was caught off guard. I have been in love before, just as I'd dated girls until the novelty wore off. She caught me by complete surprise, and it was love at first sight. Have you ever felt that couldn't be true? So did I, until I saw her. I knew that she was the girl I was going to date next. I had to have her, the attraction was instant, the chemistry intense. Just at first glance I could tell she took care of herself. The sparkle in her eyes told me she knew how to have a good time. Something was off though, like something was missing in her life.

Either way, I knew I had to have her. I figured if she lived around Union I could find her. When my manager called Cody the next day to give him a job offer I was elated because I knew I was that much closer to having a better life with my dream girl. I shocked myself, I'm not some kind of loser who falls too quickly over random girls, not in the slightest, that's how I knew she was so important to me. I'd never hit the ground hard when it came to girls, especially after what went down at my house almost daily.

Not many people knew about my home life, and I intended to keep it that way. I was there as little as possible; I was always out doing my own thing, making sure my sister, Michelle, was with her friends. After Cody started working the same shifts as I did, we got closer and started hanging out. All throughout the summer, we'd bike down to my friend Nico's to start up our band with the rest of the crew, whose members included Cody, our friend Frank Nichols, myself, and our twin friends, Nico and Kosta Eliades. We'd bike, play music, and hang at the mall trying to get Cody to meet more people besides us. Alex would come around from time to time, but she always seemed to avoid me. That made the chase even more desirable, in my mind.

The first day of school was when everything seemed to change. I had offered to pick up Cody and Alex to bring them to school because it was on my way. I was waiting out in their driveway in my old 2001 Chevy Malibu, when Alex was the first to emerge.

"Hey, Justin!" She called to me as she walked over to the car. She looked breathtaking. I had to look in my mirror and pretend to adjust it, so she wouldn't catch me staring. When she got into the back seat, I smelled her perfume. She smelled like vanilla and lavender. I turned around to greet her.

"Is Cody all ready? If not, you can sit up here you know. I'm not going to bite," I said, chuckling. She seemed to think about it for a moment before climbing over to the front seat. She was wearing black skinny jeans and a tunic top. Her hair was curled just perfectly. I thought she looked like an angel. I must've been looking at her funny because she cleared her throat.

"Is everything okay? You look kind of spaced out... you're not high are you?" she said alarmed. I shook my head.

"No, I'm not high- I don't smoke. I don't drink either," I said, my voice a little too bitter. She looked at me, her eyes questioning me. I smiled at her. "Don't worry; I'm not like your run-of-the-mill guy around here. Some people like to get caught up in drinking or smoking for a lifestyle, but the rest of us actually want to go places with our lives," I turned my head to see Cody on his way out. He came strolling out of the house and ran to the car.

"I'm sorry I'm coming out late, I forgot to grab my bag. I don't even know what we'll need for today," he remarked when I gave him an agitated look. I wasn't agitated that he was late. I was annoyed because I wanted more than forty-five seconds alone with Alex.

"It's all good, bro," I said as I turned my key in the ignition. Beside me, Alex looked at her brother.

"Cody, what happens if we don't have any classes together? I only know you, Justin and Lissa. If I'm all alone, I think I'll cry," she said. Cody grabbed his sister's hand, and playfully slapped it.

"Don't worry, sis. It'll be fine. There's going to be plenty of people to meet, and I know the guys out here will think you're pretty, you'll get the cream of the crop to pick from," he winked. I slammed on the brakes causing them to lurch forward. Cody scowled at me as he rubbed his forehead where he hit the seat in front of him. "Dude, really? How didn't you see the stop sign?" I really did see it; I just wanted the conversation to stop. I realized I'd have to tell Cody about how I felt about Alex sooner rather than later.

"Sorry, I was watching the car in front of me take a left turn, no big," I said nonchalantly. Alex, on the other hand, gave her brother a look.

"Cody, he's fine," she snapped. "Let him drive, and let us worry about the first day." I laughed when she turned her aggravated face to me. She looked sexy when she was angry.

"What are you laughing at?" she demanded.

"You," I said simply. "You're nervous. There isn't a reason to be, I promise."

"Are you sure? Have you ever gone to a new school before?"

"Of course... I was new here at the end of my freshman year," I said, turning and looking at her. "I went to a different high school before Cooper. I did perfectly fine. You're gorgeous-you'll be fine. Cody has me and the crew, so he'll meet people through us. Seriously, Al. Don't sweat it." She looked more relaxed as we turned into the student parking lot. I saw Kosta, playing air guitar next to Spencer Freedman, his long time girlfriend. I pulled up next to them and shut the car off. I climbed out of the car and walked towards the passenger side door. I opened it for Alex, who smiled.

44

"You're such a sweetheart, Justin! Thank you," she said gratefully. She stepped out of the car and grabbed her bag. On the other side, Cody got out and slapped Kosta in a handshake we taught him.

"Yo, bro! You ready for your first day?"

"About as ready as I can be, man. You know how it is," Cody replied. He said hello to Spencer and walked over to Alex and I. I grabbed Alex's bag for her and walked alongside her, ignoring her objections.

"You know," she began with her hands on her hips, making her perfect frame like an hourglass. "I can carry my bag myself, Justin. I'm a big girl." She was giving me a look, and I so badly wanted to lean over and kiss her. Her hazel eyes had a shade of yellow in them, so they looked like moons in the light. Her makeup was subtle and flattering and I noticed guys around us paying attention to the pretty, new girl.

"I'm just trying to be nice, miss. I suppose you've never had a guy treat you properly before, then, have you?" I asked her. I meant it rhetorically, but I was surprised when she mumbled an answer.

"Well... no. I can't say I have...." She looked away, and I saw that hurt flash in her eyes again. I pulled her into a hug and just held her for a moment.

"I'm sorry if I made you feel uncomfortable. I'm just trying to be a friend," I said quietly. I let her go, gave her bag back to her, and walked up to Cody. I directed them to the main office and told them where to go from there.

"After you go to the office, just report to class one. Don't worry about homeroom today. Deal with that tomorrow," I explained. "You'll need to get an idea where the classes are." He shook my hand.

"Alright, I'll see you at lunch then? If not we can meet up after school and work on our songs," he said, already retreating. I waved goodbye to the two of them and walked over to Spencer and Kosta, in time to hear them sniggering.

"Well what do you know," chuckled Spencer. She flicked her long red hair over her shoulder and looked directly in my eyes. "Justin's got a crush on the new girl already!" Kosta smiled as well and slapped me on the back.

"Way to go, J! She's a beaut. She know you got a thing for her?" he waggled his eyebrows at me. I rolled my eyes.

"No, she doesn't. Neither does her brother. I have to tell him as soon as possible. I need him on my side if I'm going to get her. Kosta, you know me. When have I ever fallen for a girl this hard before?" That statement earned a sharp look, he clearly had this down as a 'crush', because his smile vanished and he looked at me like I was speaking Egyptian.

"So you're saying you're like, in love with her? Dude, you barely know her!"

"Well, no shit Sherlock, I'm just so into her I'm going to do whatever it takes to be with her. There's something about this one. I can't let other guys get to her. I don't know too much, but I know that it'll hurt like hell if I see her with another guy." I thumbed the pocket of my jeans, not looking at Kosta. Out of my whole crew, Kosta and I were the closest when it came to talking about things like this. He understood what I'd gone through, and helped me with advice. This time, however, Spencer came to my rescue.

"Justin, she's new here. She left her whole life behind. She probably won't be looking for a guy so soon. Try talking to Cody and get his input before doing anything. What you just said about her was really sweet but don't force the issue. Good things take time," she warned. She opened her mouth to speak again, but we heard the bell ring to signal that first period was about to start. "Let me know how it goes, J! Good luck!" she hugged me, kissed Kosta quickly and then ran to meet up with her other friends as we marched, in a crowd, to get inside to our classes. I said bye to Kosta and headed to my first period on my schedule- English.

My English class didn't have many people I was close to, but I did know a few people. Jenna Feiffer and Mandy Ricker were in my class. I had dated Jenna last year; she was the only girl I'd ever been in love with, and she had ripped my heart out. After two years of dating, she had broken it off, telling me she was bisexual and that her girlfriend didn't want her dating such a masculine man. I felt them staring at me as I sat down, but I ignored them, something I'd gotten good at.

The rest of English class was uneventful. The sound of the bell let us know it was time to transition to class two- Gym. I took my time walking to my class because by now, I was getting antsy, hoping Alex and Cody made it to the office. They must've done alright because as I entered the gymnasium I saw Alex standing with Lissa DiAngelo, near the volleyball net. My heart started beating profusely; my favorite class now had the hottest girl in school. Sure, I was what people called 'popular' but even still, we got nervous too.

"Oh my god! Justin! Thank goodness you're in this class. Lissa and I were freaking out because she doesn't know anyone in this class, which meant bad news for me. Ah, I'm so relieved!" she went off in hyper speed. Lissa looked awkwardly down at the floor. I knew Lissa through my sister, Michelle. Even though she was a year younger, Michelle always got along with the older girls. When she had moved in with our grandparents, Michelle decided she'd rather be home-schooled. I smiled at the girls.

"Yeah, you have nothing to worry about. I'll tell you who the people to talk to are, follow me," I replied. I started walking around the gym. "That is Hana Wayne, "I pointed to my cousin, who was standing around with a soccer ball. She dribbled it with her feet and put it in the net. "She is my cousin, and she's really nice. You'll get along with her pretty well, I think." I continued walking around the gym and prattled off more names that she could try and befriend. Jean Newton... Farah Montana... LeAnn DiGrazia. I deliberately avoided introducing her to guys, because I couldn't let my chance slip away before it appeared. Lissa faded off into the background, mentioning something about wanting to run laps, leaving Alex and I alone.

"So, do you like Cooper so far?" I asked, clearing my throat. She nodded at me and remained silent for a few seconds before replying.

"Yeah, it's great. I mean, so far. Cody's in three of my classes apparently. I like it," she said. The bell rang about forty minutes later, so the class filtered out slowly. We weren't going to start anything until tomorrow. I watched as she walked away, a vision of beauty. Since I always believed in the 'honesty is the best policy' attitude, I was going to be up front with Cody about how I felt. I wanted his approval before saying anything to Alex.

The rest of the school day went by in a blur. I didn't have any classes with the crew, which bummed me out. Turns out, we didn't have any of the same lunches either. We met up after the last bell rang, however. We decided we were going to hang out in Nico and Kosta's garage.

"So," started Frank as we entered the man cave. "I heard from a little birdie that you got a crush on you know who!" Kosta hooted and hid behind the couch as I threw a water bottle at him, proving I knew exactly who the birdie was.

"Cody, I'm just going to tell you now, so you're hearing from me first. Your sister, Alex- she is the most beautiful girl I've ever seen, and I want to date her. What do you think?" I was suddenly nervous that Cody was going to flip on me for talking about his sister, but to my surprise, he laughed.

"Dude, I called it! Nico and I were placing bets on when you'd finally tell us. No worries. I'd rather you with her than any other guy. But, she's been burned by other dudes before. You gotta go slow and have her trust you first, that's my only advice." He looked at me, serious now. "Just don't hurt her or things will happen," he stated. I nodded in agreement. I could never hurt such a beautiful person. Someone that special deserved to be treated accordingly. The conversation ended for the day, and we continued to jam out to the song we were composing.

One thing I knew for sure was that Alex was going to be mine. I'd do whatever it takes for that to happen. I'm a genuine, honest, kind of guy. That's got to count for something, right?

CHAPTER FIVE
Alexandra

"Alex, don't start."

"Why, though?" I stared at the face of my best friend, Kat. We were video chatting once again, complaining about school already. I'd been there about a month, and I could no longer deny the fact I was seriously crushing hard on Cody's friend, Justin. What got me the most, though, was the fact he seemed to have suddenly forgotten I existed. Okay, I supposed that was a lie. He talked to me every day like usual, but those nice things he did when he first came around had stopped.

"You don't know what's going to happen, that's why!" exclaimed Kat. She was munching on some Doritos and flipping through a magazine. "It isn't going to happen, because he's your brother's best friend. It's like, some sort of guy code. Your brother won't allow him to date you, just in case he decides he wants something else. It's to protect the brotherhood," she explained.

"I mean, I don't know, Kat," I sighed. "He is so cute, and so nice. Maybe I just read the signals wrong. I have a history of that…." I trailed off. Kat changed the subject.

"Well, guess who had gotten her ultrasound this weekend," she said. Kat's smile got mischievous. I found myself instantly interested.

"Who? Is it someone we know?" I probed. Her smile got

broader.

"Of course, we do," she said wickedly. "When I heard I thought you'd get a kick out of it. Are you ready?" I fidgeted in my seat. Why wouldn't she just tell me?

"Yes, Kat. I've been waiting for you to tell me since my birthday. You've avoided the topic each time, even though you told me to ask. So, spit it out!" She put down her bag of Doritos and laughed.

"Okay, if you're sure... it's Deanna." Deanna! I was floored. There was no way my brother's ex-girlfriend was pregnant.

"What? Deanna de la Garman? That would mean..." I never finished the sentence because I had the nastiest thought. Dean Richmond, my ex-boyfriend, had gotten my brother's ex, pregnant. What. The. Eff.

"I know... I saw her and I wanted to laugh. She is by no means ready for a baby, Alex. Cody did the right thing leaving that beatch," Kat said. There were some voices over on her end of the screen, and she disappeared momentarily. When she returned, she gave me a sad face. "Sorry, mushka, but I have to go. Aunt Anya needs Dan and I to help her put away groceries. We'll talk later, and remember- Justin is off limits. Bye, love you!" she blew a kiss, which I reciprocated, and we signed off.

I sat there for a while, wondering why I was hit so hard by Cupid's arrow. Didn't I say, not six weeks ago, that I wasn't going to deal with boys here? I thought about asking Cody about what he thought, but I decided against it. I'd just have to let things pan out. I saw a lot of Justin. He was always over, hanging with Cody. On the weekends, when Cody wasn't sleeping at his "crew" hangout, Justin and this other kid, Nico, were spending the night at our place. I don't know what it was about Justin, but whatever it was, it was driving me crazy. When he smiles, he gives this little half-smirk. It's adorable.

I sat there in my reverie for what seemed like hours until I heard a knock on my door. I quickly snapped out of my daydream and went to see who it was.

"Hey, it's me," said my brother's muffled voice. I opened the door to see, no surprise- Nico, Justin and Cody standing in the hall. I felt my face smile as I saw them standing there.

"What's up, Code?" I came out from my room to face the three of them. My brother was holding a piece of paper.

"McKenzie wrote to us today," he said waving the paper at me. My sister had left last month to go to college. As much as she pretended to miss us, you could tell from her letters that she'd rather be doing something else. Not that we cared if she wrote to us or not, to be completely honest.

"Is that why you knocked? To tell me, our sister wrote to us?" I raised an eyebrow at him. "You know as well as I do that I don't want to read the crap she's trying to make us believe." Cody shook his head.

"No, I'm just saying. I actually came to see if you wanted to come to the bonfire we're having with us tonight. It's going to be fun," he said, with a sparkle in his eyes that I couldn't quite understand. Nico grinned at me.

"Yeah, come with us, Alexandra. You'll have fun!" I chuckled at the kid. Really, dude? No one called me that.

"Sure, I mean it couldn't hurt. What else is there to do on a Friday night?" Justin smiled at me and held up his hand for a high-five.

"I'll be driving, by the way. So, if you decide to drink, you'll be safe," he said.

"Good to know, but I don't drink. Thanks for the offer, though. Just give me a half hour to get ready." Cody nodded, and the three of them retreated to the first floor while I returned to my room to gather clothes. Since it was the beginning of October, it wasn't too chilly at night, but it wasn't like it was summer anymore. I opted for a flannel plaid shirt over a white lace tank top. My ripped jeans over black leggings looked especially cute paired up with my knee-high heel boots. I didn't want to make the boys wait too long, so instead of doing my hair straight, I decided on leaving my curly hair as it was. Since a girl's best friend is makeup, I wanted to make sure I got attention. When I was finished, my eyes looked smoldering.

I grabbed my wristlet and went downstairs. Justin was already in the car, so I waited for Nico and Cody before going outside. I could hear them in the kitchen talking. Being a nosy girl, I decided I was going to eavesdrop.

"We can't say anything, bro. It'll cause too much tension between them, don't you think?" came Nico's huddled voice. I heard some movement, which scared me a bit. I let my breath out a little when I realized they weren't coming my way.

"I know, but she has a right to know. I don't think anything bad will happen anyway. I told him I'd talk to her. I know my sister better than anyone else. If anyone's gonna talk to her, for him, it's me," said Cody. His voice was coming closer, so I ran over to the couch and sat down, just in time. The boys came out from the kitchen and headed over to me. Cody grabbed the house keys and made a motion with his head to the front door meaning let's get going. We were walking to the car when I suddenly realized something. They were talking about me in the kitchen! About Justin and I! I had the biggest smile on my face, which turned evil. I had to play hard to get with him tonight because if I let on how much I liked him, then he would stop being interested. I learned this back in Boston with Dean. I hated remembering what Dean had put me through, but I can thank him for teaching me more than one life lesson.

"Are you okay, Al?" asked Cody. He was looking at me smile at myself like a creep. I cleared my head of the thoughts and gave my best smile.

"Of course I am! I'm going to meet boys and have food and have fun, what more could be better?" I jumped into the back seat next him, and we were off. I caught Justin looking at me through the rearview mirror. Honestly, I don't like to play games, but I've come to realize that's the only way you don't get hurt anymore. I decided I was going to flirt with random boys and have fun, until my brother spoke to me about him. Through the radio, I could the sound of a familiar song.

"Oh! Turn that up! I love this song!" Justin laughed and rolled his eyes at me, while turning up the Kesha song. I immediately started singing. I didn't care that all of the guys were laughing at me. This song reminded me of the time Kat, Marco and I had snuck into a club back in Boston. This song came on, and it was the first time we'd heard it so we danced like crazy to the beat. I looked at Cody, who was laughing just as hard.

"Don't become a singer, Al," he said, wheezing. "You got a nice voice, but leave that song to Kesha." I playfully smacked him on the arm.

"Oh, shut up Cody. You're just jealous I'm the better twin. I'm the prettier one with the better voice. It's okay, you'll be fine, I know it," I joked. By now, all the boys were howling with laughter. "I don't get what's so funny…" I said. Justin was looking at me, by now. Well, more like staring. I guess he finally saw my outfit. I looked away from him, with the faint trace of a smile on my face.

For the remainder of the car ride, I continuously sang the most ridiculous songs that came on the radio. From Justin Bieber, to a bad rendition of The Beatles, I certainly knew how to make an audience laugh. We finally reached the place where the bonfire was being held. I could see the fire already happening. There were so many people here, so I was bound to meet new friends. Once Justin parked the car, the boys jumped out and made their way to the keg. The only one who held back was Cody.

"Alex! Wait up," he called. He walked to where I was standing and put his phone in his pocket. "I need to talk to you about something." He looked at me.

"Okay, shoot."

"Alright, so… Do you like anyone so far? Like, boys?" I started to giggle.

"Well, what else would I like, dummy? Of course I like boys. What's your issue?" I asked even though I knew what was coming.

"Well, I'm asking because I know someone who's interested in you. He's liked you for a while, and he insisted I talk to you before making a move because he wasn't sure if you felt anything."

"Are you going to tell me his name or am I going to have to guess?" I asked playfully. Cody rolled his eyes at me. Typical brother.

"I'm getting there! Alright, alright... It's Justin?"

I stared at him. I had to play it cool, otherwise history would repeat itself. "He likes me? Good joke, brother. If you told me Nico liked me, I'd believe that."

"Alex," he said seriously. "Nico likes Alessandra. I'm telling you Justin likes you. Don't be mean; just give him a chance. He's my best friend and I trust him with you. You know I wouldn't let you date someone as messed up as Dean, remember?" he gave me a dirty look that disappeared just as quickly as it came. "Just talk to him and get to know him, Alex. If you don't like him, after all, then that's fair. Please," he said. "You won't go wrong with Justin."

I shrugged at my brother. "Eh, I guess so. Now, let's go join everyone!" I said as I grabbed his arm and pulled him toward the fire.

At the clearing we saw a bunch of people chugging beers down like they were water. Cody saw a few more of his crew members so I was left to my own devices. I was thinking about what my brother had said, when I realized he told me Nico liked Lissa! Ever since we'd become friends, Lissa found that she was more socially accepted than she had anticipated. I hadn't noticed my brother's friend had taken an interest in her, though. I walked around to a table of drinks. I finally found a tub of soda cans labeled "Pop" by the edge of the assortment. I grabbed myself a ginger ale when a voice from behind me nearly made me jump out of my skin.

"Whoa! Sorry to scare you, Alex," Justin said as he held an arm out to hold me from falling.

"Jeez, here I was thinking I was completely alone. No worries, though," I said reassuringly. "Why aren't you with the rest of the crew? They all went to sit on the bales of hay near the fire."

"That would be reason enough to stay away," he joked. "Actually, I was thinking I'd rather spend time and talk to you." He looked straight at me; making me remember the time he'd caught me in my bra. Since it was night time, he couldn't see me blush.

"Why would you rather talk to me? I'm not that exciting." I twirled a piece of curl through my fingers.

"You'd be surprised," swallowed Justin, who was drinking a root beer.

"Right, I'm so exciting! I always just make everyone's day... not." I looked at him and laughed; mostly out of nervousness. He'd gotten closer to me, as though he wanted to hold me on his lap. Ever since Dean and I split up, I'd lost some of my flirting skills with boys because I was scared of being hurt again.

"You really are though, Alex. In the car earlier... you were your complete self, just having fun and not caring what anyone thought of it, and that's different around here. Most girls just care more about looks and status, and they're never truly themselves," he said. He was even closer still, almost inches from my face. "You're absolutely beautiful too, and your personality is amazing... what's not exciting about you? I like all of that about you. I like you."

And then, before I could register what was going on, our lips were together. I had never felt anything like it before. It was like fire and ice, soft yet passionate. I felt his hands on my hips, and I was lost to the world. As we pulled apart Justin's face was pink, like he was an embarrassed schoolboy caught cheating. I smiled a shy smile back at him.

"We don't have to tell anyone about this, if you don't want to," he said quietly. I was quite shocked. Why did he think I didn't want people to know how I felt?

"I don't mind telling people," I retorted. "I'd rather them know we're getting to know each other better, actually. Although we went out of order here..." I made a motion with my hand between us to represent our little kissing session.

"So, what? We got caught up in the moment, Alex, it's human. I would've preferred it if I took you out on an actual date first, though. I don't usually kiss girls before taking them out. I'm more of a gentleman than that, so I apologize," he said solemnly. I faked a gasp and covered my mouth playfully.

"Wow, is that the line you use on all the girls?" I winked. I hopped up on a bale of hay and patted the side next to me for him to sit down. He obliged. "Don't worry- I won't tell my brother."

"Well," he started. "Your brother was the first to even know I liked you. He knew I wanted to invite you tonight, to talk to you and see how you felt. I didn't know how you felt. Sometimes I'd get a reaction out of you that made me sure you felt the same, and other times you'd withdraw into yourself to the point I couldn't even tell if you wanted to be friends." He grabbed my hand. "If we were ever to be something, I want you to know I'm completely honorable, as well as painfully honest, miss. I don't keep any secrets, and I expect the same from you. I'll treat you the way a girl should be treated, and I will prove to you they ain't just words." He kissed the back of my hand and looked at me.

"We'll have to see, now won't we?" I said. I nudged him with my shoulder so that he fell off the bale of hay.

"Hey!" he exclaimed as I laughed and fell off of the bale of hay as well. He pulled himself up and held out his hand to pick me up. When I reached for his hand, he pulled too hard and we both toppled over the bale of hay with me landing on top of him.

"You're quite clumsy, Justin Barry. I thought I'd let you know that," I giggled.

"Do I have to be that asshole that says 'I'm clumsy cause I fell for you' by Fergie, or whoever?" he replied. He kissed the top of my nose, which made it twitch. "Oh my god, that was so cute. Do it again!" Immediately, I sat up and covered my nose. He found my weakness.

60

"Don't ever do that again!" I demanded. "No one's supposed to know about that! How embarrassing," I complained.

"What are you talking about? That was completely adorable, Alex." He looked at me, somewhat confused.

"Ugh, I guess I'll have to explain. Alright, when I was a little girl, I wanted to be a dog and whenever someone poked my nose, I'd twitch it. Over time, it became a habit. It's embarrassing so don't remember this. If I have to, I'll use the 'Force' on you, and I'll make you forget," I concluded. He must've thought I was joking, because he laughed and poked my nose again. "Quit it! I was serious!" I said.

"Oh, come on, Alex. It's not embarrassing. If you want, I'll give you a really awkward story about me when I was little, okay?" I nodded for him to continue. "Alright, when I was seven years old, I walked in on my parents having sex, and they told me it was a game called snake in the barn. One time I caught a garden snake and I told my mom I wanted to play the game with her too. She made me get rid of the snake, and grounded me for a month," Justin looked away, trying not to smile. I couldn't help but laugh.

"That's terrible! How didn't you know what they were doing?" I asked. He shrugged at me.

"I don't know, most people around here keep that stuff to themselves. I suppose it's more broadcasted in bigger cities. Who cares, it embarrassed me for the longest time, but I figured that you told me one, so I owed you." I heard a beeping noise, which could only be his phone. He pulled out his Blackberry and pressed the answer button.

"What's up? You guys all ready? Alright, dude. Where's Kosta... seriously? What the hell, man. Go find him and Alex and I will get the car. We're keeping the window open for him, he's not puking in my car." He hung up the phone, and looked at me. "Sorry, we have to cut this little outing short. Kosta's hammered and throwing up near the pond, and Nico and your brother want to head back to the house to play some video games.

So I need to take you out on a date, are you free Sunday night?" he asked.

"Well, I have to go to the stables and work Celtic out for a bit because I won't be able to get to ride her tomorrow. I usually go there once a day, but Sunday night I should be free. Why? What do you have in mind?" He grabbed my hand and began to walk away from the fire to where we parked.

"Oh, I don't know, maybe dinner at a restaurant of your choice and then go see a movie? If you don't want to see a movie we could cruise around and find some childish, fun things to do. I'm sure we'll be a great time no matter what we do," he said. We stopped at the car and he opened the passenger seat for me, as I climbed in. He got in the driver's side, and turned the key in the ignition.

"Sounds great to me," I smiled. He smiled back at me, as he put the car in gear to find my brother and the rest of our friends. I was on an emotional high. Finally, things were starting to look up. Maybe life in Union wasn't so bad after all. I smiled to myself while I looked out the window. Tomorrow, I decided, I was going to call Kat, Marco and Dan and let them know about what happened. Tonight was my night, and I was going to enjoy the rest of it the best I could. It wouldn't be that hard.

The car ride home passed by in a blur. Kosta never threw up in the car, even though he kept moaning about his stomach. Thankfully, he was the only one who drank this evening. Nico helped him inside when we got there, and the rest of us drove back to my house. When we got there, the lights were still off.. We went inside. The boys headed right for Cody's room to play Xbox. I, on the other hand, went into the kitchen. Inside, I saw a box of pizza with a note on the top.

'Alex and Cody,

I went out for the night. Don't wait up for me. I left the pizza for all of you to eat if you get hungry. Love you! – Mom ☺'

Wait... since when does my mother use smiley faces? She went out for the night? Where did she go, and with whom? I went to bed wondering what was going on. The last thing I remember thinking about before falling asleep was that kiss Justin and I had shared, and wondering where things would go from here. Only time would tell where things would lead.

CHAPTER SIX
Justin

If there was one thing I learned about girls, it was the fact that you had to play cat and mouse in order to get any type of sign of if they were into you or not. I hated games like that. For the last month, I'd been doing just that with Alex. Let me tell you- it worked, though. The more I chased her, the more she pushed me away. But the more I pulled away and acted disinterested, the quicker I could see if she was into me. It was hard- I wanted more than anything to just tell her I was done playing games and get to the better part. I knew, however, that wasn't the way life worked. Finally, the night of the bonfire, Cody told me he had talked to her.

"Dude, I know my sister. She's pretending she doesn't care, but I can see it in her eyes. She really likes you. You can go for it. Just don't expect everything to go smoothly. Certain things have happened in her life and she's jaded. I know she likes you, but I'm warning you- you're in for a rough journey. Who knows, though?" Cody said as he patted me on the shoulder. "Maybe she'll surprise us both." He walked away, toward Nico and Alex's friend Lissa. I had recently found out that Nico was crushing on her, and that he'd taken her on a date. I had to ask Alex on one before someone else did. So, I manned up and went to look for her.

While I was talking to her, I just couldn't keep myself away any more and I kissed her. I was more than elated when she kissed me back. I felt like the luckiest guy in the world. I knew I had to have her as my girlfriend, because she needed someone who could take care of her. Call me a hopeless romantic, but I know how not to treat a girl, as well as how to make one happy.

I made a date with her for Sunday night, just before we left the fire. I knew we were going back to her house, but it seemed inappropriate to hang with her when I was invited over to hang with the crew. We got back to their house around midnight, and we'd decided to pull an all-nighter, which failed because Nico fell asleep texting Lissa. That left me and Cody playing a war game by ourselves. Nico was our designated trash talker, and since he fell asleep, we were left to try to trash talk ourselves.

"What the hell man, you're like... worse than your grandma on life support!" I said lamely as Game tag "xZ_Man_Zx" destroyed our kill streak. I was so bad at this. "xZ_Man_Zx" quickly retorted back to us.

"Good one, dude. Seeing as I just raped your streak you shouldn't be talking." Beside me, Cody went stiff.

"Say that word again I'll come find you and kick your ass! Screw you!" he yelled angrily. Cody turned off the game, and stormed out of his room. I just stared at him, confused by his behavior. I looked over at Nico, who'd stirred from his slumber because of Cody's outburst. He blinked a few times, and rolled over and went back to sleep. I decided I'd go find Cody and see what was wrong with him. Just as I was about to get up to find him, he came back in with a bag of chips and sat back down on his bed.

"Cody, you alright man? What got you so angry?" I said, but I didn't want to press the issue if he wasn't willing to share his thoughts.

He sighed. "It's really hard to talk about because it's not anyone's business, really. I guess since you're dating my sister I can tell you, but please don't tell her you know. That'd kill her. But last year, she went out with this guy named Dean Richmond. He was the captain of my school's hockey team and he knew exactly what to say to get to my sister. They got into a fight at the end of the relationship, and things took a turn for the worse and he ended up raping her. He also beat her, and she was a bloody mess when we got to his home. My father, who's a lawyer, called the cops and he was arrested and held on charges. Dean knew my dad was cheating though, and blackballed my father with the threat of exposing the affair," he said softly. "He didn't want his daughter to live with that. Dad won the case, but Dean got a plea bargain so he got off after all. My dad lost his family and his credibility instead. That's why we're here." I looked up to see Cody's eyes were red, and it was only then I realized I had tears welling up. Their family had gone through too much in such a short time. I felt a deep hatred for Dean Richmond. Scum bags like that deserved to be shot.

"I am so sorry, Cody. I really am. I had no idea she went through that. I promise I'll make sure nothing ever happens to her again, and I mean that."

"I know you do," he said seriously. His eyes were level with mine. "I just hate hearing that word. It reminds me of how much I hate that prick, and that I wish I had beat the shit out of him when I had the chance." I sat there, with new understanding for this family. Alex was raped and beat by a guy she thought she trusted. Well, no wonder she barely trusts guys. Cody lost a father, just as his mother lost a husband. In most cases, that was a tragic thing. In my case, though, I wish my mother would lose my father...

"I'm serious, Code. Nothing will happen to your family when I'm around, I promise." I gave Cody a grip on his shoulder. For the remainder of the night, we avoided the topic, we played more games and watched movies until we passed out. The next morning, I had to get up early to drive Nico to Lissa's, because it was on the way to my grandparents' house. I was supposed to pick up Michelle and drive her to our Bi-weekly therapy session in Cincinnati. We usually spent our time there talking about our issues at home. When I got to my nana and papa's house, I saw my little sister waiting on the porch. She looked hardened for such a young girl. She waved as I pulled up.

"Hey, Justin," she called as I parked the car in the driveway. I gave her a nod as I got out of my car.

"What's up, Shelly?" I said as I hugged her. She reciprocated and looked up at me.

"I'm okay, just want to get this week over with," she said. She walked over to my car and got in, putting her headphones in. I poked my head through the door, and yelled a quick hello, but no one was there. It was Saturday morning- they would be out food shopping.

Soon, we were driving down Old Union Road toward the highway. My sister barely said anything anymore. I wished she wasn't such a loner, though. We got to the office and took our seats in the waiting room. We never got called in separately unless the therapist wanted to speak exclusively about something. When we were younger, Michelle had terrible separation anxiety from me. She'd gotten better now. They still saw us both out of habit.

"Barry, Michelle and Justin?" the receptionist called out our name to signal it was our turn. I stood up and walked to the door, Michelle tailing behind me. The room we were in looked like a children's bedroom. The only thing that was different about it was the fact that there was no bed. In replacement, the room had four squashy chairs to sit in and converse.

"So, Justin," the therapist named Marcy started. She looked at her clipboard and addressed me again. "Has anything changed in the past few weeks when we last spoke?" I shook my head.

"No, still the same old song and dance there," I said bitterly. "My mother still drinks when she's at home and my father beats her. He gets in my face when I protect her. Nothing ever changes." Marcy looked over at my sister.

"What about you, Michelle? How do you feel that your life has changed since moving out and starting the homeschool curriculum I know we missed a few meetings with you due to your grandmother's health?" My sister just looked at her.

"Life changed because I moved out," Michelle said simply. She looked out the window for a few moments before answering again. "I wish Justin would move out, too. He stays to protect our mom, but I don't think she wants to be saved," she said quietly. I looked over at my sister.

"What do you mean, Shelly?" I asked. She shrugged her shoulders.

"Well, think about it," she said. "If she really wanted to be saved from the abuse, she'd have moved out when I did. I think she likes the abuse. It might be comforting to her." As much as I didn't want to admit it, I was starting to think Michelle's hunch was correct.

"Justin, does your father still beat you or is it just your mother?" asked Marcy. She had a different tone in her voice this time. It was like she actually felt sorry for asking. I had a lump in my throat. I didn't want to answer, but I replied all the same.

"Yeah," I said. "He still hits me." Michelle's eyes bugged out wide when she heard me.

"Justin, please tell me you're lying," she said. Her eyes were rimmed with tears by now. I hated seeing my little sister cry. It was because of those tears that I started my mission to get my sister out of the house.

"I wish I could, hun. I truly wish I could, but I need to stay to protect mom."

"No!" Michelle yelled angrily. She leaped up from her chair and faced me. "You don't need to protect mom because she doesn't need it! You need it. You can't always be the hero, Justin. You're a football and basketball star, that's it. You can't always save the day, okay? Mom knew what she was getting into. She never did anything to protect us when Dad decided to hit us. Why should she be protected?" she cried. Marcy looked over at Michelle but stayed quiet.

"Justin, you need to get out of there now. I don't want my only brother getting hurt, or killed for that matter. I need you more than mom does!" Tears flooded her face and she collapsed in my arms. I held my little sister for a while as Marcy spoke to me about appropriate behavior and preemptive action. When the hour was over, Michelle and I silently left the office. The car ride remained silent as well. When I dropped Michelle off at Nana's, she gave me a look before getting out of the car.

"Please think about it, Justin. I really am worried about you," she hugged me. With that, she hopped out of my car and walked to the house without looking back. I felt a surge of hatred toward my father. I hated him for blasting apart our family. If he wasn't so controlling, my mother wouldn't have resorted to drinking to get rid of the pain. Michelle would be a normal, social teenager and have friends. I would also have a full family, something I had always dreamed of.

That was why I was determined to make my life better. I was hoping to get a basketball scholarship to the college of my dreams, and to end up being a football coach to my favorite team- the Cincinnati Bengals. I'd get married to the woman of my dreams, have kids, and never bring them up the way I was brought up.

While I was thinking about my future, I found myself at a field of flowers. I don't remember thinking about which direction

I was driving, so I was pretty sure I was lost. However, the field was connected to a horseback riding stable, the very same one that Alex's horse was stabled at. I immediately knew where I was, but I was in no rush to leave. I sat in the field for about two hours, keeping to myself and ignoring any texts and calls I had received. I got a text from Alex as well, but I ignored it too. I just didn't want to be around people right now.

A couple hours later, I finally got up and walked to my car. I decided I'd answer Nico back and tell him what we discussed at therapy, but he didn't respond to the call. I supposed he was still at Lissa's house. Since everyone had their own plans for the night, I figured I was going to have to brave and go home and just watch a movie in my room.

My shabby house on New Park Lane was empty when I got home. My mother, who was a "recovering" alcoholic, was probably at a mandatory AA meeting. Who knew, or cared where my father was. I went upstairs into my small bedroom and locked my door behind me. I secretly locked and barred my door every time I was in here so I wouldn't get attacked if my father had another one of his episodes. I sprawled myself onto my bed and popped in my favorite movie- The Fast and the Furious. I had two other favorite movies- Space Jam and Friday Night Lights. I can quote pretty much any line from any of the three movies. About an hour into the movie, I heard my front door slam open.

"Laura! Where the hell are you, woman?" James Barry stormed in angrily. I stuffed my pillow on my face and stifled a groan. Though my father doesn't drink, he's as violent as an abusive alcoholic. He stomped upstairs and I heard him shuffle around. Then, he rapped on my door.

"Boy, you know where your mother is?" he said from behind the door. Resisting the urge to open the door and punch him in the face, I took a deep breath and answered him.

"Nope, I got home an hour ago and no one was here," I said. Dad swore under his breath and he retreated downstairs to watch his hunting show. I resumed my movie.

Beside me, my blackberry started to vibrate. I had three text messages.

'Hey. R U okay? Didn't answer my text earlier ... needed help on math homework, I suck LOL. If u want to meet up for study sesh with me let me know! – Alex'

'Sup, bro. Sorry I missed your call. I was with Alessandra. Made her my girl- its official! :-D Time to double date! Woop! – Nico'

'Want to go out tonight? Super bored, and want to play a pickup game of ball. Shoot me a text if you're down. – Cody'

I didn't really feel like staying home with my dad still here, so I opted for basketball. I quickly dialed Cody's number and made some plans to ball up. As I put my sweats on I re-read my messages and sighed. As much as I liked Alex, I didn't feel like talking to her right now. I needed some time with the guys to clear my head from today. I grabbed my keys and walked downstairs. My father was sitting in his brown recliner drinking pop. He saw me heading to the door.

"Where do you think you're going?" he growled. I didn't feel like fighting tonight- I just didn't have it in me.

"Dad, I'm going out to play basketball. You know how to reach me," I said heavily. I never understood why he acted like he cared about where I was going.

"Whatever, Justin... you see your mother you best let her know I'm lookin' for her!"

"Okay, dad." I shut the door behind me. I was tempted to ask one of the boys if I could crash at their house, but I didn't want to put that burden on them. I finally got to the park and could see the boys already playing. I jogged over to where Frank and Kosta were sitting.

"Hey, buddy!" called Nico. He ran over and gave me the handshake. I nodded my hello and walked onto the court as I took my sweatshirt off. Basketball with my crew was my escape from this crappy home life. We continued to play basketball with made up scenarios well into the night.

It was about eleven PM by the time we finally stopped playing. We were all tired, and we needed to take a breather. Since it was Saturday, we all decided we were sleeping at the Cave. I dialed my mom's cell phone number to let her know I was staying out.

"Hey mom it's me. I'm just letting you know I'm staying out at Kosta and Nico's tonight."

"Alright, are you coming home tomorrow?" she said. She sounded tired and was probably eager for a drink.

"Yeah, at some point... I'm going out on a date tomorrow night so I won't be home until later, though." I waited for her answer. I could hear her drinking something and my heart sank.

"Okay, well... good night." She hung up on me, clearly not wanting to hear me anymore. Michelle's voice rang out in my head as I recalled what she had said about my mother not wanting to be saved. As much as I didn't want to admit it, it was true. She didn't need my help, because she was perfectly content with her messed up life. She didn't want her son and daughter anymore; she just wanted her drinks strong and cold.

"Justin, you okay?" asked Cody. He'd come to stand behind me while I was on the phone.

"Yeah, just family stuff... it's not a big deal." I shrugged my shoulders. I just wasn't ready to let my best friend know yet. I knew he shared painful recollections with his sister with me, and I was glad to have that insight, but this was something I had to deal with as best as possible. "When I figure all this out, I'll share it with you," I said smiling.

"Alright, man... do what you have to do. We all have your back," he said. I gave him a hug in gratitude. Kosta beeped the horn to signal Cody to get in the car. I followed in my car. After this weekend, I was hoping that I could get my work hours pushed back so I could focus on football for the last couple weeks of the season. I had to end early because we were starting basketball two weeks early. I persuaded Cody to play ball for the school since we didn't have a hockey team.

At the Cave, the boys all started talking about what they were doing for Halloween with their girlfriends. Cody and I kind of sat there, taking in the conversation. Nico and Lissa were going as a cowboy and cowgirl. Frank and Amanda were going as Batman and Robin while Kosta had tried persuading Spencer to be Ronnie and Sammy from Jersey Shore. She had laughed in his face apparently, and decided they were going as a police officer and a criminal. Nico looked at me after telling the crew about his decision.

"What are you and Alex doing for Halloween?" he asked me. I threw a pillow at him.

"Dude, I'm just taking her on a date tomorrow. I'm gonna take it day by day," I replied, even though I wished we could do the corny couple dress up. Those were my favorite parts of relationships. I'd never admit that to any of the guys, but the small, cute things boys and girls do for each other was what I loved.

"Ha-ha, alright, Justin, whatever you say." Nico threw the pillow back at me. Tomorrow, I was going on a date with the beautiful Alex. I needed to sleep, and plan where I was going to take her. I wanted to make sure that this was one of the best dates of her life, one that she'd never forget. I suddenly got the perfect idea. I smiled to myself. Maybe tomorrow would go flawlessly after all. I was one of the last of the crew to fall asleep, as I was busy planning out things to do with Alex. As long as the weather stayed mild and sunny, we wouldn't have a problem.

CHAPTER SEVEN
Alexandra

I couldn't believe how nervous I felt. We were going on an official date, and the fact that it felt right, made me jittery. I tried on several different outfits while Kat, Marco, and Dan were on chat, to get their opinions.

"Mmm, no, girl. I liked the cardigan with the scarf and leggings," said Marco. He was more flamboyant than Dan, even though Dan liked fashion more. It was irony at its best. Kat was still shell-shocked that Justin and I progressed this far with Cody's consent. She had been so sure that Cody wouldn't allow it because of the bro code. At least she was happy that I seemed more settled in Union. "Just remember, Alex," she said. "This could be a good thing or a bad thing. Take it day by day, sweetie. It's okay if you don't want to date." She was always the motherly type.

"I'll be okay, Kat," I replied. I threw off the little, knitted hat I was wearing. I'd flat ironed my curly locks so that they were completely straight. My make-up looked natural because I didn't want to look like I was overdone. On the computer, Dan was looking through magazines.

"Why don't you throw something together that looks like this?" he asked. Dan held up the page to show a fierce-looking model wearing an off the shoulder shirt paired with leggings and tall heel boots. The model's belt was around the shirt on the outside, giving the shirt just the right amount of pucker. I fell in love with the outfit.

"Dan! You might be right on this one!" I yelled. I ran to my walk-in closet, silently blessing his sense of style. Marco and Dan would never lead me astray when it came to clothing. I wished they were with me in Union because they'd come shopping with me and tell me what would flatter my figure and what wouldn't. A pang of sadness hit me because I missed them so. I didn't have a silk, off the shoulder shirt, so I opted for a cotton, long shirt that I quickly cut to make it fit appropriately. I fastened my boots up and put the knitted hat back on my head, paired with my knitted scarf. I walked out of my closet and to my webcam.

"Wow! Alex, you look gorgeous!" exclaimed the trio. I couldn't help but smile. I finally felt beautiful. Next to my sister, people would always exclaim that McKenzie was the beauty of the family. She fed into that attitude, and dyed her beautiful chestnut hair, blonde, and went tanning. She adopted this "superior" attitude and acted as if everyone else in the family wasn't good enough. When she met Justin, it was evident that she'd rather see him with her, than me. She even mentioned him in a letter she had written to Cody! 'Oh, Cody... how is that good-looking friend of yours doing? I don't remember his name, the one that made our sister a sandwich... I don't know why he would do that; she's more than capable of making food herself, the lazy girl. Anyways, give him a big hello for me! Love you!' She was stupid, for lack of a better phrase.

"Thanks, guys!" I meant it. They were the most honest

friends a girl could ever ask for, and if they didn't think I should go out on a date wearing a certain outfit, I'd listen. "You guys helped, so all the credit goes to you." Marco actually blushed. Kat and Dan, being the Russians they were, just shrugged off the compliment and changed the subject.

"So, what do you think you guys are going to do?" Kat asked. She was hungry for details - ones I couldn't divulge because I had no clue myself.

"I already told you! I have no idea..." I sighed. I wished I knew. That way, my nerves might calm themselves.

"He didn't mention anything about tonight?" probed Dan.

"He told me nothing. All he asked me was if I was free Sunday night because he wanted to take me on a date." I looked at my clock by my bed. Six fifty-five. My heart raced. He'd be here in five minutes!

"Guys! I have to go! He'll be here any minute!" I said my goodbyes quickly and signed off. I was sorting through all of the clothes on my bed looking for my purse when I heard my doorbell ring. My heart started beating faster. Cody was working tonight, and my mom was out again, suspiciously. I took a deep breath and walked down the stairs. I didn't want to seem over-eager, yet I didn't want the kid to wait too long. I stopped outside of the door and took another breath before answering.

Standing on the doorstep had to be the cutest boy I'd ever seen. Justin was wearing really nice jeans, and a dress shirt, unbuttoned with a white tee shirt underneath. In his hands was a bouquet of flowers. He smiled as he held them out to me.

"These are for you," he said shyly. I smiled, trying to keep the "aww" from coming out. I held the door open for him to come in, but he stayed where he was. "Come on, we're going out tonight."

I nodded and went to grab my keys. I put the flowers in a vase and left them on the counter in the kitchen. When I walked back out, he was waiting by the passenger side door. "After you," he said. I got in, feeling more nervous than ever. Was I really this bad with guys? I always thought that I was fairly decent around them, but with Justin, all of the presumptions flew out of the window. Once we started driving, I decided to ask what was up for tonight.

"So, what are we doing?" I looked at him from my seat. He seemed so calm about everything, like he'd done this plenty of times. He probably has, I realized with a sudden drop in my stomach. My nervousness was replaced with sadness. What if I was only meant to be a notch on his belt? I supposed I'd let the evening play out.

"I figured since you love horses so much, we'd go for an evening ride," he said smiling over at me. He'd remembered I loved horses! This was something I wasn't used to; that's for sure.

"Ah, are you sure? We're dressed up kind of nice, and we're going to smell..." I chuckled nervously. No, Alex. I couldn't be letting a boy affect me so badly... I tried not to remember what happened when I let it the last time.

"I couldn't care less," he laughed. "Clothes were made to be washed, and so were bodies. Getting dirty doesn't bother me." He looked over at me. "I mean, if that's not what you want to do, we can always find something else," he said quickly. It seemed as if Justin was pretty nervous himself, now that I took a closer look. That settled the score a little bit in my mind.

"No! I don't mind at all, silly. I was just wondering because of what we were wearing. Are we going to my stable?" I was hoping we were because I could always give Celtic another workout.

"I thought it'd be nice to go there. There's a catch though..." he said trailing off. I was suddenly on guard. There was no way my clothes were coming off.

"And what catch would that be?" I leveled.

"You need to teach me how to ride. I have no idea how to work those things," he said. I had to laugh. How does someone from Kentucky not know how to ride horses? Kentucky is horse central!

"Okay, fair enough," I giggled. "But if you fall off, don't put any blame on me!" Justin pointed a finger in my direction.

"Hey- don't laugh. If I go down, you're going down with me!" he mocked and threatened me with a wink. I rolled my eyes, but some of the nervousness was starting to disappear.

"Yeah, you can bring me down- if you can catch me!" I joked back. Justin chuckled and shook his head as a mock gesture. He pulled the car over and shut the engine off. The look of surprise must've been the reaction he was waiting for because he explained, "I think we should go out to eat first, so we don't smell like a horse at a restaurant. Is that OK?" I smiled at his thoughtfulness. We were in Cincinnati now, at a fancy looking restaurant.

He held the door open for me as we walked in. Justin walked over to the Maître' D and told him the reservation name. The man nodded briskly and led us over to our table. It was swanky, almost like something you would see in Boston. I sat down opposite Justin and looked at the menu.

The menu had a lot to choose from: Italian entrees, desserts, appetizers and more. I couldn't decide, so I opted to order whatever Justin was having. He was carefully studying the menu as well, and by the look of his face, he couldn't decide between two choices. "What do you think sounds better, Alex? Spaghetti with garlic sauce or with a side of meatballs?" I contemplated this.

"I would think spaghetti and meatballs," I said. I didn't admit to him that garlic sauce wouldn't turn out too well after the meal was over. Justin flashed me a smile and closed the menu. "Alright, spaghetti and meatballs it is, then. What're you ordering?" he asked. I placed my menu on top of his.

"I decided to get whatever you were getting. I've never been here before," I admitted, even though he knew that already. The waitress came over shortly, and we placed the order for food. She'd left us some bread and dipping oil, but it didn't really appeal to me.

"So," started Justin. He looked over at me. "Tell me something. What made you attracted to me?" At first, I thought it was a trick question, but when I looked at him, I could see the sincerity in his eyes. It was almost as if he needed to know, that he was worth liking.

"Well," I thought. What did make me start to like him? I

could count many things, but I couldn't sit there and name them. That would make me look really odd. "I liked… the fact that you were a gentleman to me from the very start. It made me feel as if I could trust you," I said carefully. The truth was, I did trust him- but only a little bit. Guys can be particularly good, or bad, at lying. I was still judging him. I felt like he could be telling the truth, seeing as Cody was his best friend. There was no way of being one hundred percent sure, though.

"My grandparents taught me how to treat girls," he said simply. "You treat a girl the way you'd want your daughter to be treated. I always treat a girl with respect, dignity and honesty. Wouldn't you want a boy to treat your daughter that way?" Justin spoke so quietly; I felt myself leaning in to hear him. What he said threw me. Where were these types of guys in Boston? I smiled back at him. "Well, of course. Your grandparents seem like very nice people, then." Justin grinned.

"Of course they are! They're the parents I never got to have," he stopped suddenly. I saw him look down at the table. Instinctively, I reached over the table and lifted his chin.

"Hey," I said softly. "Talk to me, what's wrong?" Justin turned his head away and remained silent. I didn't press the issue because, at that moment the food arrived. The look of sadness on Justin's face vanished as the plate of spaghetti was placed in front of him.

"This looks wicked good!" he exclaimed. I smiled enthusiastically and began to eat as well. For the rest of the meal, we chatted about the people around us. From the woman wearing a wig to the right of us, to the man trying way too hard to get the number of a bleach blonde girl with fake boobs And the conversation about his home life never once reappeared.

When the meal was over, Justin refused to let me pay for half of the bill. We drew the attention of the people around us because I had childishly grabbed for the bill, and he responded by tickling me on my side, so I giggled loudly. I didn't care. I was having the time of my life. We were still laughing, by the time we got to the car.

"I bet the lady with the wig was appalled," laughed Justin. He wiped his eyes. "Her mouth was seriously hanging open when we made a scene." I nodded in response, still laughing at the memory of her surprised face when Justin had tickled me and paid the bill before I could surrender my money to the waitress. We took the highway back to Union, headed to the stables. I thought about how I was going to teach Justin how to ride. It was darker out now- it was nine fifteen.

"How do you expect us to go horse riding now in the dark?" I asked as we approached a stoplight.

Justin looked at me, "Oh, you're right," he said gravely. "It's way too dark out now for learning. I guess we'll have to go on another date someday then." He winked at me, which made the butterflies start up again. "But first, would you like to come to my football game tomorrow night? We're playing Ryle High, my old high school. I'd like it if you came and supported me," he said. I grabbed his hand, which was resting on the middle compartment as if he was waiting for me to do that.

"I'd love to go! I haven't been to a game in so long, and as long as I get to wear your jacket, it's a date." I thought about my sudden boldness and wondered if I had said too much. Thankfully, however, he seemed delighted at the offer.

"Well, of course, you'll wear it. I wouldn't have it any other way!" he tickled my side once again, and I giggled. Seriously, it was funny how much Justin had an effect on me. I barely giggled before, and tonight I was full of them. It was like I was morphing from Alex- the guarded girl to Alexandra- fallen in love. I sobered at the thought of love. It was impossible, to even, think that. What good would that do me? Love wasn't something permanent. It affected you like a disease and then left you with side effects. It ended in sadness and heartbreak and in my case, pain.

We ended up at the woods area, where the bonfire was. It was different now that it was not lit with the seven-foot fire, and hundreds of kids. I liked the fact that it was peaceful. We walked hand in hand for a few moments before he spoke.

"My grandparents raised us because my parents couldn't." I looked at him, a little shocked at his sudden confession. "My father's abusive, and my mom's an alcoholic because of it," he said flatly. Justin looked at me with sad eyes. "He used to beat my sister as well, and we fought. I still live there, but I got my sister out. I live there for my mother's sake, but I'm actually not sure she wants to be saved." He laughed humorlessly. I felt the tears bead up in my eyes.

"Justin, I... I didn't know. I'm sorry," I couldn't think of anything else to say, so I decided the best way to express how sorry I felt, was to show it. I pressed my lips to his softly. It wasn't a passionate kiss, but the meaning behind it was understood. After we had broken apart, he let me hold him in an embrace for a while. Even though it was a sad thing to hear, I couldn't help but admit this was the best part of my date. It proved that he was only human and that everyone goes through their own horrific ordeals. I knew how that felt- but I could never imagine having someone as close as family harm you in any way.

I supposed he thought tickling me would lighten the mood, so I was attacked by a flurry of fingers to my sides. I laughed and tried to get away, to no avail. I laughed until I couldn't breathe, and when we stopped, we laid down on the ground to look at the stars.

"You see that one, right there?" he said pointing to a mass of stars. I squinted up at the night sky to look at a blob.

"Yeah... the one that looks like grated cheese?"

He laughed. "It's the Big Dipper. It contains the North Star, the one that leads you home," he explained. I turned so I could look at him.

"Home is where the heart is," I said. "Not a specific place, you know. So, technically it can't lead you somewhere. But, if it could, where would it lead you?" I thought about where it would lead me. Would it lead me back to Boston or Union? I waited for Justin's answer.

"Home is where the heart is..." he repeated slowly. "Well, then I guess the North Star would lead me to you." The look of utter seriousness set in his face made it known to me that he was by no means joking. I have never heard anyone say something that sweet, ever. Joking around, my friends say corny things to me. But, to be completely serious was something different. I didn't want to ruin the moment by saying, 'I meant if it could lead you somewhere not someone,' so I opted, for the kiss, he was leaning in to give me. It was like nothing I've felt before. It had passion, longing and hope mixed with desire in it. My head had found its way to his shoulder as I snuggled against him; for once in my life I was feeling safe.

All of a sudden, his phone started to ring. He fumbled for it and looked at the screen. It was his sister, Michelle.

"Hello?" he said into the receiver. He listened to what was being said on the other end. From where I was sitting, it sounded like she was really excited about something. He hung up shortly and turned to me. "I guess my grandparents got my sister and I a puppy," he explained. "Oh, and they also want to meet you. Apparently my sister heard from your friend Lissa about us, and they want to meet "Justin's girlfriend,"" I looked at him. Were we at the relationship stage yet? I didn't even know what to call us.

"Oh, is that what they say?" I teased. "That I'm your girlfriend?" Even as I said the word, I felt shivers down my spine. My body felt it before I could process what that meant- I wanted to be his girlfriend. Justin laughed.

"Don't worry, I'll clear it up. I'll have to introduce you as Alex, my future girlfriend. Is that better?" I nodded my approval and moved closer to him so I could put my head on his shoulder. We remained sitting there together, just looking at the stars. When I looked at the clock on my phone a while later, it was eleven-thirty. Justin sighed, and then stood up.

"We should probably go," he said. "We have school tomorrow." I reached for his hand, and he pulled me up. The rest of the ride home, I kept yawning. I felt bad- I didn't want him to think I was bored. It was a quarter to midnight when we finally pulled up to my house. The light in Cody's room was on, but that was it. My mother must still be out, or in bed I thought. I got out of the car, and on to my pathway. Justin came to me and gave me a hug.

"Thank you for tonight, Justin. I had a lot of fun," I said. I meant it, too. He smiled and grabbed my hand.

"Well, I'm glad as well. I had more fun with you than I have with anyone in a long time." He kissed the back of my hand. "The game is at five-thirty tomorrow. I'll give you a ride if you like, and we can plan our riding day." I confirmed my answer to him as I walked up the stairs. I waved goodbye and walked inside. I was barely to the stairs when I heard a knock on the door. Grinning, I opened it and was surprised to see, not Justin, but Deanna de la Garman standing on the doorstep. A very pregnant Deanna.

"Where's Cody? I need to speak to him," she hissed quietly. I stood there and gaped at her swollen stomach.

"What on earth do you need to speak to him for at this hour? Couldn't you have called him? Why the hell are you even here?" I asked. Deanna looked down at the ground before leveling with me.

"Because I'm pregnant, if you haven't noticed," she said dryly. "I'm six months pregnant, and I thought it was time Cody knew. He's the father."

CHAPTER EIGHT
Justin

Considering, the fact that we didn't get to go riding, I still thought that the date went really well. I'm pretty sure Alex enjoyed herself; as did I. I wanted to be sure she was comfortable around me, which made me less hesitant to tell her about my home life. Come to think of it, I never even told Jenna about my situation. I never had her over unless my family was gone, or I would take her to my grandparents' house. I wished I asked Alex about her dating past, though.

Even though Cody already mentioned it, I wanted to hear it from her. I swore to myself if I ever saw that Dean kid, I would rip him from limb to limb. After I had dropped her home, I stuck around long enough to see a pregnant-looking girl go up to their stairs. I wondered if that was their cousin from Louisville. I drove home; elated that I was a few steps closer to making Alex my girlfriend.

She had accepted my offer to come to my football game the next day, which I saw as huge. If we won tomorrow against Ryle, I could take her with me to the Victory party that all of the seniors throw each year after we defeat Ryle. Last year was rough, however. We lost in the last quarter with thirty seconds on the clock. Ryle's quarterback made a perfect throw to their tight end, and they got the touchdown. I was so angry at the fact we lost. This was the year it was going to change.

I got home around midnight and hopped into the shower. It felt good to let the warm water run down my shoulders. My parents were already asleep when I got home, so I didn't have to worry about bothering them. Once asleep, my parents wouldn't budge if a bomb blew up right next to them. When the water ran cold, I got out of the shower and changed into my sweatpants. I looked at my phone- I had two text messages.

'Guy, we have some major prep to do tomorrow to get ready for Ryle. Practice right before is cancelled, we're going to talk strategies. - Kosta.' I penned a quick reply back to him confirming that I will be there. My next text was from Alex.

'Call me as soon as you see this. Flipping out, majorly, right now.' I was worried. What could've possibly happened since I left her at her house? I called her cell phone, and she picked up immediately.

"Justin," she said. "Did Cody ever tell you about his ex-girlfriend, Deanna?" Her voice sounded strained as if this phone call wasn't supposed to happen.

"Yeah, why?"

"She came to my house tonight... She's with Cody now. She's claiming that the baby is Cody's. She can't be right, Justin. My brother would never be that careless. I know him," she finished in a whisper. I know Cody too, and I'm pretty sure he wouldn't be careless like that.

So that was the girl who I saw approaching the house. "I know that. She has to be making it up," I said, caught between trying to cheer Alex up and figuring out if it was true or not. There was silence on the other end of the phone. We were both stumped.

"What if it is true though?" Alex said slowly. "I mean, what if Deanna is telling the truth? It isn't impossible- whenever they had sex, if he didn't have condoms, they'd take other precautions. He'd tell me... Oh, Jesus. I can't be an aunt right now! He isn't even ready to be a father! Justin, what is going to happen?" I could hear the sadness in her voice. I felt so bad for her and their family. They've gone through so much, in so little time. This was not something they should be dealing with right now.

"Listen to me, she had another boyfriend since Cody right?" I asked even though I didn't know if this was true.
Alex said, "Yes. My ex-boyfriend, Dean."
My heart nearly stopped. Dean? The same boy who'd hurt Alex? I had to be careful how I addressed my words now. "Well, then it has to be his baby. When did Cody and Deanna break up?"

More silence. "I think they broke up in May. It was just before we moved here." I could hear Alex walking up stairs. "Ah, look, I'm sorry this is very abrupt. I have to go. We'll figure this out soon. Thanks for listening to me; I'll see you tomorrow! Good night, Justin!" And with that, she hung up. I was completely confused. I felt like I should contact Cody, but I decided against it. If he wanted to share with me, or the crew, he would. I didn't want to get Alex in trouble, either. I slid my phone to silent and hopped into bed. I had a big game tomorrow to focus on. My best friend's baby drama would have to wait. I drifted off into a deep slumber, with thoughts of babies playing football dancing in my mind.

The next morning, I woke up to my mother standing over me, smiling. "Good morning, sweetie!" she said brightly, as she opened my curtains to let in a stream of bright light. I groaned and covered my head with a pillow. Why was she in my room, and why was she so chipper?

"Are you alright, mom?" I asked her. "You seem.... off today." She flashed a big smile.

"Sure, honey! Today's a big day for us. Guess what?" she said, bouncing down on my bed. I looked at my clock- it was five forty-five in the morning. What could possibly make today a big day for us?

"Okay, what?" I asked, clearly humoring her. I know her well enough to know that even if I didn't ask, she'd tell me anyway.

"Justin, sweetie... We're moving! You and I will finally live in a nice house in California. I figured that would help you with your football career," said my mom. We're moving? As in, without my father? I didn't want to move to California, though.

"Mom, moving to California won't help me if I'm being scouted by colleges here. Let's move into a different house across town. Isn't Dad coming with us?" I asked. My mother's eyes fluttered down to the bedspread.

"Well, fine. We can stay local, I just... I'm done with your father... I'm sick of that monster treating us like crap," she said coldly. "I'm done drinking and I don't want a wife beater living in my life. Hurry up, and pack. I want to be out of this dump before he comes back from his hunting trip." she walked across the room to the door. She only paused long enough to look back at me and smile. I could barely believe it. My mother finally took a stand for herself! She's leaving my dad! My father left this morning around four thirty for a five-day fishing trip. That means, tonight after my game I'd have to pack and get ready. Maybe I could get the crew to help me. I got ready for school quickly and made it to Alex and Cody's house within twenty minutes. When I got there, I saw a man leaving. On guard, I approached him.

"Who are you?" I asked. The man looked to be in his late 30's, maybe even early 40's. He wore a suit and tie. His salt and pepper hair was neatly coifed.

"Ah, you must be the boyfriend. I'm Peter Bradley," he said, extending out his hand. I grasped it and shook. He had a firm grip.

"Uh, yeah. Nice to meet you, I'm Justin." I looked at him again. "Are you the landlord?" He laughed and shook his head.

"No, I'm a friend of Connie's. Nice meeting you, Justin." He smiled once more, and off he went. Confused, as usual, I shook my head and walked up to the door. Just as I was about to knock, Connie answered the door.

"Oh, Justin!" she said warmly. "How are you? I haven't seen you in a little while. Cody's up in his room. I don't think he's going to school today, though. He's got company." She didn't look too happy about his company. I headed up to Cody's room. I knocked on his door, which was slightly ajar. He called for me to come in, which I did. Sitting on his bed, was the pregnant girl I could only assume was his ex, Deanna. She smiled when she saw me.

"Oh my, aren't you a cutie," she purred. "What's his name, Cody?"

He scowled over at her. "Alex's boyfriend," he growled. "Leave my friends alone." The tone of his voice shocked me. I never saw him disrespect a girl in the months I'd been close to him. I was appalled to see his change of character. On the other hand, if she was pregnant with his kid, after all, flirting with his friends and dating his twin sister's ex-boyfriend doesn't make her look good.

"Dude, I got to talk to you," said Cody. "Alone." I nodded and followed him to the hallway, in which we went into his mother's room. I waited for him to speak.

"That's my ex-girlfriend, Deanna," he said heavily. I looked back to where his door was still slightly open. "She came last night- she thinks her kid is mine. I'm trying to rack my brain to think if it really is, but I don't know," Cody sighed, running his hands through his hair. "I dumped her in May, and it's October... Last time we even did anything was in April, which was six months ago..." Cody trailed off his sentence. This didn't look good in his favor; I had to admit.

"Cody, I need a drink! Ginger ale, please. My stomach is going crazy!" called Deanna from the other room. Cody grimaced and shook his head at me.

"I'm going to kill her. This baby cannot be mine, I am not going to be tied to her for the rest of my life." Cody opened his mother's bedroom door. "Go get one, yourself! Cranky bitch," he muttered the last part under his breath. He led me out of the room and downstairs, where I saw Alex eating a bagel at the table. I smiled. She returned the gesture and waved.

"Hey, Justin!" She jumped down off of her chair and walked over to me. She looked drained, as though she'd been up all night. She gave me a quick hug and addressed her brother. "You stay home today, and take care of her. Text me if you need anything. We'll figure this out, I know it's not yours." Cody nodded in her direction and gave me the handshake.

"Have fun today, and good luck against Ryle tonight man," he said. He walked up the stairs, and the muffled yelling began almost instantly. I felt so bad for Cody. I now understood why he broke up with her. I turned my attention to Alex, who was looking at the mail on the table.

"Oh, I guess my sister has a boyfriend now," she said conversationally. She put her hair behind her ears and continued to read her sister's letter. "It says here that his name is Michael, and he's in ... Oh, he's in a fraternity." Alex frowned. "Typical McKenzie. She will forever be the stupidest girl I have ever met." She threw the letter down and walked to the door. "Are we ready to go?" she asked. I nodded and followed her out to the car.

Once we were on the way to school, I decided to ask if she was alright.

"I mean, I'm okay," she started. " It's just.... My brother can't be having a baby right now. Especially, not with her. Did Cody ever tell you she tried fighting me the last day of school for me in Boston?" The alarmed look on my face clearly told her Cody never told me.

"Wait, you got into a fight with your Brother's ex-girlfriend?"

94

That was definitely news to me. Alex didn't seem like the type of girl to try to fight another person.

Alex chuckled. "Yeah. She pulled my hair back and tried to go at my face. All I had to do was duck and uppercut her in the face. I broke her nose, and she had to plug it up with a tampon," she said as she burst out laughing. I couldn't help but laugh too because the thought of that pompous girl having a tampon up her nose was pretty funny.

When we got to school, we saw Kosta and Spencer sitting on the back of his pick-up truck. When he saw me get out of the car, he ran over to me and barreled into me.

"Yo! Are you ready to cream Ryle today? I am so PUMPED!" Kosta jumped off me and helped me off the ground. I got up, and gingerly rubbed my butt. Ever since Cody had moved here from Boston, we'd picked up on some of his words.

"Yeah, I'm ready. Either way, the season's over for me if we win or lose because I have to move." Everyone, including Alex, looked at me with open mouths.

"Wait, where are you moving to?" asked Spencer. She slid off of the back of the truck and came up to me. "You're not moving out of state are you? What about Alex? Your friends?" She said quietly to me. I shook my head.

"We're staying in Union. My mother's leaving my dad, so we're just getting a different place to stay." I figured no one would really know about what was going on- except Alex. It was a little weird having someone know the truth about the family, but at the same time, it was a relief. I had someone to talk to if I needed to. The bell to signal school was in session rang, and we all went our separate ways for classes. I reminded Kosta that I would be there right after school was over, so we could talk strategies with the team. Kosta and I were named captains back in the end of July. Since I played basketball as well as football, I had to stop the season once November hit so I could get ready for my real sport.

School went by so slowly. All day long, people kept wishing us our good lucks. But by the end of third class, it was getting unbearable. I didn't want to hear about us beating Ryle; I wanted to actually do it. In English class, I heard Mandy and Jenna talking about the game. From what I heard, Jenna was single again. But I didn't care. Alex was better than any girl I've ever met.

"Hey, Justin." Mandy called to me from the opposite side of the room. We were in study groups, and she was paired up with Jenna. "Can we talk to you for a minute?" No, you can't, I thought to myself, but I decided to be polite.

"Uh, yeah sure." I got out of my seat and walked to their table. They exchanged a whisper as I was making my way over. "What's up?"

"I decided to give you another chance at being my friend," Jenna said. "I feel like you've earned it, and seeing as Isabel, and I split, it would be okay." She looked at me. "And besides, you've gotten even cuter since last year." She looked over at Mandy and smiled while turning to give me a wink. I was floored. Was she really stupid?

"Yeah, that's alright. I'm all set, with the girl I'm seeing now. Thanks, though. Give my regards to your future girlfriend!" I turned around and walked away. When I got to my seat, I could see Jenna's face beet red, and she was glaring in my direction. Whatever. I had Alex, and there was no way I was going to give her up for Jenna.

Thankfully, the rest of the school day went by a lot quicker than the first half. I couldn't wait to see Alex. Since I had a strategy meeting right before the game, I could only see her at the lockers as school ended. That's where I found myself heading as soon as the last bell chimed. I spotted Alex standing near Nico's locker, with Lissa. Now that they were an official couple, everyone was waiting to see when I would make it the same with Alex. I didn't want to do that in their time, though. I wanted to make sure it was on our time.

"Hey, beautiful! You all ready to get going? I can drop you off at your house on the way to the strategy meeting, or I can take you with me. You'll be about an hour early for the game, though. What would you like to do?" I handed her my captain's jacket. "It's all yours," I kissed her forehead.

Alex laughed softly. "Thanks, I'll be sure to wear it tonight! Um, if you can drop me off at my house, I'll just take the car over to the game. I want to see if Cody wants some freedom, anyway." She put the jacket on over her sweater, which in my opinion, made her look ten times more beautiful. "Just give me a few, Lissa and I need to use the bathroom before we head out," Alex said. The girls walked away, leaving me, and Nico standing there.

"When are you going to admit that you're in love with Alex?" asked Nico. He leaned against the locker, to get more comfortable as we waited for the girls to come back.

"What are you talking about, man? I'm not in love with her; I haven't even made her my girlfriend yet," I said defensively. The truth was, I could see myself falling for her. I just didn't want to cross that bridge just yet. Nico must've known what I was thinking because he dropped the issue. Unless it was the fact the girls were coming back, which it probably was.

"Sorry that took a little while," said Alex. "We saw your cousin Hana, and we started talking. If you're ready to go, I am too." She gave Lissa a hug goodbye and waved to Nico. We left the school and found that a light drizzle had started to fall. This type of weather wasn't uncommon, and it made for better games, in my opinion. It had a challenging feel to me. I unlocked my car and told Alex to wait in there for a moment while I went to see if Kosta was bringing the papers and waters.

I couldn't find him anywhere, and it was getting late. I decided to just wait and talk to him at the meeting and proceeded to walk to my car. In the parking lot, I spotted Jenna near her Buick. She gave me a dirty look and stalked away. I shook my head. Thank God I wasn't with her anymore. I smiled at Alex as I hopped into the car and drove away.

"You know Jenna Feiffer?" asked Alex. She was looking through her bag to find something.

"Uh, yeah I used to date her last year... Why?" I asked, somewhat alarmed. How did she meet Jenna? She contemplated her answer.

"I heard her talk about you in the girl's bathroom this morning; that's all. I didn't know you two had a past. Isn't she a lesbian now?" I didn't know how to answer, seeing as I didn't talk to Jenna. I just shrugged my shoulders and turned some music on. I hoped Jenna wasn't going to drive a wedge between Alex and me already. Alex's phone started to ring. "It's Cody!" she exclaimed. "Hello?"

I couldn't hear what he was saying, but from the tone of his voice, he still sounded aggravated. Alex's face registered confusion momentarily before relaxing into relief. I tried to ignore their conversation, but I was worried for him too. Cody was one of my best friends, so of course I wanted to know what's going on with psycho and him. Shortly after, Alex hung up the phone and turned to me.

"He's going to take her to court after he's taken a paternity test. Cody said that if it's not his child, he is going to try and get her charged with entrapment and false accusations," she said smiling. I breathed a sigh of relief as well. He must really be sure that it wasn't his kid.

"Good, this girl needs some psychological help," I agreed. "Just try not to fight her anytime soon, babe. If it is Cody's kid, we don't want to mess it up, so it turns out like her, do we?" I winked, giving her a nudge. She rolled her eyes at me but laughed.

"Either way, it's going to come out messed up, it's Deanna's kid! But, thank you for the ride. I'm going to see if Cody wants to come tonight. Deanna is going maternity clothes shopping with my mom today anyway," Alex said dryly. "My mom doesn't like her at all, but I think if she thinks the baby is really Cody's, then it's her grandchild." I pulled up to her beautiful house. She grabbed her bags and kissed me on the cheek. "Good luck tonight! I'll be the one in the jacket rooting for you," she smiled. I smiled back at her as she got out of the car and retreated into her house.

I'm usually a good driver and follow the rules of the road, but I was running late for the captain's strategy meeting. Being one of the captains, I should be there. I sped down the road to the football field. When I got there, I was five minutes late. I ran over to the field house just as Nico was getting there.

"At least I'm not the only one late," said Nico. "You ready to wipe the floor with Ryle?" I nodded back, and we entered the field house to assess strategies that could help us win. This year, it was our year. Ryle had an air of arrogance when it came to us Cooper kids. I should know- I went there my freshman year. It's not like I hated the school, but the rivalry was so high during this time; it was hard not to get caught up in it.

If we won tonight, I'd have made my senior year as football captain the absolute best. All other thoughts in my mind, including Alex, disappeared from my mind, as I got ready to prepare for the biggest game of the season.

CHAPTER NINE
Alexandra

The whistle blew loudly as Randall K. Cooper High School trekked back on the field after they used their last time out. There were seven minutes to go in the last quarter, and Ryle was up 28-24. Tensions were high as they got into their formation. I was sitting with Spencer and Amanda, Frank's girlfriend. Since everyone, minus Cody, in the crew played football, we would tend to group together for events.

Amanda was pacing back and forth, while Spencer remained stony-faced. If you asked me to tell you the rules of baseball or hockey, I could commentate for you. Football, on the other hand, was like another language to me. Spencer had to explain some of the rules to me throughout the game. I watched Justin try to rush the ball past Ryle's defensive line and fail. If they could get just one touchdown, we'd win by two points. Kosta, who was a wide receiver, was trying to call for Justin's attention. He was wide open, and he had a clear shot at Ryle's end zone.

Why isn't Justin responding? I said to myself. Looking at the clock, we had three minutes left. "Justin! Pass the ball!" I yelled. He couldn't hear me from where I was standing, but it was like he did. No sooner did the words pass from my lips did he throw the ball to Kosta who jumped up and caught the ball. He ran the last twenty yards and threw the ball down in the end zone with a yell. The crowd responded ecstatically. They did it- it was 30-28!

They needed to get this PAT and hold the score for the next two minutes, and they'd win!

Both teams got ready at Ryle's end zone. The field goal kicker, a sophomore named Roland, prepared to make the kick. Since they didn't stop the clock when they were getting ready, it was now forty-five seconds until game over. Roland nodded to the punter, who held the ball for him, and kicked. It was like it was moving in slow motion. Everyone's heads turned slowly to follow the ball as it soared through the air. When it passed through the end zone, everyone held their breath for a second. The noise was deafening.

Amanda, Spencer and I were screaming as loudly as the rest of the crowd. I hugged Spencer and we ran down to the field to congratulate the boys. We made our way through the ruckus and I ran smack into Justin.

"Whoa, sorry! I didn't mean to-" I stopped short when I found out he was exactly the person I was looking for. "Justin! You did it! We saw everything; you guys did amazing at the end!" I gushed. Since I knew next to nothing about football, I decided I was going to play it safe when recounting to him. He smiled at me and picked me up in a big hug. Justin twirled me around and set me down.

"No, I think it was my lucky jacket. We wouldn't have won if my beautiful girlfriend hadn't been wearing it," he replied. My heart skipped a beat. Girlfriend? He grabbed my hand. "That is if she'll have me." I looked into his hazel eyes. Right then and there, I think I decided I could trust him. I smiled and gave him a kiss. Justin seemed to think that was a good enough answer because he held onto my hand and led me to the rest of the team.

"Do you want to go to the victory party with me? We won't stay long," he asked me.

"Oh, I wish I could," I said sadly. "I promised Cody we would get some homework done. He hasn't had time because he's been dealing with Deanna." Justin looked disappointed but understanding. He kissed me on the cheek and offered to drive me home, which I declined. I had driven here myself, and he should be celebrating instead.

"I'm keeping your jacket, though," I told him. He smiled at me and playfully shoved me toward my car.

"Gosh, miss. Only ten minutes into dating and you're already mesmerizing me into staying away from friends," he winked. "Go on, get outta here and go do homework. Call you later?" I smiled and nodded. Yes, he could definitely call me later.

When I got home, Cody and Deanna weren't in sight. Since I promised Cody I'd help with homework, I waited for a little bit and then decided I was going to call Kat and tell her about what happened. I felt as though I lied to Justin. I know I hadn't, but I still could've gone to the party with him. When I logged on, I saw a few others, but Kat, Marco, and Dan were offline. A hollow pit in my stomach formed. It was a Monday night, I realized.

Back when I lived in Boston, every Monday night we'd go out to eat at a restaurant in the North End. It was our way of making the beginning of the week less painful. That's why none of them were online right now. I signed off and picked up my cell phone. I dialed my brother's number and waited for him to answer.

"Hi, Cody's not here right now, so go away and bother someone else." Deanna's voice was shrill, almost like she'd been crying. I seriously did not like this girl.

"Hi, give the phone to my brother or I'll find you and punch you in the nose again," I replied coldly. I heard her suck in air in surprise, but I didn't care. I was sick and tired of her being rude to me. "I'm waiting, Deanna. Seriously, you're not his girlfriend. You're not his baby mama, even if your sick mind wants to believe that. That's Dean's kid. Stop pretending it's Cody's because we figured it out. You cheated on my brother with my ex, and you don't want to admit it, so you came here pretending that the baby is Cody's. It's not!" I yelled. I heard her sniffling, but I continued anyway.

"You think whoring around makes people like you, but it doesn't, Deanna! It makes you a slut. Okay? You're a big, nasty slut that no one likes, because she's as rude, as she is slutty. Do you think dressing like a hooker makes guys want to fall in love with you? Well, it doesn't. It makes them want to use you. Congratulations, Deanna. You've been used. So, don't take it out on my brother and the rest of my family and use us because you know we're nice enough. Go home, Deanna. Stop making my brother's life a living nightmare!" I breathed deeply. Everything I'd wanted to say to her had finally come out.

By now, I could hear Deanna sobbing. Truthfully, I started to feel bad for her. I couldn't say sorry, though. She needed to hear the truth. I heard muffled noises at the other end, and then I heard my brother's voice.

"Jeez, Alex. What did you say to her that made her that upset?" Cody sounded indifferent.

"Well, I just told her the truth, honestly. I told her that her kid isn't yours. It's Dean's." I heard him breathe in as if getting ready to argue this. "No, Cody. Don't even fight it; it's the truth. She cheated on you remember? One of the reasons you broke up with her? She cheated with Dean- that's how I figured out it's his kid, not yours. Besides, I didn't even call to talk about this. I called you to see when you'd be home so we could do homework like we planned." Straining my hearing, I realized there were people in the background. Cody said something to someone before answering.

"Uh, we can later Alex. I took Deanna to the doctors. After I take her to the hotel room, I'm going to the victory party. I thought you'd be there already, anyway."

"I bailed because I promised you I'd help with homework... Thanks for bailing on me instead. Have fun with your girlfriend, bye." I'd hung up the phone before he said anything. Deanna always brought out the worst in Cody. We'd always been close, but, the period when he was with her was when we fought the most. She never liked me, and I never liked her because of her attitude and how she treated my brother and my family.

I felt bad now; my brother was going to the same party I skipped out on for him. I sent a quick message to Lissa and Justin telling them the situation, but neither of them replied. I wasn't bothered by it, though. It was his night to celebrate with his team and his friends. He didn't need me around to babysit. I didn't drink or smoke, so I'd be sitting there while he mingled with those who did. It was weird to call him my boyfriend now, however. I found myself wondering how long it would last. Would we fight? Would we break up? How would we break up? I knew I shouldn't be thinking those thoughts, but given my past, I didn't have much room for a positive outlook on relationships.

I went on the family computer for a little while watching movies online.. It was the latest craze and everyone was hooked. I watched trashy reality shows for a little while, but eventually I got bored. After an hour, I'd showered, braided my hair, and gave myself acrylic nails. I flopped on my bed, completely bored. Cosmo magazine had nothing in it, and I'd already ordered and received my Halloween costume for tomorrow. The clock told me it was eight thirty. By now, the sun was going down. I had no time to visit Celtic.

I told my mom I was skipping school tomorrow to catch up on sleep. She originally said no, but she's working until seven, tomorrow night. How would she know?

I heard the front door open, and voices filled the air. It sounded like my mother and a male voice. I wondered who that possibly could be. I remember my mom had a guy over this morning, but I was under the impression he was just a colleague. I was seriously starting to doubt that, judging by the laughter coming from my mother.

I crept near the stairs so I could get a better angle to listen from. Hearing the words they spoke gave me the impression they had no inclination anyone was home. The voices were getting louder, and with horror, I realized they were coming upstairs! I ran into my room and shut the light off just before the man from this morning walked past, carrying my mother in a sultry way. He was kissing her neck, and I heard the bedroom door shut and rustling sounds. That was the most disgusting thing ever. NO kid, whether you are eighteen or forty, wants to hear their mother getting it on.

I quietly padded my way downstairs and into the kitchen. Why did I have no clue about my mother's new love life? I figured after my father, she'd just live her life alone. It never occurred to me that she would find someone else.

On the kitchen table, I saw another letter from McKenzie. I didn't even bother to read it, but instead I decided to give her a call and see if she knew what was going on.

"Hey, you've reached McKenzie's voicemail. I'm obviously too busy to answer right now, so leave a message after the beep and I'll get back to you. Ciao!" - BEEP.

"Uh, hey McKenzie, it's Alex. Your, uh... Sister. Anyway, um so mom has a guy over. Sleeping here. I was wondering if you had an idea as to what was going on. Give me a call when you can, I guess. Love you, bye." I hung up, feeling stupid. I obviously knew what was going on upstairs, but my question was: who was this man and why else was he here?

The next thought that ran through my head was how I'm going to pull off skipping school now? Was she still going to work? I sighed to myself. This man was already ruining my Halloween plans. I heard the front door open. Cody, Justin and

Frank walked in. They started to say hello, but I cut them off with a finger to my mouth.

"Shhh, she'll hear you!" I pointed to the upper level. "Mom's in bed with some guy... She came home like twenty minutes ago," I said. Cody's mouth dropped in confusion.

"Like, she's having sex with him?" he asked. I rolled my eyes at him.

"No, I thought they were just playing Sudoku," I replied drily. "Obviously, she is. I mean, he carried her up the stairs kissing her neck. I was scarred for life." Frank and Justin laughed. Justin walked over to me and engulfed me in a hug.

"Well, be scarred no more, princess. I'm here to save you!" He chuckled, but I was honestly glad they were all there. When he let me go, I looked at my brother.

"Are you going to school tomorrow?" I asked. He shook his head.

"I'm taking Deanna to the airport. She needs to go home, and I told her we're doing a paternity test as soon as the baby's born. She said no at first, but I told her if not; I won't even pay child support." I had to hand it to Cody. He was being so strong about this. The boys went into Cody's room, leaving me alone once again. I decided I was going to attempt to go up to my room; hopefully whatever my mother and that man were doing was over.

I was just about to go upstairs when I heard someone call my name quietly. It was Frank. He motioned for me to come over, so I walked over to him.

"Does your brother know Justin made you his girlfriend?" he asked. I shook my head. "Please don't hurt Justin; he's been hurt before, more than you know. We all think he's in love with you- he won't admit it, but we think it's true. So please go easy on him."

He was in love with me? What? That couldn't be possible. People don't fall in love with me. I'm not good enough to fall in love with. People always fall in love with my sister because she is gorgeous and outspoken. Girls fall in love with my brother because he is a romantic. I wasn't any of those things, so why would anyone want to fall in love with me?

"Don't worry, Frank. Nothing is going to happen." I walked away from my brother's friend and retreated to my room.

I must've fallen asleep, because when I came to, it was seven forty A.M. I groggily rubbed my eyes and rolled over in bed. Since I never formally got ready for bed, my window was still open, showing it was a sunny but crisp day. I shivered under my blanket. I decided the best way to see if I was able to skip school was if my mother went to work or not. If she didn't, I was going to tell her I was going, with Cody, to take Deanna to the airport with him.

Jumping into some slippers, I opened my bedroom door as quietly as possible. My mother's bedroom door was open, and I sighed a breath of relief that she had work today. I went back into my room to grab my bathrobe and headed downstairs. Cody must be making Deanna breakfast, I thought. I smelled bacon. I went to go say hi to my brother, but I stopped short.

"Hi, honey!" my mother's cheery voice cut through my foggy head like a knife. "Hurry up and get dressed! You'll be late for school." My mother smiled at the man sitting in my brother's chair, and put French toast on his plate with bacon. He smiled back and looked at me.

"Hey there, Alex. I'm Peter, your mother's boyfriend. It's nice to formally meet you." I gave him a polite smile, but that was all. My mother had a boyfriend now? Since when? I decided to address my mother about school instead.

"I'm not going to school today, Mom. I told Cody I would take Deanna back to the airport with him, so he doesn't have to make the drive back to Union alone." I meandered over to the bread container, hoping my mother would offer me French toast. She didn't. Instead, she gave me a stern look.

"Get it out of your head, Alexandra. You're not staying home," she said with finality. I wasn't going to back down.

"But, mom!" I whined. "Cody's stayed home twice already, and I haven't even missed a day! I'm not going. I need to get things done for tonight. Why do you have to play favoritism? If I wanted to deal with that, I'd have stayed with dad!" I stormed off, not caring whether or not if I hurt her feelings. I wasn't usually a mean person, but everyone always got what they wanted, except me. If Cody needed a personal day, he could stay home. But if I needed one, I was forced to go to school.

I went up to my room and slammed the door. In the end, I showered and got ready for the day. Since it was Halloween, I dressed up in black jean leggings and an orange tunic top. I straightened my hair and fish tail braided my bangs to the side of my head. I placed Dan's earrings on my dresser and traded them for pearl studs. I didn't want to chance anything happening to them. I normally don't act in defiance, but I walked straight down to my mother and her boyfriend to tell them I was staying home.

When I got to the kitchen, my mother and Peter had already left for work. In their place sat Justin, Frank and Cody. They were eating bagels while talking about yesterday's victory party.

"You know, it's crazy to think Deanna's finally leaving Union today," remarked Cody in between bites of his cinnamon bagel. "Too bad she's leaving. If she wasn't so rude all the time, she'd be likable." Frank nodded in agreement.

"Oh, I know. Amanda was telling me that she was going around with a glass of champagne yelling at some of the girls who were standing with their boyfriends," he chuckled. "I thought pregnant girls aren't supposed to drink though."

"They're not," Cody frowned. "She was drinking ginger ale because she was complaining of morning sickness feelings. I thought that only happened in the morning." While they were discussing pregnant girl details, I sidled next to Justin, who was remaining unusually silent. I nudged him as I sat down.

"Everything okay?" I asked. He nodded silently and continued to eat his raisin bagel. I knew better than to press the issue, so I let it go and ate my toast as silently as he was. A few moments passed before he spoke.

"I can't go out tonight, Als," he sighed. "My mother wants to move out of the house before my father gets home on Friday, so we need to pack quickly. Frank and Cody are going to help me after we take back Deanna to CVG. I'm sorry- I know you wanted to dress up and go out." Justin looked genuinely disappointed. I felt my heart tug.

"Hey, no. Shhh. Don't worry about it. I'll help if you like. I want to meet your mother anyway; I bet she's a nice woman." I smiled at him, hoping my eagerness to meet his family would show him that I understood how he felt. Not too long ago my family uprooted from Boston to here, so I was no stranger.

"Thanks, I'm sure she'll be happy to meet you." He kissed my forehead and grabbed our plates.

Cody grabbed his keys and went out to start the car. The three of us filed behind him, climbing into the back seat. Deanna came out shortly with her bags and a pout on her face. The ride to CVG was a quiet, awkward one. Deanna kept shooting me evil looks, and the boys kept glancing at one another through the rear view mirror.

"So.... How's Boston, Deanna?" Justin asked. She glared at me again before turning to answer him.

"Oh, you know. City life never sleeps with parties, clubbing and nightlife. Something you guys would have no clue about," she said sweetly. Cody looked at her.

"Stop, Dee. You don't need to be rude to my friends." She pulled her face in a look of shock.

"Whatever do you mean, Codykins? I was just being honest." I gritted my teeth. It was time for the sister to step in.

"Stop with the superior attitude. If you've realized, we are bringing you back to the airport because no one in this car wants you here. You open your mouth, and people don't like you. Learn to be nicer, and maybe you'd have a chance." Deanna's face actually registered real shock for a moment. She opened her mouth to speak, but then closed it again. For once in her life, Deanna de la Garman was speechless.

Cody chuckled quietly in the driver's seat. He turned the music up so the drama would cease. Justin reached for my hand, and gently held it with his own. I looked up at him, embarrassed by my behavior. He surprised me by giving me a wink, however. I smiled and turned my head to look out the window.

We waited in the car while Cody took her to the terminal she had to leave from. The boys thought it'd be funny to park the car somewhere else, so Frank hopped in the seat and moved the car two rows back. We all enjoyed the laughter from the confused look on Cody's face when we tried to open the door of someone else's Prius. Frank moved over to the passenger side to avoid being slapped on the head. He failed.

"Very funny guys, you're such the comedians," Cody muttered. I decided this would be the perfect opportunity to ask him about what was going on with Deanna and him.

"Well, it's complicated, Alex. Deanna was my first love, and that can't change. But I do not have any romantic feelings for her whatsoever. She can't handle that. She thinks she can come in and out of a relationship as often as she wants without any reaction by me. She cheated on me with Dean, and now she's pregnant. Half of me believes it's Dean's. The other half of me, unfortunately, believes that the baby's mine. The timing would be correct. I'm doing a paternity test just to be sure though," he sighed.

"Well, is there anyone in Union that caught your eye, then?" I asked. I wanted my brother to be happy. He didn't deserve all of this misery. Frank and Justin looked at him as well.

"Well, uh, no. No, there isn't. Sadly the ladies don't want me," Cody replied. Something about his answer was off, I realized. Call it twin-tuition but he was hiding something it seemed.

When we got to Justin's, I was surprised at his mother's appearance. She was thin, and she looked like she was sixty years old. Earlier, he had told me she was only forty-eight. It must have been all the years of drinking that had made her look older.

"It's very nice to meet you, Mrs. Barry," I said politely. She smiled back at me and said, "Oh, no, the pleasure's all mine, dearie! You can call me Laura. Mrs. Barry is Justin's grandmother." Justin rolled his eyes, but smiled and gave his mother a hug. She nodded her head toward the house.

"Come on, let's get going. We only have a short amount of time." we followed her up the stairs and into the house.

Seven hours later, we finally got the last of Justin's bed onto the pick-up truck. Laura had made us some pink lemonade, my favorite drink, and we relaxed as we watched little kids and their parents walking from house to house trick or treating.

"Will you kids be alright to walk to the new house?" asked Laura. She wiped the sweat off of her brow and took a sip of the lemonade. When no one was looking, I caught Justin sniffing his mother's cup to make sure it was still non-alcoholic.

"I brought my car, ma'am," Cody quipped. "If you want, I'll drive us all over there, and we can walk back and wheel the stuff over that won't fit in our cars." Laura beamed at my brother, and we were off. The sun was setting by now, and the air had turned chilly. I shivered in my tunic top. Justin must've noticed, because he slipped his arms around me and guided me to a box near the trunk of our car to pull out a sweatshirt. I gratefully gave him a kiss, and snuggled into the warmth of his sweatshirt. Frank had elected to take the Prius over to the new house so that Cody, Justin and I could wheel the last bit over.

"Once we get done wheeling this over, you guys can go. I'm sorry I kept you guys from having a fun Halloween," Justin apologized as we walked down a woodsy path.

"Are you kidding me? Who trick or treats now anyway? Not like we were going to go to any parties. I got to spend the day with my brother, my friend, and my boyfriend. What more fun could I have had elsewhere?" Smiling, he grabbed my hand and kissed it. Cody pretended to gag, but he was smiling too. I grabbed some leaves off of the ground and tossed them over at the boys.

"Hey, what was that...?" I said out loud to myself. I squinted my eyes into the distance because I swore I saw someone watching us. Cody looked around too, but saw nothing. We kept walking for a quarter of a mile before we saw anything else.

"Look guys- it's shiny!" I picked the shiny something off of the ground to inspect it. "It looks like a bullet shell," I muttered.

Just as I was about to turn around to show the boys, I heard a gunshot. I froze and turned around in alarm to see Justin fall to the ground with blood dripping out of a wound on his chest.

I screamed. "Justin!" I ran over to where he'd fallen and grabbed his head. Cody stared in shock. "Please, stay with me! Justin don't close your eyes, it will be okay. It has to be okay," I said over and over, crying. "Cody! Call 911! Hurry!" The tears down my face didn't stop. Justin looked up at me dazed and confused.

"I'm not.... going anywhere," he panted. It took a lot of effort for him to breathe. "Don't leave me..." he whispered before he lost consciousness. I broke down then and stayed with him until the ambulances came and took him away from me, making me have to break my promise. My brother held me in his arms as I cried, hoping that when the hospital called, it wouldn't be too late.

CHAPTER TEN
Justin

The last thing I remember before everything went dark was her face. The light surrounding her made her look like an angel. Maybe it was an angel, I was seeing. I felt cold, like the warmth draining out of my body was a virus. The area surrounding me was getting dimmer. I faded in and out of consciousness. I tried to hold on for as long as I could before the darkness overcame me.

When I was coming to, I could hear distorted voices coming from all around me. I could feel a dull pain in my chest. Opening my eyes was a chore, but once I managed they adjusted to the light, I saw people huddled around my bed. Faces that seemed familiar, but my brain was foggy from the medicine tap I was connected to, so everyone's names evaded me.

Then, I saw her. It was the angel I remembered from what seemed like so long ago. They noticed I was stirring, and the girl rushed over to me.

"Justin! You're awake, it's a miracle!" She hugged me tightly, and when she pulled away, I saw her face was shining with tears. The girl smiled at me. I racked my brain trying to remember her name as she spoke again. "How are you feeling?"

I was feeling confused and groggy, but I don't think that was the answer she would want to hear. "I'm feeling a little better, thanks." My answer made her smile wider while her tears kept falling. I didn't get it; why was everyone crying in relief?

The girl leaned in and gently kissed me. And then it hit me. Every memory came flooding back with the kiss. Alex. I remembered her name, remembered Cody and the boys. I remembered moving. I remembered getting shot.

"Alex," I whispered. She looked at me and nodded.

"I'm here, honey. I'm here. I didn't leave you once. I was by your side the whole time. I had to admit we got worried you would never wake up at some point," she admitted quietly. I was puzzled. How long was I out?

"Wait, so what happened? All I remember was getting shot," I said. Alex and my mother exchanged a glance.

"Well, honey," my mother started. "You were shot in the chest, and by the time you got to the hospital, you'd lost so much blood, you needed a transfusion. Cody and Alex, luckily, had the same blood type as you, so they alternated donating blood until you had what you needed." My mother took a breath before continuing. "The doctors couldn't get your body to cooperate with healing, so they kept you in a medically induced coma so your body could heal."

I looked at Alex, who had gauze pads on her arms. "You really donated blood for me? Why?" She looked around, embarrassed.

"Well, I mean I figured if it were the other way around, you'd do the same for me. I couldn't let you die," she whispered. She bit her lip and walked out of the hospital room as Cody came in. He looked back at her before laughing to himself. My mother excused herself, leaving us alone.

"I love Alex!" I blurted out before I could help it. "Her hair, her eyes, her freckles. I love it all. I love her personality and everything about her. I am so in love with your sister, man." I couldn't believe what I just admitted, but if I had almost died, there wouldn't be a better time.

Cody looked at me for a moment before answering me. "Yeah, I know. We all do, bro. And we all know she loves you too." Quizzically, I thought for a moment. She loved me too? I mean, it certainly seemed like she cared about me if she donated her blood to save my life, but at the same time, it seemed as if she still was closed off.

"Yeah? She told you this?" I asked him. He shook his head.

"No, but I'm her twin brother. I know her better than she knows herself at times. I've never seen her look at anyone the way she looks at you. When you were in the coma, she literally only left to go to school and to shower." I sat up suddenly, causing me to wince in pain.

"How long was I in the coma, Cody?" He bit his lip, trying to think of the best way to answer me.

"Three weeks." I stared at him. "You were shot Halloween, and today is November twenty-first. We thought your heart had stopped twice because your pulse was so faint," he added. I was in disbelief. I was in a coma for three weeks?

"When is Thanksgiving?" I asked him. Cody got up and looked at the nearest calendar.

"It's the twenty-fifth," he answered. He sat back down and looked at his phone. I slumped back into my bed. I couldn't believe that. Why did this have to happen?

"So, you said Alex never left here?" Cody nodded.

"She didn't want to leave. She thought your attacker was coming to finish you off," he chuckled. "Either way, whether that was her true reason or not, she stayed." I attempted to laugh, but it hurt my chest. It was a dull pain, like it was weeks into healing, but it was truly uncomfortable.

"Do you guys know who my attacker was?" Now that I asked, I wasn't so sure I wanted to know. I think Cody felt the same, because he hesitated a while before looking at me.

"Well, here's the thing," he started. "They caught him a while after you were in the hospital, but he escaped. They tried to catch him, but they're still searching." I was starting to get antsy. That was all well and good, but who was it?

"Well, they'll find him, but who was it, Cody? Was it someone I know?" Cody didn't look me in the eyes when he answered.

"It was your father, Justin...." He trailed off quietly.

"What? You've got to be kidding me, why would he shoot me? Is this a sick joke?" My dad was abusive, but would he truly shoot his own son? "Besides, he's away on a five-day trip."

Cody grabbed a piece of paper from the box next to my bed. "I know, but one of your father's friends found out you and your mom were leaving, so he came home to stop you. He wasn't in time, so he went looking for you. Remember the shiny something Alex found? It was his bullet shell. He saw us watching, and he aimed for Alex. He wanted you to be punished too, but he missed and hit you. Both your mother and mine are pressing charges for attempted murder." I looked at his face, searching for a joke, but I saw none. Instead, I saw regret and anger.

"How do you know all of this?" I asked slowly. Cody handed me the piece of paper.

"Your father admitted to everything after they arrested him. The affidavit was scripted by the police. When they were transferring him from the station, he bolted. Your mother has a copy, and so does ours." It was taking me a while to take all of this in. My father wanted to kill Alex? He didn't even know about her. My only guess was he saw us holding hands, and instead of killing me, he wanted me to suffer. In the end, he missed and shot me anyway.

"Why did this have to happen?" I said again sadly. "I mean, I'd rather be in this bed than Alex. But still, she shouldn't have to worry about herself."

"I don't think she's worried about herself. She's worried about you, even though she refuses to admit it. Try talking to her when she comes back, and see what you can get." Cody stood up and stretched. "I uh, have to be somewhere soon. I'll come back later after everything is settled. You good, man?" I gave him the handshake and watched him walk down the hall. Leaning back into bed, I drifted off into a nap, dead to the world.

When I woke up a few hours later, the sun had set. I called the nurse so I could get some food, but she had told me I needed to be introduced to solid foods slowly. Alex was there as well, quietly napping on the couch. Her homework was strewn everywhere, and her books were heaped in a pile of disorder.

I sat there and watched her sleep. She looked so peaceful; it was like she was from heaven. And when I was with her, it felt like heaven on earth. I knew that ever since I laid eyes on her at papa's, I'd fall in love with her. I never knew how quickly and how true that statement was until now.

She stirred a little while later. Her eyes fluttered open and she slowly looked around to see if I was awake.

"Good evening, sleepy," she said sleepily. She stretched and walked over to the side of my bed. I patted it and made room for her to sit down. "Did you have a nice nap?"

"I could ask you the same thing," I said chuckling. "How was school?"

"It was okay, I guess. Everyone is just waiting for you to come home. Your fever seems to have broken," she said as she felt my forehead.

"I had a fever?" I asked. She nodded. And for the next few hours, Alex told me every little thing I've missed since being in the coma.

By the end of the night, I learned that everyone at Cooper had heard about my getting shot, and who had attacked me. People were sending care packages to my mother's new house for us. Alex and Cody were doing fundraisers to help my recovery. I felt my eyes brim with tears when I heard how much they were doing for me.

"Really Alex, you don't have to do any of this for me," I said. "I'll heal anyway. The doctors told me that since I came out of my coma, my body has been responding to the medicine and my wound is almost fully closed." She shook her head.

"I don't care. I want to help. It was my fault you got shot to begin with, and I can't live with the fact that you almost died." I laughed.

"How do you figure it's your fault? You didn't do anything wrong. My dad just doesn't want me, or my mother, to be happy without him. He could tell I cared about you, and he didn't want me to feel that," I said quietly. "But he missed you and got me. I'm glad he hit me. I can get him back for that. I couldn't imagine what would happen if you got hit by that bullet." She held up a finger to my lips to quiet me.

"Shhh. I doubt your father wanted to take away your happiness," she replied. Alex kissed my forehead. "Your happiness can only come and go from you. No man or woman can get rid of that- only you." She smiled at me. I was getting aggravated. She wasn't making sense; nor, did she understand what I was saying.

"Yeah, I get that," I said impatiently. "But you don't know my father. He hit my mother and sister. He hit me. Seeing me happy with a girl I love would be the perfect opportunity to make me miserable." I saw her eyes widen when I mentioned the word 'love'. Her surprise was only there for a moment, and then was gone just as quickly.

"I know, I know. Shhh. I'm not trying to make you mad, Justin. I'm just trying to help you rationalize. I feel like it's my fault because I wanted us all to walk instead of driving and because we were in the woods, he got that chance. I could've lost you...." she shook her head. "Look, I'm sorry. I'm just going to go. I'll be back tomorrow after school. You need to rest. I'll see you then." Alex gave me a quick kiss and left the room.

Somehow, I felt relieved that I admitted to her how I felt. At the same time, I felt confused at her reaction. Was Cody right when he said she felt the same? I just couldn't read her sometimes. I wasn't tired because of the nap I had taken earlier, so I paged a nurse to help me shower.

Taking off the wound dressings, I saw raw, pink skin around where I was shot. It was healing fine, but it would leave a scar. I remembered when I first came out of the coma, I heard the doctors tell my mother that it was a miracle I was alive because of where I'd been shot. Once it closed, however, it would heal fairly quickly.

The shower was refreshing, but exhausting. Once I was showered, I was so tired that I fell straight asleep, dreaming of finally being home.

In the days that followed, I did school work with Cody, Frank, Nico and Alex. The flux of people visiting kept me busy from when I woke up until I fell asleep. Kosta and Spencer visited from time to time, but he worked more than the rest of us. Cody took my doctors' note to Papa's, so I was excused from missing work.

The nurse told me on Wednesday I was able to go home Black Friday. I was pretty disappointed that I couldn't spend Thanksgiving with my sister and grandparents like I usually did.

The next day, Alex and my mother surprised me with a turkey dinner in my hospital room. Cody, Alex, my mother, Michelle, and my grandmother huddled, in my room, to eat.

"I'd like to give thanks to the Lord above for saving my grandson so that he can continue a life for himself and keeping our dysfunctional family together," my Grandmother prayed. We were saying Grace, something that my family always did every

Thanksgiving. Alex was sitting on the bed with me while Cody and the rest of my family had chairs.

"I want to give thanks, too," I said as I grabbed Alex's hand. "I want to thank God for a beautiful, amazing girl who stuck by me when I needed her most." I turned and looked at her. "You have impacted my life for the better since meeting you this summer, and I am wholeheartedly thankful that I can call you my girl. I love you, Alex." I kissed her cheek as the rest of the room all smiled and said "aw". I looked at her face to see her reaction. She was smiling and had tears in her eyes. She didn't say a word, but the smile she gave me said it all. In my opinion, that was enough.

For the rest of the day, we ate turkey and watched football on the small television. Cody and my mother talked about colleges and where he wanted to go. Alex and Michelle chatted about horse-back riding. Alex agreed to teach Michelle how to ride horses if she taught Alex how to bake Apple Pie. My grandmother came over to me.

"Have a seat, Nana," I said as I moved over for her to sit on the bed. She shook her head.

"No, it's okay darling. I have to get going, but I wanted to say I'm proud of you. You did good holding on to our family and bringing your mama out of that mess. You also held on when your life depended on it, and you stayed around for Alex and the rest of your friends and family. You have a good one," she nodded in Alex's direction. "But you put her on the spot. Don't worry if she doesn't say I love you just yet. If she ain't ready to say it yet, it might put a strain on the relationship. Keep that in mind, Justin, baby." She kissed my forehead, and touched my cheek. My grandmother taught me almost everything I knew about life and love. I nodded.

"Sure, Nana. Thanks for coming today. It means a lot." She waved good-bye to the rest of the crowd and left.

"Your grandmother is something else," said a voice fondly, from next to me. I turned my head to see Alex standing there. My face grew hot; she had probably heard what Nana was saying about her.

"Yeah, she is. I'm sorry if I put you in an awkward moment back there. I wasn't thinking," I apologized.

"It's alright. You can't change how you feel. I respect your feelings, but that means you have to respect mine too. I care about you a lot, obviously, but I'm not quite there yet. Loving means leaving to me, and I'm not ready to lose anyone just yet. Please bear with me," she said. That troubled look was in her eyes again.

"Hey, it's no big deal, Al. I understand perfectly. There isn't a rush. I'm not into taking things fast, anyway," I joked, even though I was disappointed. She looked grateful, though. I couldn't help but feel happy that at least she was mine.

Even after everyone left that night, I laid awake just thinking of the future. I knew I had to have Alex in my life. I wasn't going to force her to love me, but I could be a better man to prove we weren't all the same. I was determined to get back at my father, too. All the pent up hate I had toward him, exceeded my tolerance limit when he aimed to kill. How far was this man going to go before he succeeded? I wasn't going to find out.

CHAPTER ELEVEN

Alexandra

Ever since Justin and I became official, I had noticed a rise in my popularity. Both Cody and I made more friends now that we were friends with the "now complete" crew.

Justin got out of the hospital the day after Thanksgiving. It was Cody and I's first holiday away from family. My mother had to work, and her boyfriend Peter invited us over. We politely declined. Cody and I came up with the idea to spend Thanksgiving with Justin because he was still in the hospital.

During the period when everyone said Grace, Justin announced to everyone that he loved me. It was a shock. I knew what would come next- a breakup. Isn't it that always how it went? They tell you they loved you, get what they want, and then leave you in the dust. Justin seemed to be different, but every case turns out the same. Boys never know what they truly want.

The day he got out of the hospital, I dismissed myself from school to go and get him. His mother, Laura, had to find a job so they could pay rent for the beautiful lando they'd moved into. I drove out of the parking lot and nearly hit Jenna Feiffer as she was pulling in. She slammed on the breaks and got out of the car.

"Are you blind?" she yelled at me. "Can't you see this is an entrance only? God, you Bostonians are so stupid!" I looked at her.

"You've got to be kidding me, right? There is no sign that

says 'Entrance Only,' and just because I'm from Boston doesn't mean we're stupid. It just proves you're ignorant...." I shook my head in disgust as I defended myself. She took a deep breath, and the hysterics began.

"YOU HAVE NO RIGHT TO BE CALLING ME IGNORANT, YOU GHETTO BIMBO! YOU'RE ONLY POPULAR BECAUSE YOU'RE DATING THE MOST WANTED GUY IN THE WHOLE SCHOOL! Don't worry, though. You'll be dropped to the curb in no time. He leaves girls after he sleeps with them. He's not even that good, anyway. Don't say I didn't warn you." She got up to my open window and was inches from my face. My first instinct was to hit her for down talking Boston, but instead, I pulled the ultimate act of satisfaction.

I slowly rolled up the window on her and drove away. I was pretty angry. Angry at Jenna for talking about my hometown, angry at Justin for being the exact type of boy that I didn't want to deal with and angry with myself for letting it get to me this bad. By the time I got to the hospital for Justin, I was fuming.

"What's wrong?" was the first thing out of his mouth when he got in the car.

"Nothing."

"I know you better than that, tell me what's wrong," he said gently. I drove away and let it out.

"I spent the last three weeks of my life, day in and day out, caring for you at that hospital, not knowing if I was even going to see you open your eyes again. And I find out that all you do is sweet talk girls into thinking you care about them, sleep with them and leave them! What kind of scumbag are you? I was so wrong to think you were different!" I erupted. He looked at me in absolute shock.

"I don't sweet talk girls into doing anything? I don't sleep with girls and then leave them, I slept with a total of ONE girl, and she left me shortly afterward, for another girl. I've only loved a total of two girls, one of them being you. I have never asked you, nor forced you to do anything with me, or even brought the subject up. Where are you getting this from?" he asked me. I suddenly felt horrible. Here I was, accusing him of something his bitter ex-girlfriend said when he has never lied to me before.

"Oh my god, I am so sorry. I should never have listened to her." I felt my face turn red from embarrassment. His face was still shocked, but his voice softened.

"Who? You shouldn't have listened to who?" I sat there for a while, debating on whether or not to tell him. In the end, I decided just to be honest.

"Jenna Feiffer," I said in a small voice.

"Jenna Feiffer," he repeated to me. "You really think listening to her is a good idea?. She was always manipulative and sneaky. She got mad because the day I asked you to be mine, she wanted to pick things up again, and I told her to take a hike. Why would you talk to her?"

"She almost hit me when I was leaving school, and said it was my fault. I'm sorry, Justin." I felt really bad. I could see the hurt in his eyes when I brought it up, and knew Jenna was lying. Why did I keep messing up?

"It's alright, I guess I would've questioned it too if I were in your position," Justin replied. He looked out the window to end the conversation.

The car ride to his new house was quiet. I couldn't tell if he was still angry with me, or if I was just over-reacting. When I pulled into the driveway, we both tensed up. His father was sitting on the steps.

"Well, well. She is a beauty, after all, Justin. Good choice," he called arrogantly. I got out of the car and walked right up to him, even though the very essence of my body screamed in protest.

"Don't you dare talk to him," I said in a low, dangerous voice. I could see amusement register on Mr. Barry's face. I turned around to see Justin trying to climb out of the car, but I shook my head.

"No. I'll take care of this," I said to him. I turned my attention back to Mr. Barry. He looked frail, like he hadn't eaten in months. His face was juvenile in appearance, almost like the face of a child on an older man's body.

"You'll take care of this? What is the problem, miss?" he smirked at me. I felt the anger boil inside of me.

"Do you realize you almost murdered your own son?" I shrieked. "You almost took the life of someone you brought into the world. How messed up is that?" I was in disbelief. He was laughing at me.

My phone started ringing.

"Go ahead and pick it up. I'll wait for you to continue," he said. I fumed on the inside once again. It was Justin on the phone.

"Do you need me to come out and deal with him?" he asked.

I felt it was better if Mr. Barry didn't know Justin was calling.

"No, Mom. It's perfectly fine. I'm just with Justin at his house. He has some company," I responded. I prayed Justin would play along.

"Stall him, then. I'm going to call the cops." I silently thanked Justin a million times over.

"Sounds good. I'll see you later!" I hung up the phone and turned to face Mr. Barry.

"Why are you even here?" I asked him. He lit up a cigarette and blew the smoke in my face. That made Justin angry because he came out of the car and walked over to us.

"Do you have any respect? Blowing smoke in a girl's face, you're pathetic. I've always wanted to tell you how much I hated you, and finally I can. I can't believe you wanted me dead!" Justin screamed. I was alarmed at how loud he was yelling, but held back as I realized he was finally letting out his feelings about all those years of abuse.

"You are the worst father I have ever known! Nico and Kosta's father is more of a dad to me than you ever will! When was the last time you congratulated me on winning a sports game, huh? When did you ever say, 'I love you, son!' You haven't. You hit me, Michelle, and mom. You're the type of person who deserves to rot in jail!" Justin was shaking with anger. I looked between the two guys. Justin's dad had a steely resolve to his face now.

"You really think I wanted you to die? Naw, that'd be too easy. That's a weak man's way out. I wanted you and your mother to suffer for what you've done to me," he huffed. I could only wonder what Laura saw in this man. "I wanted you to lose the one thing you loved more than anything, so you could see what you did. I wanted her dead and gone." Mr. Barry pointed right at me. I felt the color drain out of my cheeks. He wanted to kill me?

"You hold your tongue, you filthy excuse of life," Justin said in a deadly voice. I looked up in time to see Justin swing at his father. Fist hitting flesh, James Barry tried fighting back, but after a few well-placed punches, he fell down to the ground, knocked out by the strength of the blows. Justin kneeled over to catch his breath before vomiting into the grass. When he was done retching, he stood up and shakily walked over to me.

"Are you okay?" I asked. He nodded and looked over at the crumpled heap that was Mr. Barry.

"Yeah, the adrenaline rush was a little too much for me, but I'll be okay. The cops should be here any moment." I stood with Justin on the sidewalk keeping an eye on his father to make sure he didn't escape.

Ten minutes went by until the first police car appeared. Justin went over to the police officer and told them the situation. I got into my car and cried. Ever since arriving in Union, I've dealt with drama. I thought in a smaller town there would be less. I felt alone. My best friends hadn't contacted me in almost two weeks, Justin's father had attempted to kill me, and I didn't even have the slightest clue why. I sobbed harder, thinking more about the drama that passed. My family's move to Kentucky, Deanna and the baby, and Justin and his family issues. I heard a knock at my window. It was a police officer.

"Are you alright, miss?" he asked. I shook my head.

"I'll be fine, it's just a lot to handle right now," I replied. The officer told me to head home, shower, and take a nice nap to clear my head. I said good-bye to Justin, and went to the stables. Naps never cleared my head, but riding did.

I saw Celtic laying down resting, but she stood up when she saw me. I patted her velvety nose and handed her a treat before brushing her down. I rode her for a good two hours before I brought her in. By now, I could hear the rumble of thunder in the distance. I checked my phone. I had two voicemails from Justin.

"Hey, you called earlier?" I said as he answered the phone.

"Yeah, I wanted to make sure you were alright. I had no idea you didn't know about my father... Cody made it seem like you did," he apologized. "I want you to know you're always going to be safe with me. I won't let anything happen."

"I know."

"Do you want to come over? My mom isn't home from job hunting yet, and I know Cody and your mother won't be home for a while." I could hear a genuine tone to his voice.

I realized I didn't want to be alone. "Yeah, I'll come. I'm at the stables right now, mind if I shower there?"

"Of course not. I will unpack a towel for you," he replied. I smiled and hung up the phone. I must smell awful, I thought to myself. I got into the car and drove back to his new house as the rumbling clouds became more ominous.

As I pulled into his driveway, the rain hit hard. It was a torrential downpour, and for the first time in a while, I laughed just as hard. Justin came to the door and gave me a look of bewilderment as I stood in the rain.

"Come inside, Alex! You're soaked!" he yelled to me.

"What's the difference between this and a shower?" I called back. I ran to him and pulled him in the rain too. "I don't know why, but this kind of rain is my favorite." I twirled in the puddles that already formed.

"How so?" he asked. I smiled at him.

"Ever since I read the scene in *The Notebook* around this type of storm, I always wanted to run in the rain during one," I answered.

"I read that book too, and I don't remember them running around in any rain. I do remember something happening, though. I think it went like this." He picked me up and leaned me against the car and kissed me.

I wrapped my legs around his waist so he didn't have to hold all of my weight, and I kissed him back with enthusiasm.

It never occurred to me until we went back inside a half an hour later that he mentioned he read the book. I always pictured Justin to be that kind of guy who would watch the movie because some girlfriend made him, but I never pegged him to be one to read a romance novel.

"Yeah, it's kind of a guilty pleasure," he admitted. He peeled off his soaked shirt to reveal a six-pack that I never knew was there. I looked away, but he caught my expression. "I play sports and work out. You didn't expect me to be fat, eh?" I laughed.

"Of course not, but it caught me off guard is all. Do you have anything I can put on until my clothes are dry?"

He threw me a shirt and a pair of basketball shorts. I quickly undressed and threw my clothes in with Justin's in the dryer. We went back upstairs to make some hot chocolate.

"Have you ever tried hot cocoa with cinnamon and whipped cream?" he asked me. "It's my favorite way to drink cocoa. I won't have it any other way." I looked at him and bit my lip.

"It sounds amazing, but whipped cream can't be in it. Add the cinnamon, though. I'd like to try that." I sat down on the couch we had moved only three weeks ago.

"Why can't whipped cream be in your cocoa?" Justin asked. He grabbed the box of hot chocolate and stirred the packet into the water.

"I don't like whipped cream. I choked on it when I was five, and ever since then I've been turned off by it," I said. My father had sprayed each of us with whipped cream for us to eat, but it shot down my throat and I spluttered, almost certain I was going to die. I haven't eaten it since.

"Oh, well then no whipped cream for Alex, then. How about marshmallow fluff?"

"I absolutely adore fluff! Did you know it's only made in Massachusetts?" I asked him. He shook his head and spooned a few scoops of fluff into my caramel cocoa.

"I didn't until now," he laughed. Justin handed me my cup and went to turn on the television.

"Justin," I started. "Why did your father want me to die? Did I offend him?" I just couldn't understand it.

Justin grabbed my hands and moved my wet hair from my face.

"No, you didn't offend him. My father is a sick individual who thinks the world is only there to please him, and that's it. He didn't like the fact my mother stood up for us and left him, and he wanted to hurt the one thing I love. He believes in his mind that it's justice, but it will never get that far," he stated. "I won't let it, my mother won't let it. You mean the world to me, and I don't care who knows it. Maybe I declared my feelings for you a little early, but once you almost die, there is no time like the present." He looked into my eyes.

"I know you don't believe it, but there are good guys out here, Alex. I'm one of them." He kissed my forehead and went to go turn the shower on for me while I finished my hot chocolate.

"Waters ready!" he called from upstairs. I climbed the stairs and was handed a towel and facecloth. I stepped in the warm water and felt my stress disappear. The rain hitting the window made me almost want to fall asleep. I washed my hair with some sweet smelling shampoo and turned off the showerhead.

I just put Justin's clothes on again and went back downstairs. I saw him looking out the window at the storm.

"It's almost beautiful," he said. I walked over to him.

"What's beautiful? The rain?" I asked. He nodded.

"Yeah, it sounds nice. I could fall asleep to it. Care to join me for a nap?"

"Sure, I'm pretty tired." I replied. He walked over to the couch and pushed a couple ottomans to create a long enough space for us. I grabbed a blanket and cuddled up next to him. The sound of his breathing, accompanied by the rain, helped create the perfect lullaby to put me to sleep. Had I stayed awake for just five more minutes, I wouldn't have missed the phone call from Cody.

"Alex... wake up," called Justin, but it seemed off. It was like he was far away. I felt someone shake me and I jolted awake.

"Wh-what's going on? Where's the fire," I said sleepily. Justin answered by tossing my clothes over to me.

"Your brother has been trying to call you. He just called telling me Deanna had the baby." I sat straight up.

"Seriously? What is it?"

"He doesn't know. She is going to call when she gets time. The baby was born prematurely so it's got lots of problems." I looked at Justin's face.

"Should we go find Cody?" I asked. He nodded and opened the door. The rain was still pouring heavily, so we got soaked walking to the car.

When we got ahold of him, he told us he was at Frank's house. We rushed over to see him and ask what else was going on.

When we arrived, Frank and Cody were sitting at the table.

"How'd you make it through all of this rain?" asked Frank. We were sopping wet once again.

"Didn't you know? I bought a boat," joked Justin. He hung up his jacket and we sat down next to my twin.

I hadn't seen Cody this nervous since he was waiting to see what rank his hockey team back in Boston made.

"She said she was going to call me back an hour ago," he said. "I'm still waiting." As much as Cody disliked Deanna, a part of me couldn't help but wonder if he wanted the baby to be his. We all sat in silence for half an hour. No one wanted to say anything because he was already nervous enough.

Another quarter of an hour had passed before his phone rang.

"It's Deanna! Shhh!" he told us as he turned the speaker on. "Hello?"

"Barnes," came a voice from the phone. I felt my smile disappear, just as it always did when Dean's voice was heard.

"Where's Deanna?" asked Cody. There was static on the other end of the phone due to the storm, so Cody had to repeat his question. Meanwhile, I slid myself into the other room and covered my ears.

'No one has to know about this, Alex. Keep your mouth shut.'

The words hashed through my mind. I willed myself to listen to the conversation happening in the kitchen. Dean was yelling at my brother, and Cody was yelling back. Cody never liked Dean, especially when we dated. Cody was the only one besides Kat, who knew everything that had happened. I thought about sharing my secret with Justin, but I couldn't. He'd probably laugh at my weakness. That, or take advantage. I put those thoughts out of my head and quietly walked into the kitchen just as Cody slammed his phone down on the table, smashing the screen to pieces.

"Cody!" I said, shocked. He looked up at me, eyes red. I knew that look- he was furious.

"He only called to taunt me. Deanna is still in the room, and the tests are being done now..." he trailed off.

"What did he say?" My voice was barely a whisper. I didn't know what else to say. Dean was toying with this family. I looked around at Cody and Frank and realized Justin was no longer in the kitchen. "Where did Justin go?" I looked at Frank.

"He went outside. His sister called and I don't think what Dean was saying made him any happier," he said.

"What did Dean say, Frank?" I demanded. Frank opened his mouth to answer, but Cody stopped him.

"Don't worry, Allie. It isn't the truth, so don't worry about it," he said. Cody only called me Allie when he was trying to protect me from something.

"Well, I'm going out to find Justin," I said trying to keep my voice normal. But for the first time in over a year, I found myself wanting someone to tell me everything was going to be okay. I was just about to go outside, when a huge clap of thunder caused the power to go out. Kosta, Nico and Justin all ran inside as another wave of thunder hit.

"What a storm!" called Kosta. He threw his jacket on the floor and slid into the booth seat next to Cody. Cody handed him his broken cell phone. "Dude, what'd you do to your phone?" He started telling Nico and Kosta the story of what happened, but stopped.

"Allie, could you go into the other room, please?" Cody's eyes looked hauntingly at me. I was going to protest- say that he could say what happened in front of me, but Justin grabbed my hand and guided me into the dining room with him.

"What is going on?" I asked. When Justin didn't answer, I

turned around and walked back into the kitchen.

".... and Dean was just causing trouble, reminding me of what happened to Alex. He got into detail, too. About how he held my sister down and raped her, even though she was screaming. When she didn't stop shouting, he hit her with a beer bottle. He hit her over and over. Why would he go through telling me that again? He said he told the whole school we moved because she got pregnant by him and she was disturbed that he left her, despite her claims of love. Why would he do that to my sister?" I heard Cody sigh. Angered because of what Dean had put me, and our family through.

They knew. I stood there with my mouth open, frozen. Nico looked up and saw me standing there.

"Alex!" His voice was filled with genuine shock. Cody looked right up and saw my face.

"I told you not to be in here!" I just continued to stare, no emotion registering on my face, but a thousand running through my mind. I felt Justin's hand on my shoulder, but I shrugged it away.

"No one was supposed to know," I whispered. Cody got up and tried to hug me, but I stepped away.

"I know, Allie. I'm sorry. They overheard everything when he was on speaker. I didn't want you out here, because I didn't want Dean to get to you. I was telling the others because Frank and Justin heard it to begin with, and I don't want to keep things from them. They're our friends. You don't need to relive it. He was saying it to get to me, not you. I wish you listened to me," he said. I stepped closer to the door slowly.

"You didn't want me to relive it? Cody, I relive it every day. Every time I close my eyes, it's there. Every time I hear Dean's name, I think of him. Of what happened. Who are you trying to protect, Cody? Me or you?" I looked at him and shook my head. "Don't bother any more, it's over." I walked past Justin, not even giving him a second glance. I walked out of the door and ran.

The rain and thunder became my ally during my run home. It drowned out the many thoughts in my head that threatened to make me break down. I didn't stop running until I reached my house. As usual, the lights were off except the porch light. I unlocked my door and trudged up the stairs until I reached my room. I turned on the shower and got in, clothes and all. I wordlessly changed into dry clothes after and walked back downstairs.

Mom had left a note saying she was at Peter's and would be home around ten. It was nine thirty now. I picked up the phone and dialed without thinking.

"Hello?" I heard the voice as they picked up. I needed someone to talk to, and this was the only person I felt I could right now. The tears started to fall.

"Daddy? I need you."

CHAPTER TWELVE
Alexandra

"Honey, are you okay?" I was sobbing uncontrollably, and my father's voice was filled with concern.

"No, Daddy. They found out, they know." I took a deep breath to try and stabilize myself. I told him everything, from meeting Justin up until now. It felt good to get today's drama off of my chest. He asked the right questions at the right time and let me vent without judgment. It was like my old father was back.

"I'm so sorry, honey. I wished he'd gone to jail where the pervert belongs. Unfortunately, he got off easily. Try your best to ignore the taunts, sweetheart." I could hear him sighing on the other end of the phone.

"It's hard, Dad," I started to explain. "Justin knows, and all of our new friends know now. They'll look at me differently. I'm a freak," I muttered.

"Hey, now! You're not a freak. You're not the one who hurt anyone, or got off on it. You were a victim, but you came out stronger in the long run. If they're real friends, they won't treat you any differently." my dad said sternly. "You know you're better than that. Do you need to come home? You know you are always welcome here at any time. I'll book a flight for you, and Cody too." The offer sounded wonderful- to head back to Boston where my old friends and old life were waiting for me.

"I can't, Daddy. I have friends, school and Justin here, if I didn't, I'd be on the first flight back to Logan." My Dad laughed.

142

"I know, sweetie. I have to go, though. We're going out to dinner, but if you need me, I will always be available for you. I love you," he said. I said I loved him back and hung up. I felt better, but just wanted today to be over. There was barely any food in the cupboards, so I made a grocery list for my mother to go food shopping. I made a bag of popcorn and sat in the living room silently.

After what seemed like hours, I heard the front door open and saw my mother come in.

"Hey, honey. You're home early, is everything okay?" She had a rosy pink color in her cheeks, like she had the time of her life tonight. I didn't want to ruin that.

"Yeah, it's okay. I spoke to Dad and he said he would get flights for Cody and me to go visit whenever," I answered. Her smile faltered, but was back in a moment.

"Oh, that's nice! I'm going to go to bed. Hopefully the storm will pass by tomorrow. Goodnight!" she called as she retreated upstairs. I felt terrible for lying to my mother, but I didn't want her to worry about me either. As it was, I had enough people doing that for me.

A little while later, I heard the door open again and Cody appeared in the living room with the rest of the crew.

"Hey, you okay, sissy?" he asked. I nodded and offered the boys some popcorn.

"No thanks, Al. We're going down in Cody's room, see ya!" said Nico. He followed Frank, Kosta and Cody downstairs so only Justin remained. I didn't look him in the eyes.

"Hey," I said to him. It almost felt awkward, considering all that we went through today. He walked over to me and pulled me up into a tight hug. "Everything okay, Justin?"

"No, I'm worried about you," came his muffled voice. He let go of me and sat down on the couch, so I followed. "I've seen you close yourself off to certain feelings, but you scared me tonight. I thought I lost the Alex I know. Please don't disappear on me, I don't think I could deal with that." His voice was soft, but I could sense the urgency in it. "Talk to me, Alex. Get it off of your chest. I want to know your side of the story. I'm not going to lie to you- Cody told me about this a while back, but I didn't say anything because I wanted you to trust me and tell me on your own time. You were there for me in my time of need, so now I want to be there in yours." I stared at him for a moment. He already knew?

"If you already knew, why were you acting differently at Frank's earlier?" I asked.

"Knowing about what happened was rough enough, but hearing it in detail, and to see how worked up your brother was getting, got to me. I don't like seeing people hurting. I care about people, especially you guys. It bothered me that I couldn't be there to comfort you when it happened. All I can do is make you comfortable now. The guys laugh at me and say I'm soft for being like this, but I don't care. You need you to know you mean something," he said. He was right, I wasn't used to the constant flow of generosity.

"Fine, I'll tell you. Please don't think different of me, though," I pleaded. He touched my hand.

"Nothing could make me do that. It wasn't your fault," he

replied. So I told him everything.

"Look, Alex. I'm sick and tired of you always getting mad at me whenever I go and party," Dean said angrily. I stood there at my locker, scared. I'd seen him angry plenty of times, but this was completely different.

"I'm not angry because you party, Dean. It's keeping it from me. You never tell me what you're doing, but you expect me to tell you every little detail of my life. Why is that?" I said back. He walked away from me toward the parking lot.

"Well, are you coming?" he asked. Since he was my ride, I had no choice but to accept. For the last month and a half, it seemed like all we ever did was fight. Most of it came from me turning down sex. I wasn't ready for it, and he didn't understand it.

"Don't you realize I wouldn't need to go out and get drunk all the time if only you'd stop fighting and just have sex with me? I'm a guy, damn it. I have needs too. We've been dating for six months now. Can't you cut me a little slack?" he rolled down the window of the beamer and turned the ignition.

"You're unbelievable," I snorted. "Six months isn't enough time to be ready, Dean. Why can't you cut me a little slack? You know I'm not comfortable with it just yet." I wished he was only dropping me off at my house, but no one was home and I didn't have any keys. Cody was hanging with Deanna and her little sister, and he was picking me up afterwards.

"How isn't six months enough time? You say you love me, but you won't even do that for me. Why do you think it's called 'making love'? People do it if they're in love. You and I, we're in love. Why do we have to wait?" He looked over at me. His eyes were like razors cutting into my soul. "Baby, please. You know how much this means to me." His voice was like butter. I almost felt like I should give in.

"I couldn't today, anyway. Cody's getting me in an hour, and I'd rather take it slow, Dean. I'm sorry." By now, we'd reached his apartment. Since he lived on the first floor, we went through the window because it was easier for Dean to get to his bedroom. I sat on his bed while he got some macaroni and cheese. When he came back in the room, he was drinking a beer as well.

"Dean, you know you shouldn't touch your dad's beers. He gets angry. You remember what he did with your hockey stick the last time you took one," I said. He shrugged and put the beer down.

"Eh, it's whatever. I had this one open anyway." He crossed the room and lay on his bed next to me. He leaned over and kissed me, breath smelling like beer. Something was off about him, I realized. I backed away.

"What is wrong with you today, Alex?" he demanded. He sat up and stared.

"Nothing, I just don't think you're in your right mind, and maybe I should just wait outside for my brother," I replied. He ignored me and turned the TV on.

"Come lay down, babe. Your favorite show is on." Hoping he had settled down, I laid down to watch TV.

He leaned over and started kissing me again. I tried to get up, but Dean lay on top of me, pinning me down. He started kissing my neck, which was a turn on. I knew better, however.

"Dean, stop!" But he didn't stop. While he was laying over me, I could feel his hands undoing my belt. "Did you hear me? Stop, you lunatic!" I yelled louder. By now, his hands were near my underwear. I knew where this was going, so I yelled at the top of my lungs. "STOP!"

Twenty minutes later, when he was done pleasing himself amongst my screams, he got off of me. My eyes were filled with tears of pain and anger. I tried to see where he was going, but my eyesight was blurry.

"I told you plenty of times to shut up, Alex. Now, you're going to be quiet like a good girl." I felt cold glass hitting the side of my temple, which made me cry out in pain. He got on top of me once again, and continued bashing the sides of my head along with my chest while he was having his way. All I could think about was how I was going to die.

Finally, he stopped. He replaced my clothes loosely and got dressed as well.

"No one has to know about this, Alex. Keep your mouth shut, okay? I love you, baby. I'm sorry, though. It's over between us." He got up and walked out of his room, leaving the window open. I laid there paralyzed in fear. I faintly heard my brother walk through the open door, and swear loudly when he saw me. I felt his hands pull my head up, and asking me if I was okay, but I couldn't answer.

"Alex, I called the cops. Dad and Mom are on their way too. Stay with me, Allie. Please." He wiped the blood from my face mixed with tears.

After the hospital cleaned me up and checked me for a concussion, which I thankfully didn't have, they made me tell them everything. The look on my family's faces when I told them about the rape was heartbreaking. My brother swore he'd pay, but my father got to him first. The last thing I remembered before passing out due to exertion was my father's teary eyes, asking the doctor if everything was going to be okay.

When I finished my story, I looked at Justin's face for a reaction. He sat there for a long time before saying anything.

"I'm going to kill this kid," he muttered. He sat up, and I reached over and hugged him. After all of this was said, I realized how much better I felt about it now that someone knew.

"Yeah, I mean it happened a year ago by now, so it's okay," I said to him. He shook his head.

"It's not okay! Your brother is so upset over what this kid said to him. Cody wasn't there for it, and now he feels like he watched his little sister get raped, Alex. Don't deny it, I know that doesn't help. Look what happened to my father and I." Justin got up from the couch and pulled me up. "It's late, you should go to bed," he said gently. I was going to protest, but I realized I was exhausted. The little nap I had earlier had worn off.

"Fine, but stay with me? The boys can be fine without you tonight, I need you," I said. I felt vulnerable, but I trusted him. He responded with holding my hand and walking upstairs to my room.

"I'll stay with you as long as you need me to," he said. I

looked at him and gave him a grateful kiss.

"You can leave after I fall asleep," I said thoughtfully. "I just don't want to be alone."

"You won't be, I'll be right here," He replied. I climbed up on to my bed and got under the covers. Justin followed. Since he was in sweatpants, he didn't need to change. I thought about putting some on as well, but I decided to just wear my shorts. I leaned into his arms and listened to his heartbeat until I drifted off into sleep.

I woke up the next morning still in his arms. I looked up at him, sleeping peacefully. He must've been so comfortable that he'd fallen asleep as well. The day before had been so stressful on all of us, so I decided I'd let him stay there, sleeping.

I crawled out of bed and looked out the window. It was a mess out there. The rain had stopped sometime last night, but there were branches and twigs strewn everywhere. I didn't hear anyone upstairs, so I went down to the kitchen to see if anyone was awake.

In the kitchen, Frank, Nico, Kosta, my brother, my mom, Peter, and a girl I didn't know were all sitting around the table eating pancakes.

"Alex, where's Justin?" asked my mother. I bit my lip.

"Asleep," I answered back. "Upstairs." My mother didn't yell at me, but she put a plate of pancakes and bacon down at an empty spot next to me.

"Want to wake him up and tell him it's time to eat?"

"Sure," I said. Why didn't she yell at me? I thought to myself as I walked up the stairway. Justin was still asleep when I went in my room, so I crawled across my bed and kissed him until he stirred.

"What's going on?" Justin said startled. I chuckled and got off of the bed.

"My mom made breakfast for everyone. She wanted you to be awake to have yours, so get your butt up. She made pancakes!" I taunted, hoping this would wake him up. It seemed to do the trick, and shortly after he was following me down the stairs towards the kitchen.

When we got there, my mother was telling the boys about how she was taking a break from work.

"Oh, Alex! I want you and Justin to meet Brooke," she chittered happily. Justin and I exchanged looks at Brooke, who'd mumbled a hello, embarrassed by my mother's attention. Brooke looked to be about fifteen years old. She had medium length brown hair with pretty pink highlights throughout. She had blue eyes like my sister, but hers seemed to be much kinder.

"Nice to meet you, Brooke! I'm Alex, Connie's d-" I stopped dead in my words. "Mom, what is that?"

My mother's smile got wider as she flashed her hand around. Cody snatched it out of the air.

"Ma, is that what I think it is?" he asked. I looked from Brooke to Peter to my mother.

"You two aren't...."

"Getting married, are you?" Cody finished for me. She smiled wider and nodded.

"Yes! He proposed last night, and I said yes! They're moving in with us this weekend!" she gushed absolute happiness. I was happy for her, but we didn't need another family.

"Don't you think you two are, um... rushing things a bit?" I speculated. Peter took the time to finally, address me.

"Well, I've been seeing your mother since March and I've fallen for her. We aren't getting married any time soon, I don't think. But we hope to have a long and happy engagement and I'm proud to say I'll be your new step-father!" Peter drew himself up like he was looking in a mirror. I looked over at Brooke

"Where is she going to be staying?" I asked my mother.

"Right now, we're going to give her McKenzie's room. When, and if, she decides to come home, after college, we're going to split the downstairs to create two rooms instead of just one," she explained. I looked over at Brooke again, who didn't seem too happy about this either.

"Congratulations, Mrs. Barnes. Or Mrs. Bradley," said Nico. She gave the boys a warm smile and looked at the clock.

"Oh! I have to run; I told Roberta I'd meet her at the spa at ten. Be good kids, see you!" she kissed Peter goodbye and rushed out the door. I caught my brother's eye and we looked at each other in confusion. Well, it made sense to me now why she didn't care Justin slept in my room last night.

"Do you guys want to ball up for a little bit?" Frank asked. The crew thought that would be a fun idea, so a little while later, all the boys were dressed for basketball.

"Have fun bonding with Brooke," Justin winked at me.

"Yeah, yeah, yeah," I said rolling my eyes. I had brought Brooke with me to the court where all of the boys played ball. She had stayed in the Prius, refusing to come out to meet anyone. Justin laughed and kissed me.

"Be nice to your new step-sister," he stated. "You never know how lucky you are to have her until it's too late." I snorted.

"I have a sister already, remember? One I'm perfectly happy to forget about. I don't need another snob living in my house. I wish I could have another brother," I said thoughtfully. Justin threw the basketball down in front of me and sat on it.

"Technically, you have Nico, Kosta and Frank for brothers. Once you're in the crew, you're family for life," he said. Now it was my turn to laugh.

"The crew is for guys only. I'm just the girlfriend. We're not as cool," I replied. He stuck his tongue out at me before running to catch up with the guys playing already.

I shook my head at him, laughing, and turned back to the car. When I got inside, I saw Brooke looking through the window quietly.

"You must hate us," I said. She didn't acknowledge me, but I continued to talk. "You're part of a family, just like us. It isn't fair for them to throw this on us, and I understand. But being miserable around us isn't going to bring us together. We might as well get used to hanging around together, you know." She turned and looked at me.

"I don't hate you guys, honest. I'm just not used to the fact I'm going to have another mother. Mine died two years ago, and I'm not over it yet. My dad clearly didn't love her like he said he did if he's marrying your mama already," she said. I cocked my head in interest.

"Oh, I'm sorry. I had no idea," I said somberly. She shook

her head.

"Don't be. It's not your problem. I just think he's rushing too fast into this." She looked out the window once again. I tried making more small talk with her, but she ignored me. I sighed in defeat and headed home. I wasn't going to bother with her if she was going to be like that. I knew she was having a hard time, so I tried not to judge. But it was hard.

Considering I got the last of my drama off of my chest, I didn't need to deal with anyone else's. I helped her move what little things she brought with her into Kenzie's old room. She murmured a thank you, but not before I stood there waiting for one. She was just like a little McKenzie. I texted my sister telling her about the proposal, but she never answered, like usual. I know she got the messages because it told me when she read them. I stopped caring about interacting with her long ago. I couldn't control her, only how I carried myself.

I made my way to the stables to give Celtic a workout, but she was asleep. Maybe I could find a job; I thought to myself, as I headed to the place I now called home.

CHAPTER THIRTEEN
Justin

The winter holidays approached too quickly in my opinion. December spread through Union like fog. Everyone was decorating their houses in festive lights and decorations. The crew helped my mother decorate our new house as well. School became intense with random homework papers and tests. A few workers called out for the holiday, meaning Cody and I had to work double time, so between school and work, Alex and I barely had time to hang out.

"Why is it the older people get to go away and us young people, who have school and lives you know, have to work our holiday away?" grumbled Cody as he cleaned off the counter. I was sweeping the shop after a long day of working.

"Probably because we're young and nowhere near retirement," I laughed. It was a slow day, but we had barely gotten anything done. Our manager, named Turk, usually stayed in the back room which meant we could goof off most of the time. Today we'd had problems with the flour machine, which resulted in us being completely covered from head to toe in the stuff. Thankfully, I swept up the last of the flour just as Turk came out of the office.

"You guys did a good job today, handling the rush," he said in his nasally voice. He reminded me of one of those Steve Urkel guys. Turk had mousy brown hair that was thinning. His voice sounded as if he always had a head cold, and he was shorter than Cody, who was only five foot seven.

"Oh, it was no problem at all," snickered Cody. We always mimicked Turk behind his back, trying to sound and walk like him. Whenever he spoke, we would try not to laugh.

"Oh yeah," I said. "No problem. Can we go now?" Turk gave me a look.

"Now hold on, Jovan. It's only eight o' clock. We close tonight at eight thirty." He pushed his glasses back up on his nose. I couldn't help it. I laughed. "What's so funny?" he barked.

"Sorry, Turk. It's just funny because it's only a half an hour. Why can't we close early? That way we can go home and get homework done. Besides, I heard there was a star trek marathon on tonight, and I'm really excited to watch it," I remarked. I caught Cody's eye, and we tried to hold our laughter in. We watched Turk's eyes light up.

"St-star trek?" he said. I nodded.

"Oh yeah, it's my favorite too! I can't wait!" Cody quipped. Turk pulled at his bow tie.

"Alright, fine. Don't let this happen again or I'll be forced to write you both up. Have a good night," Turk said. He shut the light off, and we walked out. Once Turk had left, we burst out laughing.

"Dude! Did you see his face?" Cody said in between breaths. "He thought you were being serious. Ah, that was hysterical." I continued to laugh as we got in my car.

"I know, I know. I hate that guy; he thinks he's the best because he's the manager at Papa Murphy's. Give me a break," I snorted. "He can't even get my name straight. He even writes 'Jovan' on my paychecks. It's a nightmare!" We were still laughing about it when we got to Cody's house. Alex was at Lissa's for the night with Spencer and Amanda, so I didn't bother going in, it was just Cody and his soon to be stepsister, Brooke.

Two weeks ago, Deanna finally called Cody about the baby. It was a girl, which she named Vanessa. She had a DNA test done on the baby to determine whether or not Cody was the father. Turns out, Dean wasn't the dad either. She had a one-night stand with a guy she'd met at a nightclub named Mark, and she had conveniently forgotten about him until the results came back. When Cody got that call, he'd been so happy. I personally just think he was happy that he wasn't tied to her anymore.

"Hey, man... Do you think I'll ever find someone who cares about me as much as Alex cares about you?" asked Cody suddenly.

"Absolutely. So many girls like you from school, Code, why don't you try for one of them?"

Cody bit his lip. "Eh, I don't know. I thought Deanna actually loved me, but she just loved all of this," he said as he slid his hand up his leg like a model, which made me start to laugh.

"Are you sure about that?" I asked. "I thought she only liked you for your charming personality." He laughed along with me for a few moments before suddenly standing up.

"I gotta go, Justin. I forgot I had, uh.... homework I had to do... Thanks for the ride, though," He said. I nodded to him.

"Yeah sure, no problem. See ya!" I drove away from the

house and turned on some music.

I was confused by Cody's attitude. Since when did he care about homework? As usual, I was lost.

By the time I got to my house, my mother was already asleep. I sat down at my table and jotted some gift ideas for Alex. I decided against a necklace and earring set. She always wore her best friend's set of earrings and the same diamond necklace. She wouldn't wear rings, so that was out of the question. Frustrated, I sat back and ran my fingers through my hair. It was a lot longer now; as I didn't need to cut it for basketball. I was contemplating getting it cut, but Alex had hinted she liked it longer.

"'It's cuter that way," she had said. What can I say? I'm a sucker for love.

I threw the papers away in defeat. I flopped down on my bed, and as my face hit the pillow, it hit me. Literally.

"Ow," I said rubbing my cheek. I lifted my pillow to see a scrapbook my sister and I had made when I was ten. The perfect gift idea came straight to me. I e-mailed the Dean of my school to tell him I wasn't going to be in class tomorrow and went right to bed. I needed to be up early if I was going to get this done for tomorrow night.

The next morning, I woke up to a bit of surprise. Alex sent me a picture of her standing in the snow sticking her tiny tongue out at me. Snow? I ran to the window in the hallway overlooking the front yard. It was covered in white powder! I yelled in excitement, accidentally waking Michelle up, who had moved back now that dad was out of the picture.

"Meesh! It's a snow day!" I called to her. I heard her grumble and tell me to shut up, but I didn't care. It was snowing on the last day of school before Christmas break. I replied to Alex's picture with 'Snowball fight l8r?' and hopped in the shower. I threw on some Christmas tunes while I cleaned up. Inevitably, getting out of the shower caused me to believe I had attained hypothermia.

I looked outside, as I was getting ready to leave, and the snow was falling even harder. My mother had the fireplace going, and Michelle was sitting at the breakfast table.

"No school in Union today," Michelle said to me. "Oh, and Alex called when you were in the shower. I answered for you." I sat down at the table.

"Oh yeah? What'd she say?" I took the box of Krispy's from her and poured myself a bowl.

"Nothing, she was just looking for you to see if tonight was still on and if you wanted to hang out. I told her you'd call her back." She drank the milk out of her bowl and went upstairs to go back to bed.

I didn't call Alex back right away; I wanted to finish eating and figure out what stores I needed to go to at the mall. Once I had a mental map, I dialed her number.

"Good morning!" came Alex's voice on the second ring. I instantly smiled.

"Good morning to you, too! Sorry, I missed your call earlier. I was in the shower." She laughed.

"No worries here. Cody said the crew meeting was being held in the function hall tonight?" I wrinkled my brows.

"No? What function hall.... it was supposed to be at Kosta and Nico's house. What?" I felt so out of the loop. All through the end of November as well as December, I'd been in some sort of haze. My memory couldn't retain as much information as it was receiving. Everything about college, Christmas, what had happened before Thanksgiving, the crew, and Cody's weird behavior had gotten me in such a muddle.

"I have no idea. Kosta called Cody last night and told him. How come you dropped him off so late last night? I had to get a ride from Amanda." Now I was completely throttled. I dropped him off at eight-fifteen.

"Are you kidding me? He told me he had homework to do, so I brought him home right after we got out of work at eight. Whatever, so the function hall at seven, right?" I asked her.

"Yep. I still want that snowball fight, though," she said teasingly. "I want to kick your butt. I was always good at those in Boston."

"Eh, we'll see about that, my dear. I have a mean fastball," I said. "I have to do a few errands this morning, though. I don't know when the snow will stop so I want to be sure all of this is taken care of."

"Deal, pick me up at one, then?" she asked. I loved how she could tell me what she wanted without sounding like she was trying to control me.

"One-thirty it is," I smirked. I hung up the phone and grabbed my jacket. My mother was doing the dishes as I walked by.

"I'm going out to the mall for a little bit to get Alex's gift and then I'm gonna' get her too. We're coming back here, until the party at seven, is that okay?" She nodded.

"You know I like her, baby boy. Just don't be stupid." I opened my mouth to attempt to correct her, but she cut me off. "I mean it, Justin. Don't do anything stupid. You don't want to end up like that ex-girl of Cody's, now do you?"

"Ma, do you realize that is impossible, right? You make no sense. Whatever, bye." She waved her goodbyes to me and continued singing Elvis Presley songs as she washed the dishes. As I hopped in the car, I heard my phone ring. It was Frank.

"I need someone to come with me to help me get Alex's gift done, wanna come help?"

"I was just calling to see if you wanted to help me with Amanda's. I'll help you if you help me. I need help choosing a necklace set for her," he replied.

"Aright, cool. Mine needs a little more work than that, so we'll go get Amanda's first, I'm on my way."

Two and a half hours later, Amanda's gift was wrapped neatly in the back of my car. Alex's gift was only half done. I needed two more items from Cincinnati first, and then I had to go home and assemble it. I dropped Frank off at his house with his girlfriend's gift and made the drive to Ohio.

It took me a good forty-five minutes instead of twenty to get to the restaurant that we went to on our first official date. The snow here was falling a bit faster, and it made people drive cautiously. I went in to talk to the Maître'D about a few things. It was pretty busy inside. I was tempted to get lunch here before heading back, but I knew I'd be late to get Alex. She was going to be with me until the party. That left me with little time to finish the project. The main part of the gift I originally had, though so that would take less time. Cody and the crew had helped over the months without realizing.

Because of all the pictures of the crew and the girls, I had enough substantial photos of Alex and me throughout the time we knew each other. Since I knew Alex well enough to know she'd be mad at me if I bought her something expensive, I knew this would be one gift she'd love.

I left the restaurant with a take home menu, salt and pepper packets, and a mock 'bill' to represent the bill we'd playfully fought over when we ate there. I decided a scrapbook would be the perfect gift because as time passed, we could add to it, to record our growing love. Or at least I hoped.

By the time I got back to my house, it was twelve-fifteen. I had about an hour before leaving to get Alex. I took out the blank scrapbook I had bought from the craft store and began creating the magic.

Once or twice, Michelle had stopped in and helped me come up with a few ingenious ways to place things, as she was naturally good at crafting. When the final product was complete, I couldn't help myself from feeling proud of what I'd done. I'd never gone out of my way to make something like this for a girl before. When I was with Jenna, she was very materialistic and always wanted things. I would try to make her happy by buying her whatever she wanted. Good riddance.

When I was with Alex, I always could felt I could act like I do with the crew and be myself around her, too. I loved that. When

Jenna was around, I noticed I acted differently. It was almost as if I was justifying myself to her, and I didn't like that.

I wrapped up the scrapbook as best as I could and hid it under my bed. I had to go out and scrape my car off after because the snow was building up more and more.

Alex didn't answer when I called her, so I figured she was getting ready. I headed down the road slowly. At the red light, I caught sight of my old football coach from when I was eleven.

"Hey, coach!" I yelled. He squinted at me before recognizing who I was.

"Justin! Hey buddy, how's it going?" He called back. He trudged up through the snow to the red light. Apart from my car, there was no one on the road.

"It's good, just going to get someone for a Christmas party tonight. You still coaching the kids?" I asked.

"Yeah, we almost went to Florida this year. I remember the last time we almost got there was when you were on the team. You're a great player, Barry! Keep it up. I gotta get home, my feet are freezing! See ya," he waved. I watched him walk away and realized the light was turning yellow again. I drove off in the nick of time.

A short while later, I arrived at Alex's house. One-thirty-two. Hopefully, she was still in the shower. From the movement of her window curtain, I could tell I was wrong. She came out a little while later.

"Hey, you!" she said. I kissed her as she climbed into the car. She smiled at me.

"We have a problem, Justin." Her face turned serious. I

pulled away and tried to think of what was wrong.

"Okay... shoot?"

"You were two minutes late getting me, and now I'm going to have to kick your butt," she smiled devilishly. I relaxed a bit and laughed.

"Yeah, right. Good luck with that one, Alex." I turned onto a street, and the car slid to the other side. "Shit, hold on!" I tried to turn into the skid, but we kept sliding for about twenty-feet. Alex's face went from terrified to amused.

"That was the most fun thing I've experienced in such a long time!" she thrilled. "Can you believe that? We could've died if there were any cars out here!"
I snorted. "Fun? What if my car tipped over and we did die? I'm not trying to almost-die again." Alex stopped smiling. She looked down at the dashboard.

"I know, sorry. I didn't mean it like that, Justin. I just meant it was a thrill, and I haven't had that in a long time." She looked up at me.

"Don't be sorry, I'm just saying. You're sorry a lot, you know that?" I winked at her. That got her to cheer up. She scoffed.

"Really?" she exclaimed. "We'll see about that. We'll see who's sorry after this snowball fight." Alex opened the window and grabbed some snow off of the car and tossed it at me. I felt the ice, falling down my collar.

"Ah! It's cold!" I squirmed. The snow melted down to cold water and trickled down my shirt. "That's it!" I swerved the car to the side of the road and shut it off. I jumped out and ran to the passenger side door and pulled her out and tossed some snow at her. She ducked in time, and it missed.

Laughing, I threw some more snow at her. This time it hit her in the shoulder, and she fell over. She got up and made a baseball sized snowball and threw it so hard, it knocked my hat off of my head. I stared at her, mouth open wide.

"Did you really just knock off my hat?" I asked incredulously. She looked just as shocked as I did.

"I think so," she whispered. Then, she started laughing uncontrollably. She fell to the ground, tears coming out of her eyes from laughing so hard. I walked over to her to help her, but she pulled me down to the ground too.

"Are you okay, Alex?" I asked. She was beginning to make me laugh too like it was some sort of contagion.

She nodded and took a deep breath. Out of nowhere, she stuffed snow right in my face. It was like being hit with a thousand crystal daggers. I jumped up and wiped my face as fast as I could, but the snow that was falling kept slicing my face. I had to get her back somehow; I thought to myself.

For about an hour and a half, we had a rag tag snowball fight in the middle of the road. It was getting darker, and the snow was picking up once again, so we climbed into my car, cold and soaked, and drove back to my house to sit next to the fireplace.

"Can we exchange gifts here?" asked Alex. I put down my hot chocolate and shrugged.

"Why don't you want to wait until the Christmas party?" I said.

"I don't think we're going to have one by the looks of

outside," she replied. "It's getting worse by the minute." I sighed.

"Of course it would snow the night of the Christmas party," I grumbled. I couldn't let my perfect night go to waste.

"What's wrong with it just being the two of us?" she asked defensively. I had to immediately back-track.

"No, that's not what I mean. I just had a few things planned out, don't be so nervous, Alex. Just breathe," I said. "Do you want to exchange them now, or wait until tonight?"

"Hmm, let's see... we could put Frosty on, cuddle up next to the fire and watch the snow fall, or we could open presents. How about both?" She smiled so sweetly, my heart melted. I wanted to give her the world. I just had to wait until she accepted it.

"Deal. If you put Frosty on, I'll go and get my gift for you. No peeking, though!" She nodded and went to work stoking the fire and getting the movie ready. When I got upstairs, I realized my mother and sister were gone. I didn't have the slightest idea where they were, but I pushed it out of my head.

Alex's gift was hidden under my bed, along with my most prized possessions. I quickly thought through the way I was going to present this to her.

"Justin! Are you still up there?" she called. "I have the movie waiting!" I took a deep breath and went downstairs.

Now, let me assure you I normally don't get weak for girls, no matter who they were. Alex was someone that was entirely different to me. It was like playing a sport you've read about, but never learned the rules.

As I walked downstairs, the lights flickered for a moment, and then went off completely. I heard a crash, so I leapt off of the last few stairs and ran into the living room.

"Alex, are you okay?" I shouted. I heard a rustle from the right corner.

"Y-yeah, I'm okay. I just tripped over something on my way back from the kitchen, and I dropped the drinks. I'm sorry," she replied. I pulled out my phone and held it up for some light. Alex stood in the doorway with two cups of something on the ground. Beside her, an end table lay knocked over on its side.

"Let's get some candles lit so we can see what we're doing, and we'll just sit by the fire, to open gifts," I said. She nodded, so while I got the candles out of the cabinet, she cleaned up the cups and fixed the end table. I lit them with a spare zippo lighter of my mom's and set them up on the tables in the living room.

Alex grabbed some pillows and throw-blankets and put them on the floor next to the crackling fire. I grabbed her present and sat down next to her.

"Merry Christmas, my love," I said to her. She looked at me and smiled.

"You too, Justin," she said. She grabbed her bag and pulled out a small, ornately wrapped box and held it out to me. "This is for you. I hope you like it." She looked into my eyes; the flames of the fire flickered over her yellow-brown eyes and sent shivers down my spine.

"Thank you, should I open it first?" I asked. She nodded, so I proceeded to rip open the paper as carefully as possible. I hoped she would like her gift, as much as I did, so that I could add the paper into the December section.

When I got down to the box, I opened it slowly for dramatic

effect. It made her laugh, so I opened it quickly. I couldn't help but smile.

"Wow, thank you so much!" I said genuinely. I held up my gift so she could see my reaction to it. It was a white gold chain with a little note connected to it. I took it off and read it aloud.

"*Dear Justin, ever since you came into my life this summer, things haven't been the same for me. You taught me what it was like to finally trust another guy, as well as learn to let go of the past. Being with you is like riding my horse- it's a type of bliss words cannot describe. Even though I get guarded and mess things up for us, you're always there to fix it and make it all okay again. For me, that's huge because no one has ever invested any time in me- not even family. You being here is simply magical, and if this is a dream, I hope I never wake up. Merry Christmas, darling.*

Always, Alex"

"That's sweet, Alex," I said, quickly wiping away my wet eyes before they betrayed my emotions. She smiled at me shyly and replied,

"I'm glad you like it! I didn't really know what else to get you, as you have everything you need," she held up her fingers to make air quotes on the last part. "I just wanted to make sure you had something to carry with you, to remind you of me."

I wrapped my arms around her tightly as my gesture of thanks. I pulled out the package I wrapped for her and handed it to her.

"It's your turn," I said. She gingerly grabbed the parcel and opened my card. It was a simple Christmas card- I didn't want the card to overshadow the actual gift.

When she had ripped the last of the paper away, her eyes scrunched up in confusion.

"A photo album?" Alex asked. I shook my head.

"How about opening it up and seeing what's inside," I replied. She turned to the first page and gasped.

"A scrapbook! Justin, you made this? Oh my, that is the sweetest thing ever! And you remembered not to buy me anything! Aw, thank you so much!" I saw tears in her eyes, so I smiled and wiped them away.

"Well, I'd be lying if I said I didn't spend any money, but look through it! Tell me if you can picture each memory." I moved closer to her to get a view of everything.

The first page had a picture of us two sitting on my grandparents' porch swing. I remember that day vividly. It was in August, and I had just found out that I was going to be starting varsity in basketball this coming fall. In the picture, she was wearing her hair, naturally curly with a white shirt tied in the front, and jeans and boots. I sat next to her, arm around her waist. Cody was sitting next to her in the original picture, but for the sake of my gift, I cut him out.

She flipped through the rest of the pages, commenting on each memory. I included random photos that we had taken throughout the school year, little items from places we went on dates, dried flower from the bouquet I bought her.

"There's still blank pages," she said to me.

"Uh, that's so we can add on to it each time we do something worth remembering," I responded. She blushed a little at my response.

"Right, what a lovely idea. It was a beautiful gift, Justin. I really love it. This has been the best Christmas ever." Alex snuggled closer to me and shortly fell asleep.

Outside, the wind picked up and blew snow around in swirls of pearly white. I knew there was no way I was getting her home, so I decided just to curl up next to her and fall asleep. The fire was warm, even though the power was still out. I blew out the candles we had around us and nodded off myself.

That night, I had a dream about Cody. He was running from something, and in the dark folds of my mind, it was beginning to trouble me. He was acting so mysteriously lately, and it was clear, even subconsciously that I wanted to figure out what it was he was hiding. Alex didn't even notice his strange behavior, so asking her to help wasn't going to get me anywhere. I shook the dream from my head and fell back asleep. I never even noticed his two missed calls, because at that moment, I really did have everything I needed.

CHAPTER FOURTEEN
Alexandra

Have you ever felt so strongly for someone that words couldn't describe the joy you felt when you saw them? When I woke up next to Justin the day after we exchanged our gifts, I felt elated. I smiled softly and curled into him, trying to preserve the warmth we shared under the blankets. He rustled next to me, still in his own little world. I didn't want to wake him, so I quietly got off of the made up mattress and walked to the window.

It was freezing in his parlor room, and by the looks of it, neither his mother nor sister, had come home until late last night. Their snores could be heard like whispers from the upstairs. The embers of last night's fire still smoldered in the ashes of the logs inside the fireplace. I'd have to remember to ask him to make another fire once he woke up, I thought with a shiver.

I looked out of the window to see Union covered under a thick white blanket of snow. Snow like this was very unusual for a place such as Union. Back in Boston, it was normal to see a foot or so on the ground because we were on the coast. Union, on the other hand, was far more inland than Massachusetts, so I hadn't expected it.

With the weak, winter sun, the snow glistened like it was a sheet of glass. I had to admit- it was a beautiful sight.

I couldn't find my cell phone near where we were sleeping. I finally found it in the kitchen, almost dead. I had seven missed calls and three voice messages, from Spencer, Amanda, my brother and.... McKenzie? I listened to the voicemails, and to my surprise, learned that McKenzie had moved in with her newest beau, Liam. The message said they'd been dating for four months now, but I wasn't sure if I believed her. I seemed to remember the last time she'd written to us; she'd had a different guy.

I called my brother back, but he didn't answer. It was nine-thirty; he would definitely be asleep still. I shut off my phone to preserve the rest of its life and headed back into the parlor room. The lights were still off, which could only mean the power was still out.

Justin was still huddled under the blankets, shivering slightly. I felt bad for leaving him cold, so I hopped in next to him and inadvertently startled him awake.

"Hey, are you okay?" he asked groggily.

"I was just checking my phone; I'm sorry. I didn't mean to wake you," I replied. Justin rubbed his eyes and searched around for his phone. I glanced at the screen and saw my brother had called him as well. "Cody called you too?"

"I guess so, but he didn't leave a message or anything," he said. I shrugged. "Is the power still out, Alex?"

"Yeah," I nodded. "There's so much snow on the ground, I almost feel like I'm back in Boston."

"I bet, I've always wondered what it was like to be in Boston. I have never been there before; hopefully I'll be able to go after I go to college," said Justin.

He walked over to the window and stared at the icy ground

before him. "It really is beautiful," said Justin. I made my way over to him and put my arm on his.

"It was one of the things that I loved best about Boston," I said softly. I walked away from Justin and grabbed a blanket. I sat down again next to the fire, which has been all but burned down.

"Do you want me to relight another fire?" He asked. I shook my head, even though the frosty air had left chills down my skin.

"Nah, I think I'm good. Come sit down next to me," I replied, patting the side of the bed. He obliged and proceeded to sit down. I wrapped my arms around his body and snuggled closer to him. I loved this feeling of being close to him, even though he expected more of me. I wish I could admit my true feelings to him, but if I did so, I knew I'd be walking into a death trap. No guy ever sticks around long enough to hear your true feelings anyway.

Suddenly, my phone started ringing. I was momentarily surprised because I had thought I'd shut it off. I glanced at the screen and realized it was my mother.

"Honey, where are you? We have been wondering where you were since last night. Is everything okay?" My mother's frantic voice registered concern on my face. Justin looked over at me, but I shushed him.

"Mom, I'm fine! " I said. "I stayed at Justin's last night because I didn't want to get caught out in the storm."

"Cody went out looking for you around eleven," said my mom. I felt bad. I should have called them last night.

"I am so sorry, mom," I said sadly. "I just figured it would be easier if I stayed out here so that you wouldn't worry."

"Well," she scoffed. "That doesn't seem to have done a whole lot of good, now does it?"

This steely resolve in her voice led me to believe that she was far more infuriated with me than she was letting on.

"Okay, would you like me to come home then?" I asked her. She's shuffled around on the phone for a minute, then answered.

"Yeah! I don't think it's wise to be staying out late at some boys house," she said. I sighed. She was purposely, being difficult.

"Fine," I said exasperated. I hung up the phone and went to retrieve my things next to the couch. Justin was quiet, but he helped me collect my things. We walked out quietly to the car, just as I fell on a patch of ice. Before I had time to react or scream, Justin was beside me holding me up.

"Are you okay, babe?" asked Justin. I gave him a weak smile and nodded my head. "Please be careful, I don't want to see you get hurt."

"I'll be fine, Justin. Don't worry about me." I picked up what I had dropped, and proceeded to the car. "Thank you, by the way."

He shrugged. "It's no big deal; I love you." He had said it again. I had no idea how to respond and began to feel awkward when I was saved, by his phone ringing.

"Hey, Nico!" Justin remarked. "What are you up to today?" I opened up my door and sat in the cold car, waiting for him to turn it on. I looked out the car window and saw him laughing on the phone. I wanted to get home- my mother was very angry with me. I didn't want her to be even more pissed that I was not home on time.

Justin came to the car and opened the door quietly. He looked at me apologetically.

"I'm sorry about talking on the phone," he said. " Nico called to see what we were up to, but I told him that you got in trouble. I hope that's okay with you." I put on my best fake smile and nodded.

"Yeah, totally." I looked out the window and realized that the sun had shined a little bit brighter showing patches of black ice. "Please be careful though, Justin. I see a lot of black ice out on the road. I don't want you to slip and end up crashing."

He looked at me sweetly and put the car in drive. "We'll be fine, just relax and don't worry. I'm a good driver; I know what I'm doing."

The car ride was short but very quiet. No one had turned on any music, and we didn't talk. It was mostly awkward. My brother's car was in the driveway, along with my mother and her fiancé's. The lights were off, however. I wondered why.

"I think the power is still out at my house," I said to Justin.

"Are you sure you're going to be okay?" He asked.

I nodded once again and got out of the car. I looked back at his sad face. I giggled and ran over to the driver's side. I pulled him out of the car and promptly kissed him. I felt his lips curl into a smile on mine.

"Couldn't stay away?" He said softly. It was my turn to smile.

"Caught on, have you? I could never stay away," I laughed. He smiled too and gave me one quick hug before letting me go.

"Meet me at my stables tonight? I want to show you something," I whispered. He nodded curtly and left. Somehow, I felt this was the only way I was going to be seeing him for a while.

When I got in the house, my suspicions were correct. My mother yelled at me for a quarter of an hour, and then ranted on for another twenty minutes. I was grounded for a week. Since my Christmas break was only ten days, that left me virtually no time to hang out with anyone.

I supposed I deserved it. No, I knew I deserved it. I should have called them to let them know where I was.

At seven thirty that evening, I told my mother I was going to the stables, to work Celtic. Just because I was grounded, I couldn't let her suffer. Cody dropped me off because I had apparently lost my car privileges too. I didn't care, though. I had until ten this evening to ride without any inhibitions. I couldn't call Justin since my phone was confiscated, but I hoped he would be here when I asked.

I was just grooming Celtic's soft fur when I heard his voice.

"So, uh, what did you have in mind for tonight?" He asked. I smiled and ran to give him a kiss.

"I'm sorry I couldn't talk to you today," I started to explain. "My mother took away my phone, car and leaving the house is a no-no for me until next Saturday." He grimaced.

"Alex, are you serious? Were they that mad? Why didn't you let them talk to me, I could've vouched for you! I feel so bad, this is all my fault." I immediately held up a finger to his lips to silence him.

"It isn't your fault, meathead. It's mine for shutting off my phone. I usually tell them where I'm going and when I'll be back. Remember what happened last time?" The hardened look on his face notified me that he definitely remembered.

"Well, okay. So we'll just have to meet here in secret for the week, I suppose. Can you teach me?" He asked.

"Why do you think I brought you here? To sit here and watch me? Hah, I don't think so. Grab a saddle and let's get you started."

Twenty minutes later, I had Celtic all tacked up and ready. I had Justin on a bay gelding named Rufus. He was a docile old thing and was very sweet for novices like Justin. If the owners knew what we were doing, they might have made a scene, so I kept my mouth shut when I first got there.

"I'll teach you just the basics of riding tonight," I said to him. "That includes walking, standing and basic exercises. You'll be sore tomorrow, so we'll keep it simple."

His face registered nervousness, but he kept his cool. "Right, so how do I get on this big guy?"

I laughed. "Um, we take the horses to the arena and get on them there. We aren't going to get on them in here. Follow my lead."

I watched him as he attempted to lead Rufus to the door, but a bale of straw had caught the old horse's attention. He pulled his head down to the pile so sharply that Justin lost the control on the reins and fell over. I stifled a laugh and ran over to help him gain his pride back.

"Rufus does that to everyone," I explained. "That's why you need to use the riding crop I gave you, to gently nudge him to move along."

"Right, maybe you could do that for me, and I can stay next to Celtic?" He asked, clearly embarrassed. I felt bad for Justin, so I nodded and went to retrieve the runaway.

Rufus was munching on the remains of the big bale when I got to him. I clicked my tongue quietly to gain his attention. He looked over at me and plodded his way to my hand, thinking I had a treat for him. I grabbed the reins and walked him towards the door, trying not to smirk at Justin's astonished face. I even offered to take Celtic too, but he wanted to walk her.

When we got in the arena, I climbed onto my saddle. The cold air hurt the seat of my butt against the cold leather, but I knew once we started going; we'd warm up.

"Make sure you climb up from the left side," I said. He was clearly new to all of this, so I had to make sure nothing bad happened to him. "Put your left foot in the stirrup, and swing yourself over like you're getting on a bicycle."

"Right, like a bike," Justin muttered. He propped himself up against the saddle and hoisted himself up.

"Good job, baby!" I exclaimed. He rolled his eyes at my enthusiasm, but I ignored him.

"To walk, all you need to do is gently nudge him with your legs like this." I demonstrated, and watched him do the same. I started to lead the horses out of the arena, as I saw the flash of someone's headlights. I panicked, thinking it was my mother.

"Quick! Justin, jump off and hide in those bushes!" But it was too late. The driver stepped out of the car and walked over to us. I breathed a sigh of relief. It was just Lissa.

"Hey, guys! I didn't know y'all were here. Alex, why did you get grounded? Nico heard from Cody that you got busted!" She walked over to the arena gate and sat down on the step stool.

"Yeah," I grimaced. "My phone almost died in that freak storm last night, so I crashed at Justin's and didn't tell them. My whole Christmas break is ruined. I'm going to be grounded on Christmas day!"

"That totally sucks, Alex. I'm sorry. But, hey- I have to go pick up some of my stuff to bring home. I won't keep you two any longer, see ya!" She jumped the fence and was gone.

Turning back to my lesson, I instructed Justin to walk along the corners of the arena to warm Rufus and Celtic up. I decided against taking him into the field until I was sure he could master the basics, and besides, there was a little bit too much snow on the ground for the horses to do anything more than just walk. I loved the snow, but I hoped that it would melt down a little before the poor horses froze.

Around nine thirty, I ended our mini lesson. Justin had improved drastically since the beginning of the night. He was able to progress to a sitting trot, a kind of gait where you stay seated instead of posting up and down. It was a little difficult, but he managed to stay on just fine.

"Thanks for taking the time to teach me how to ride," he said quietly, as we untacked the horses. I blushed.

"Well, it was nothing. I won't be able to see you this vacation otherwise, so I figured I'd put you to work so we can bond over animals," I laughed. He smiled back at me and slid the saddle off of Rufus' back.

We continued to unpack the gear for a few more minutes before I heard a car pull up. My heart froze in my throat. I pushed Justin into a bale of hay as my mother and Brooke came into the stable. I tried hard not to let my nervous giggle give me away. The near hysteria of almost getting caught gave me such an adrenaline rush. I smiled to myself and followed my mother and soon-to-be stepsister out. I turned around as we walked out and winked at Justin. He smiled and gave me a thumbs-up.

For the rest of the vacation, we continued to meet in secret. I taught him as much as I could about horseback riding. He progressed greatly, even though I don't think he enjoyed it too much. The thought that he was willing to try something I loved, for the sake of making me happy, warmed my heart greatly. Something else burned inside of my heart as well, but I pushed that away. I couldn't handle falling in love. That's, usually when I'd get hurt.

Christmas passed by uneventfully. Cody and I each got new clothes, an iPad from Brooke and her father, gift cards from my sister, and countless stocking candy. Everything was sweet, but my favorite gift was up in my bedroom filled with pictures and mementos. I was still not speaking to my mother for not letting me see Justin for Christmas.

She had tried to explain this would keep me from making the same mistake again, and that I'd learn. It wasn't a mistake to begin with, and I began to shut her out. She didn't need my input now that she had her fiancé. Cody spent most of his time at work or out. I figured he was with the crew, or so I thought.

The night before New Year's Eve, Brooke came into my room, clearly troubled. She claimed she had seen him leaving the house around one-thirty the morning before. He looked suspicious, getting into a blue car of some sort. Brooke mumbled fast and almost too low for me to catch. I asked her if she knew who the driver was, and she shook her head so fast I swear it was going to fly off. She ran out of my room and slammed the door to the bathroom. Cody was sneaking out, huh? I knew he was hiding something, but what was he hiding? What was the big deal? I needed to get my questions answered before I went insane.

CHAPTER FIFTEEN
Justin

The fact that Alex was grounded for the whole vacation was a bummer, but sneaking out to meet one another, was kind of fun. I'd never had to do that before, so it was refreshing to change things up a bit.

It was tougher to plan times to meet at the stables around my job. Regardless of my busy schedule, I would always try to make time for my girl.

One sunny afternoon at work, I asked Cody about what he thought of Alex and I. I didn't want to seem overzealous, or let on we were seeing each other secretly, but I didn't want to lie to my best friend.

"She's good, I guess. I don't really see much of her," Cody responded. We were sweeping the floors after the last rush of customers came in.

"Does she, you know, talk about me at all? Has she said anything about missing me?" I hate sounding like one of those annoying, clingy boyfriends, but if I didn't act like I missed her, someone would catch on.

"Dude, she loves you. Don't let her actions or words confuse you. She's scared, and she doesn't know why. She misses you." Cody turned around and started sweeping, clearly ending the conversation.

That type of contact with Cody was the norm for the next few months. New Year's passed, with him distancing himself from the group, little by little. He barely spoke when he was with us; he was too absorbed with his phone. The guys and I wanted to have a talk with him, but with work, school, and homework, we found we couldn't find the right time. Alex and I discussed it many times as well, but she couldn't figure out what was wrong with her twin.

By the time we caught a break in our schedules, it was almost Valentine's Day. Every girl in Cooper was ecstatic about the dance that the school had thrown last minute. My crew wasn't that into it, thankfully. We had all decided that we were going to go out for a movie and some dinner and then gatecrash the dance if we felt like it.

The Friday before Valentine's Day, I headed to school late because I wanted to pick up Alex's gift. I thought long and hard about it because I knew I wanted to make the day special for her. She still had her guard up at little, so when I found a necklace with a heart lock pendant and a key, I knew that it was the perfect gift. It just seemed so... her. It was a pretty hefty price, but I didn't care. She was worth every penny I had.

I drove to school, blasting some Kanye and stopped to get myself an iced coffee.

"Could I have a mocha iced coffee with extra caramel swirl please?"

"That'll be two nineteen, sir," said the voice back. I dredged up the change I had in my pocket and handed it to the lady standing at the drive-thru window. She patiently waited for the money and handed back the coffee. I sipped on mine in total bliss; it tasted like heaven.

By the time I got to school, fourth period had just started. I quietly took my seat in class and ignored Jenna's dagger-like stare. It was almost as if she could tell I had Alex's gift in my bag, and she was mad because it wasn't her getting it this year. Oh well, was all I could think. She left me for another girl.

I had to force myself to pay attention to what my teacher was saying, but I couldn't concentrate. I just wanted to be out of school already and with my friends making plans. Needless to say, the rest of the school day went by about as fast as a snail going backwards. Before lunch break, I stopped by my locker to grab the afternoon classes' books when I heard a voice behind me.

"You don't really think coming to school late makes you look like a hero, do you?" said Jenna. She walked toward me, adjusting her shirt so that anyone who had eyes could see the top of her cleavage. She flipped her hair to the side and smiled at me.

"Since when do I care about what people think, Jenna? You don't know me anymore so leave me alone," I pushed past her and walked down the hall. I didn't even bother to turn around and see where she went because my eyes could only focus on one thing.

Alex looked absolutely beautiful today. She was wearing a navy blue top with dark jeans. She never piled makeup on like a lot of other girls here did. A little mascara and lip gloss goes a long way, ladies. Believe us when we tell you.

"Hey, gorgeous!" I hugged her from behind and kissed her cheek. I felt her smile as she turned around to face me.

"Hey! Why were you late today, Justin?" I adjusted the straps on my backpack and took a while to answer.

"I picked up a few things and ran late, that's all. I got it cleared up with the office anyway, so it's all good," I assured her. I looked up to meet her eyes, but they were staring behind me. I turned around to see what she was glaring at when I saw Jenna coming our way. I sighed in agitation. What has gotten into her?

"Hey, Jenna," Alex said coolly. Her steely gaze pierced the air as Jenna smirked and stopped in front of us. Her shirt was still down low enough for anyone to see down it, so I turned to look at Alex.

"Barnes," she snipped. Turning to me, she said sweetly, "Hey Justin. Can't wait for class later!" She winked at me and walked away, shaking her butt while she retreated. I shook my head. Why?

Beside me, Alex laughed. "That girl really sucks, Justin. I'm sorry you had to endure that for two years."

I shrugged. "No worries, Al. She was a bitch and treated me horrible the whole time. I have someone now who is ten times better. Don't stress, babe." I grabbed her into my arms and kissed her quickly. I didn't want her thinking Jenna was going to ruin something because there wasn't a chance in hell that could happen. Alex gave me a wistful smile as she picked her handbag up off of the floor. She grabbed my hand, and together we walked down the hallway to our next classes. While I was not happy to have more classes with Jenna, it gave me the opportunity to find out why she was acting like this.

I said my goodbyes to Alex and continued, on my way to lunch. My schedule was perfect on Fridays. I had lunch before my last few classes so I could make up work while I ate. Since I got food right before I came to school, I wasn't that hungry. I decided to sit in the cafeteria and work on my homework. It distracted my mind from thinking of Alex and Jenna and all the weirdness happening lately.

I heard a move near the end of the table, which jolted me awake. I looked quickly at my watch to realize I had fallen asleep for twenty minutes. The noise that had woken me up was a girl I'd not seen before, and I wondered if she was new. She stared at me with big, saucer-like eyes. Her hair kind of reminded me of Alex's, except this girl had pink streaks under her hair. Her bright blue eyes had a shimmer of something inside them, and her lips curved into a full pout. She was pretty, I'd admit. But, she was not Alex.

"Do I know you?" I asked out of courtesy. The girl shook her head at me and chewed her lip before answering.

"No, but I'm being transferred into your class," she said. "My name is Shayla Ceratto. I was new here last year." She grabbed her stuff. "It was nice meeting you. What did you say your name was?"

"I didn't. I'm Justin. Which class of mine are you being transferred into? I mean, I do have seven of them," I said with a laugh. Shayla laughed too and threw her hair up into a ponytail. I got to see the full view of her face and realized she was beautiful.

"Oops, I guess I forgot to mention which one. I'll be taking Governmental History with you, which we have five minutes to get to. Want to walk together?" She picked her bag up and headed to the door and waited for me. I figured this would make things awkward if I declined so to be nice; I obliged. "Thanks, I could really use the friends in this class," she replied with a chuckle.

"No problem at all, Shayla," I responded. The two of us quickly walked to class and sat down just as the bell rang. The class fell into its usual torpor when the teacher lectured. I found myself thinking about Valentine's Day and how much I hoped Alex liked her gift.

Finally, two hours and two classes later, the final bell rang. I jumped out of my seat and hurried along to my locker. I threw the bag inside and shut it quickly. I didn't have any homework this weekend, so there was no point in taking it home with me. As I walked out of the school, I saw Kosta and Nico standing by their truck. I waved to them and walked over.

"Ah, just the men I wanted to see!" I mused as I returned their handshake.

"What's up, man?" asked Nico. He turned to Kosta and handed him an envelope. "Finally got Lissa tickets to that Taylor girl's concert that she's always obsessing over. Hopefully, she'll like it. What did you get- oh, hey Alex!" Alex came up quietly behind me. Thankfully Nico had said hello to her, or my whole surprise would have been ruined.

"Yeah, what Are you getting Alex for Valentine's Day?" she asked jokingly.

"I didn't get you a thing girl!" I winked back. Oh, no. I'm not ruining this surprise; I thought to myself.

She laughed and gave the boys a hug as a car beeped from behind. We all turned to see Cody in his Prius waving to us.

"Hey, stranger, where you been?" called Kosta. Cody laughed inaudibly and replied,

"I've been sick, man. Sick, school, and work. No life, right? Listen, we're all still hanging out V-Day right?"

Alex looked back at me as if I was supposed to answer for the whole group. I looked at Kosta and Nico, who nodded.

"Yeah, wouldn't have you miss it for the world," I called in response. He smiled and waved Alex to the car. She kissed me goodbye quickly and ran.

"Love you," I called softly, but I knew she didn't hear me. I turned back to the boys who gave me a melancholy smile. I tried to shrug it off, but they knew.

"Give her time, Justin. She'll say it when she's ready. You don't want to push it, or you'll push her away," Kosta cautioned. I nodded but kept my thoughts to myself.

It was hard. I knew what she had gone through, and what we've gone through as a couple. I didn't know why it was so hard for her to say it back? I'd known her for eight months now, and I could tell she felt something special between us. I knew that. But, even Lissa had told Nico she loved him, already. I wasn't going to use that as a valid point in an argument, though. I knew I'd lose. I supposed the only way I'd get through it was just to wait.

"What time are we meeting Monday after school?" Kosta asked me. Oh, yeah. What a dumb ass I was. I forgot about Monday.

"We can probably meet at Cody's house around five and go from there," I replied. That way, I could pick up Alex, and we could all go out to eat right from the house.

"That sounds good," chimed Nico. He stuffed the rest of the banana he was eating into his mouth and carried on. "Ith we ah 'poeth to mee' dere," he swallowed. "Are we going to go in the same vehicle?"

That was a good question. "Um, well were going to have to take at least two cars because there are nine of us. Five in one, four in another," I reasoned. Nico nodded and hopped into Kosta's truck.

"Alright, brother. We out! See you Monday," Kosta said. He turned the truck on, and it came to life. He peeled out of the spot and raced away. I headed to my Malibu and retreated home as well.

Halfway home, I realized I left Alex's gift in my bag. "Shit!" I swerved around a median and raced back to the school. I knew it was probably safe in my locker, but I didn't want to take a chance on losing it or it being stolen. I parked my car and ran up the stairs to the school, not even bothering to turn the Malibu off. Running up to the door, I knocked loudly. I hoped the janitor was around; he loved me.

After standing there for what seemed like hours, I decided to give up. No one was answering the door. I sighed in defeat and walked back toward my car. Out of the corner of my eye, I spied a cheerleader leaving through the door.

"Wait!" I called to her. She reached quickly for the door and held it out for me. I ran over to her and saw that it was the girl from lunch, Shayla.

"Thanks, Shay. I appreciate you holding the door for me," I said gratefully, as I walked up the stairs. Shayla smiled at me and shrugged.

"Forget your homework?" she asked.

"Nope, my girlfriend's gift," I explained. "It's moderately expensive, so I don't want to leave it here over the weekend." When I mentioned Alex, her face fell. It was so quick, though, I pretended I didn't notice.

"Oh, right. Well, don't want to keep your precious girl waiting," she said flatly. She walked down the stairs and off to the parking lot. I ran quickly to my locker and grabbed the little silver box. I walked quietly through the deserted hallways back towards the main door when I heard a giggle in one of the rooms. Feigning ignorance, I dropped to the floor and started to untie and retie my shoelaces.

Normally I didn't care about drama, but for some reason, I was intrigued. I sneakily looked through the door and saw my ex, Jenna, and one of our male teachers! He had his pants undone, and she was kneeling in front of him. I heard him groan with pleasure, and before I knew what I was doing, I jumped in the class and took a picture. I ran out just as Jenna opened her eyes and gasped. I'm not sure how much of me she saw, but I was in my car and driving away as fast as possible.

Holy shit! I thought to myself. Thank God she wasn't my girlfriend any longer, that slut. I then realized the importance of not taking advantage of what I had. I had an amazing girl now, and she treated me right. Sure, we had our minor issues like everyone else, but what we have for each other is true. That's why I went out of my way to spoil her sometimes. I want her to know that not all boys who say they love a girl are lying. Some of us tell the truth and mean it with all of our hearts.

That was such a repulsive picture in my head. Regardless of who it was, what honorable teacher lets a high school girl suck his dick? Whatever, I thought with a chuckle. The crew would have a laugh at that story. I safely tucked the necklace box into my boxer drawer when I got home and headed to the shower. The warm water felt wonderful on my shoulders.

I had to work all weekend, so I wouldn't even see the crew until our Valentine's Day festivities. I mean, I had work with Cody tomorrow, but I was beginning to wonder if he really wanted to be a part of our crew anymore. He never showed up for band practice, he didn't include himself in on hanging out and playing ball. He was there maybe once or twice a week; if that.

I realized I'd been in the shower a while just lost in my thoughts, and the water had gone cold on me. I jumped out and changed quickly into my work clothes. I had time just to grab a bagel to eat, and I was on my way. I had to work until close tonight, and then a double Saturday and Sunday, which meant open to close both days, a busy few days ahead.

The next few days passed by in a slow blur. The longest day was Sunday because no one seemed to want home cooked pizza. Working with Cody was actually fun, for a change. He seemed like his normal self, which was a breath of relief. At the end of the night, he said he was more than happy to come out with us Monday night, and asked if it would be alright if he brought someone.

"I mean, I've been talking to her for a while now," Cody said. We were just sweeping and getting ready to close up shop.

"What's her name, man?" I asked, eager to finally share what was going on in my long lost best friends life. He explained to me that that was why he'd been shady the past few months. He had wanted to get to know this girl without the rest of us knowing because he felt like he could be serious with her.

"I don't know; she's perfect to me. Everything makes sense when I'm with her. Is that how you felt when you met Alex?" he asked me. I stopped sweeping for a second and contemplated this.

"Well, yeah. When I laid eyes on her, I knew there was something different about her. You can just tell that things with her are going to last. She's my missing puzzle piece if you want to get corny for a minute. Does your mystery mama have a name?" Cody grinned at me.

"Yeah, it's such a beautiful name. Her names-"

"I don't pay you guys to talk! I pay you to feed customers with pizza and clean. Shut up and get back to work!" barked a nasally voice from behind us. I stifled a laugh and looked at my boss, Turk. He wore a Pac-man tie today with pin-stripe business pants. Oh man, this guy needed to learn how to dress.

"Sorry, sir. Why can't we talk while we're cleaning?" asked Cody. Turk frowned and scratched his head.

"Well, uh... because I said so! Barney, you get into the kitchen and clean the appliances. Jovan, you can finish cleaning the front area." Turk turned on his heels and walked back toward his office. Cody frowned but went, obediently. Before he went into the kitchen, he turned around to face me.

"Apparently he's given me a nickname as well. Turd. Anyway, I think you'll like her. I'm excited for you to meet her. I call her La La." Cody smiled fondly, as if remembering an inside joke. He walked away wistfully, leaving me to my confused thoughts. La La? I'm pretty sure there was no girl at our school who went by that name. I tried to think as I finished sweeping. Laura, maybe? There was a Laura Steadman in our grade. Maybe that was the mystery girl! I was pretty excited to have finally figured it out.

I got out of work Sunday night and realized I'd completely forgotten about telling the crew about what I saw after school on Friday. Not that it actually mattered, but I just wanted to make the point that I had dodged a bullet with her. I also realized that I'd have to face Jenna in about four of my classes. Suppose she had seen me, then what? I wasn't going to hold it over her head; that would be cruel. But it would be interesting to see what she might do to make sure I didn't say anything?

I debated going to the principal, but in the end decided against it. I'd have to wait and see if she knew it was me, or not.

The only way I'd know for sure was to wait and see tomorrow. I called it an early night and fell asleep like a rock.

The next morning I was jolted awake by the sound of thunder. Great, I thought groggily to myself. It was raining. Rain always put a mood damper on events, and today was Valentine's Day. I climbed out of bed and grabbed my clothes. I looked around for my bag, momentarily forgetting that I left it in school on Friday. There was no point in taking the gift with me, either. We were all meeting up at Cody's later.

School went by in a haze. Both my teacher and Jenna were absent today, which led me to believe that they were scared I was going to do something, I realized with grim satisfaction. Cody was out too, surprisingly. I had asked Alex where he was, but she had no idea. I sent him a quick text, but the only reply I got, was him saying he was sick. Just when I thought that things were going back to normal. I finished picking out my outfit for the night and thought I looked, as the people say, "sharp."

I was wearing my black boots and a flannel with nice, crisp jeans. It was low key, but it seemed like the perfect outfit. I put the little box in my pocket and got into my car.

When I arrived at Alex and Cody's house, I saw that Nico, Kosta, and Frank were there. Lissa and Amanda were as well, but Spencer was nowhere to be found. I hopped out of the Malibu and walked over to where my friends were.

"Where's Spencer?" I asked. Kosta turned his head around and patted me on the back.

"She's with Alex helping her finish her hair," he said. My heart fluttered at the sound of her name.

"Actually, I'm right here," Spencer said from the stairs next to us. "Alex is almost done. She said she'd be out in five minutes." Spencer looked absolutely stunning as well. Her long, red hair was curled into little ringlets and was pulled into a low ponytail. I could see the adoration in Kosta's eyes when he looked at her. I was happy for my friends.

"Are we all ready to go?" asked Alex quickly. I turned around and nearly gasped. Have you ever heard the old cliché of the girls in red? Well, let me tell you it is true. She had a sparkly red shirt on with leggings and thigh high boots. Her hair was pulled back into a low bun, with a few pieces framing her face.

"Wow," I breathed. I shook my head immediately realizing how much I sounded like an inarticulate prick. "Yeah, we're ready." I reached for her hand and walked her to my car. I promptly opened the door for her.

"Are you okay, Justin? You seem out of sorts tonight," she asked me quietly as I climbed in the driver's seat.

"No, I'm fine. You really look beautiful, and it caught me at a loss for words," I said truthfully. I saw her fight back a smile but kept silent.

When we got to the restaurant, we were seated early. Since Cody and Laura didn't make it, there were eight instead of ten. They sat us at a round table and gave us menus. I was busy looking at what the place had to offer, so I elected to go last. Everyone fired off their orders while I pondered.

"Can I have a sprite with a dash of grenadine, please?" asked Alex. "Oh, and I'd like the filet mignon well done, with a side of mashed potatoes and gravy." Across the table, Frank laughed.

"Isn't that a Shirley Temple, then?" he asked her. Alex smiled for a moment.

"I guess so. I don't want a lot of the grenadine, though. I just like enough to give it a nice flavor," she replied. Frank considered this and answered her with a shrug.

"I'll have a glass of Perrier and the Bacon Burger with lettuce, cheese, pickles, onions, and tomatoes," I ordered. I looked up to give the waitress our menus. "Shayla? I didn't know you worked here," I said to the girl serving us.

"Yep, got the job about two months ago," she replied sweetly. She gave me a smile that I couldn't quite understand, which made Alex look a little irritated. I impulsively grabbed her hand and gave her a reassuring smile. She pulled her hand out of mine and looked at her plate. Shayla looked over at Alex.

"This must be the girlfriend! Nice to meet you," she said and extended her hand out to Alex.

"It's Alex," she said frostily. "Girlfriend has a name." She stared Shayla down, and to her credit, she didn't flinch.

"Well, I'll get your drinks and put your food order in! Enjoy your night." She walked away quickly, and I looked over at Alex.

"Really? Why did you have to be rude to her, Alex?" I asked incredulously. Beside me, the rest of the crew shifted uneasily. Maybe it was wrong to chastise Alex in front of our friends, but why did she act that way?

Alex looked at me and said nothing. Just then, Shayla came back and delivered our drinks and walked away, but not before giving me a swift wink. Ah. That would explain the cold demeanor that had overcome Alex. I leaned over and whispered in her ear.

"I'm sorry. I didn't realize she was flirting with me so openly. Let's just have a good night and forget the drama."

"Sure, Justin. We'll do just that," she said with a quick smile. I knew there would be an aftermath; I thought with a sigh. But for now, I hoped, we would all just enjoy the evening.

CHAPTER SIXTEEN
Alexandra

"I have to go to the bathroom," I remarked. I just wanted to get away for a few moments and collect my thoughts.

"I'll go with you if you like," chirped Spencer. I nodded in agreement, and together we got up and walked toward the ladies' room. We walked past the slew of tables and through the doors. As soon as we got inside, Spencer pounced.

"What's wrong, Alex?" she demanded. She sat up on the sink and looked at me. I instantly felt scrutinized, and I withdrew.

"It's nothing," I said. "That server was blatantly flirting with Justin and had the balls to say 'Ooh that must be girlfriend!' Hah. You see him here with a girl and more couples, why would you flirt with him." I realized I was pacing, so I halted. Spencer was looking at me and thinking hard. I had always liked Spencer, mainly because she was so honest.

"Justin is a big boy, though. None of us saw him flirt with her. He only had eyes for you, Alex. I saw him apologize to you after he spoke to you that way when he realized what was going on. It's natural to feel jealous when something like this happens. You love him," she said bluntly.

"Whoa. Back it up a step, Spence. I don't love him. And, for the record, I am not jealous." I shook my head. I had nothing to be jealous of, so why was I acting this way? Was she right? Was I really jealous? Spencer jumped down from the sink and checked herself out in the mirror before walking to the door.

"Suit yourself," she remarked. "Coming?" I felt a blush creeping up my neck to my cheeks, but I nodded and followed her out to the restaurant anyway. I wanted to smack myself. I made myself look like the biggest bitch in that bathroom just now. I shouldn't have said what I did. It's not that I don't love him; I mean, I don't. I care about him immensely, however. I don't know; it's just all so confusing. I promised myself I'd never fall in love again.

He was so sweet to me and treated me well. It's actually really hard not to fall for a guy when they do that. That is also the reason you need to be most careful. How long would that last? I mean, look at what happened with Dean...

"Hey! Sorry, it took a little longer than we thought. We ended up chatting for a few minutes and lost track of time," Spencer said cheerily to the group, which interrupted my reverie. I snapped out quickly and sat down next to Justin. I gave him a small smile, in apology, which he returned quickly. I sighed. I really did have it wonderfully, so why on God's green earth did I always have to have this guard up?

"So, guys. I think it's time we can give our ladies their small trinkets now," said Nico with a furtive smile. Kosta, Frank and Justin all looked at Nico and shared the same smile. The girls and I looked on in curiosity. Amanda and Lissa were practically holding hands in excitement. I stifled a laugh at them. They were too cute. Frank pulled a J.C Penney shopping bag onto the table and pulled out boxes.

"This one is for.... Spencer! Here you go, Spence. Uhhhh...Amanda, here you go, baby. Alex, this one's yours.

Lissa, for you." He finished handing out our gifts and threw the bag on the floor next to him. We all looked around waiting until we could open them. Justin shyly smiled at me.

"I looked high and low for your gift, so I hope you like it." I smiled back.

"Well, you've done a great job so far so I'm sure I will!" I gently tugged off the ribbon and removed the top of the box.

Inside was a small necklace. On it, was a beautiful, white-gold heart lock pendant, with a key to its side.

"The key unlocks the heart," Justin said softly. "Go on, open it." With trembling hands, I took the tiny skeleton key and turned it into the pendant. I heard a soft click, and gently pried it open. I gasped. In it, was a picture of us, which I never knew was taken. Justin and I were sitting in a field holding hands, but Justin was in one side of the heart reaching towards the middle, and I was in the other, reaching out to him. He must've had someone take that picture during the fall.

"Do you like it?" Justin asked. I jumped on him immediately and gave him a huge hug.

"I do! I really, really do. Justin, it's beautiful I love it! Thank you so much!" I kissed his cheek. Around us, I heard the others laughing. Embarrassed, I sat down in my seat and looked around. I had forgotten they were there. I was lost in my own little world. I looked around at what my friends had gotten for gifts. Lissa was crying and hugging Nico for getting her the Taylor concert tickets. Spencer was admiring a new promise ring from Kosta, and Amanda had received a pair of diamond earrings. They were all nice gifts.

Pretty soon, the food runner dropped our food off at the table, and we began to eat.

"Everything taste okay?" the server named Shayla asked. Part of me wanted to lie and say the food was awful to make her have to work harder, but I decided against it. He was mine, after all.

"Yes, everything is good," said Nico. He took a bite from his breadstick to show her. "Mmmmm!" We laughed. I ate my steak with a rejuvenated feeling. I shouldn't have let my anger out towards Justin. I was feeling good.

After dinner, everyone decided they wanted to skip the movie and just hang back at our house. My mother and her fiancé had flown to Boston, to get something from my father and plan their honeymoon. I took out my phone to check the time- it was eight in the evening. I found a text from Kat:

Hey, girl! Hope you're having a nice V-Day! Dan and Marco want to have a video date soon! Let me know when! xox- K.

I had forgotten about them.... how was that possible? My best friends back in Boston were the nicest people and I hadn't talked to them since right before Christmas. Jeez, Barnes. Guess I was disappointing more people than just Justin.

We drove in silence as we headed back to my house. It was a comforting silence, though. The lights were off in my house except for my brother's room. I was assuming that he was playing Xbox or something, due to the flickering lights in the background. I hopped out of the car and went to unlock the door for my friends. Justin went to go park across the street so Frank and Kosta could park in our driveway.

I opened the door to see the chandelier dimly lit. The ambience of the light gave my foyer a romantic glow. I smiled to myself; thinking about how long it'd already been since we came to Union. I was in such a romantic mood- it was actually a bit freaky. The rest of the group came in, and we went into the parlor room.

"We should go downstairs to see Cody and see how he's feeling," said Kosta. I scrunched my face up in disgust.
"You realize he has the flu, right?" I asked him. Kosta shrugged.

"He's still my friend. His single ass needs some loving tonight, eh?" he cackled. Nico laughed and Justin and Frank joined in. The girls and I sat there, staring dumbly at the guys. Their friendship bond had turned into a "bromance". While it was completely normal for us, people tended to think they were all more than friends in public.

"What are you talking about, K? Cody's got a girl now!" explained Justin. I looked over at him quickly.

"Wait, he actually admitted it to you?" I practically shouted. It took Justin by surprise.

"Y-yeah? We were working last weekend, and he told me about her. He's fallen hard for this chick. He didn't want us knowing because he knew we'd make a big deal out of it. He only told me her nickname." He swallowed. I felt a cold numbness float through me. Cody was my twin brother, my best friend.... he didn't even tell me about this girl. I was only guessing this whole time. I felt hurt. Betrayed, even.

"What's her name, J?" asked Spencer, clearly trying to ease the tension that had wafted in the room.

"He only had time to tell me her nickname... said it was La La. I figured out who it really was, though. You guys remember Laura Steadman, right? It's her. He didn't want to tell me right out, though." He grabbed me in a small embrace, but I couldn't return it with much enthusiasm. He sensed I wasn't very happy, so he quietly whispered in my ear.

"Everything okay?" I nodded silently. I had a flood of emotions running through me, and I didn't want to say the wrong thing. He smiled at me and walked over to the guys. Amanda and Lissa were heading out the door because they had homework to do. Frank and Nico walked them to the cars, leaving Justin and Kosta inside with us.

"We're gonna' head out too, man," Kosta said wearily. "I want to shower and Spencer needs to write her college essay." Justin gave Kosta the handshake and hugged Spencer goodbye.

"Bye, guys! See you in school tomorrow," I called to them with a wave. Justin walked them to the door and then turned back to me.

"Okay, so what's really going on?" he demanded. I was about to speak, as we heard a knock at the door. "I'll get it," he murmured.

"Hey! What are you doing here?" McKenzie? I hopped up from the couch and ran over to the door to find my sister and a man standing there. A *pregnant* sister, might I add.

"Wh-what happened?" I stuttered dumbly. McKenzie rolled her eyes and pushed past Justin and I. The guy followed suit quietly.

"If you don't understand how a baby is made, I am not going to explain it to you. I'm five months pregnant now. Liam and I are moving, to Cincinnati to find an apartment, but for the meantime we're going to stay in my bedroom. Stanford just wasn't for me, and now that I have a little one on the way, I needed to be closer to home." She sat down at the kitchen table and poured herself a glass of seltzer water. So, my sister was finally pregnant. Before I could stop myself, I exploded.

"So is this the baby's father?" McKenzie's jaw dropped, and Liam and Justin stared at me in shock. I kept going. "You know, you don't give me any credit at all. I'm not stupid, McKenzie. I am eighteen years old and yes, I do know how a baby is made. I also know that you're really stupid for dropping out of a frigging university. You're. Having. A baby! Don't you think you need an education so you can get a job to pay for it? It's a living creature, Kenz! It's not a doll or an accessory you carry around when you feel like it! This baby is a living creature that you made! I honestly feel sorry for it. Its mother is ignorant, and the father, is stuck with a girl who jumps from guy to guy, on a freaking whim! Oh, mom is going to rip you a new ass when she finds out," I shrieked.

I took a few deep breaths to calm and steady myself. McKenzie was icy pale. When she spoke, she spoke in a deadly whisper.

"Yes, Liam is the father. Mother already knows. Why the hell do you think we're here? Money? No, we have that. I actually have a job as an intern for a company in Cincinnati who, when the baby comes, said they'd promote me to full time with benefits. I haven't jumped from guy to guy, seriously? I had one other guy I saw at the beginning of the year, but I called it off because I went steady with Liam. I'm so very glad you think that highly of me, Alexandra. Where is all of this coming from? I heard from Cody about how you screamed at Deanna and now me? What's gotten into you?" She had tears pearled up near her crystal blue eyes. Liam sat down next to her and patted her hand. Beside me, Justin remained silent. I could tell he was silently willing me to back down, but I stood tall.

"You're upset of how I think of you?" I said incredulously. "You constantly put me down and call me stupid and air-headed, and that I make all the wrong choices but really, McKenzie? How else am I going to think of you? We were never close because you never cared to get to know who I was. Belittling your little sister because it makes you feel superior, who does that? I can't think highly of you because there are no expectations with you. I don't know what else to tell you, Kenz, I don't. As for "giving it" to you and Deanna, I finally learned to stand up for myself for once in my life." I looked at her face once more.

"Congratulations, though," I said as I retreated to my room. To hell with them. My night was perfectly fine until...No, they didn't ruin my mood. All my pent up anger at that Shayla girl, and anger that my brother didn't include me was channeled and directed at my sister and her boyfriend. I felt bad. Tears welled up in my own eyes, and I cried. I was crying so hard, I never noticed Justin coming into my room until he was just sitting there with me, rubbing my back. I sniffled and tried to give him a smile.

"I'm sorry, Justin. I wish you didn't have to see that." Justin shook his head.

"Don't worry about it, Al. Things happen. You think I wanted you to see what happened back with my dad a few months ago? Of course not, but you can't change how things happen. I can tell you haven't been yourself all night, and then they came and stirred the pot some more too. Do you want to talk about it?" He asked softly. I started crying again, but I nodded. I knew the best way to feel better was to vent it out, and then to let it go.

"My brother has been my best friend since the day we were born. We tell each other everything. Well, almost everything. But usually he'd tell me if he were dating someone, and the fact that he didn't tell me this time.... well, no offense to you, but I'm just hurt that he didn't come to me. McKenzie and I never got along, because I was always a little afraid of her. But, for some reason, whenever you're around, I feel much stronger and sure of myself." I knew I sounded pathetic. Hell, I probably looked pathetic too. But Justin never batted an eyelash. He grabbed me in a tight embrace and held me there.

"It's natural to feel jealousy sometimes, honey. You're not used to having to share your brother with your friends or have girls openly flirt with me in front of you.... yes, Spencer told me.

Please don't worry. Shayla is in my government class at school. I never even realized she had a thing for me until she gave me that wink. It was harmless, but I could tell you we're bothered by it. It's probably just her nature, but please think nothing of it. Cody has been in his head for a long time, and I highly doubt he wanted to keep Laura from you, but he wanted to figure things out. He's clearly serious about her. Give him time. I don't know about your sister, but I wouldn't worry about her, either. She has issues, so let her boyfriend and your mother deal with them. You just keep on being the you that I love." He cupped my face in his hands and gently kissed me. I felt... different. At that moment, I realized everyone had been right all along.

"I love you," I whispered through the rest of my tears. Justin looked at me quickly and hugged me once more.

"I know, baby. I know. I love you too," he whispered back. We stood in the embrace until I gently broke free. When we separated, I started to laugh. I had left make-up lines on his jacket. I felt bad, even though it was washable.

"What's so funny, woman?" he asked. I couldn't stop laughing so I pointed to his jacket. He looked down and saw the black marks. He looked up at my face and started laughing as well. "Oh, you look amazing right now!" I covered my face in mock embarrassment but continued to laugh. Suddenly, I pushed him down on my bed. He tried to hold his balance, but he couldn't hold himself and fell back onto my mattress.

"That wasn't very nice of you," he growled. Before I knew what was happening, he lashed out and grabbed my arm and pulled me down next to him, mushing my face into the bed. I giggled as he started to tickle me. He was stronger than me, so he had me pinned down while he was tickling at my sides. I had more tears down my face as I howled with laughter because of this attack. I tried to reach around to tickle him, but within a second, my arms were tucked under me.

"I surrender!" I yelled. "I surrender!" Justin jumped up and pulled me to my feet.

"I win, and you lose. Chalk it up to Justin Barry, winner of the century!" His hands were cupped in applause as he waved them around.

"Shut up, no, you don't. You cheated and used brute force to win. Disqualification!" I waved my finger menacingly. "I'll have to report you to the authorities if you don't rescind that," I said. Justin laughed and grabbed my finger.

"I am the authorities. I do what I want, and what I want is to tickle my woman. So, therefore I will," he yelled and pushed me down again tickling me once more. As I laughed, the hurt and pain of the night had dissolved and my life was whole.

CHAPTER SEVENTEEN
Justin

It was a dream. It had to be. I couldn't believe it when I woke up the next morning. There she was, lying peacefully next to me. The memories from the night before replayed in my head. I've been waiting to hear her say that for a long time. I didn't even mind that she was saying it to comfort herself. All that mattered to me was the fact, that she finally admitted her true feelings.

I wasn't going to do her any wrong. I couldn't hurt such a beautiful angel like Alex. I knew she was afraid of what the future held because of her past, but I was part of her present. I'd make it so that her future would look brighter.

She stirred softly, and for a moment, I thought I'd awakened her. She yawned daintily, and her slow rhythmic breathing returned. Alex was exhausted. I'd wrestled with her far into the night, and although she was a good sport about it, I could tell she was happy when I finally stopped.

I got out of bed and walked over to the window. The rain had stopped sometime overnight, and the day broke with a pale blue sky with the sun shining brightly above. Behind me, I heard the rustle of the bed sheets, and I turned around to see Alex stretching.

"When did we fall asleep?" she asked, still groggy. Getting a better look at her, made me chuckle. Alex had a serious case of bed head, but the way she cocked her head to the side made her look like a confused puppy.

"Not entirely sure, but I do know that it's almost eleven in the morning. We should make breakfast. Pancakes?"

Alex smiled. "That is an obvious yes!" She jumped up and slipped into her sweatshirt. It was amazing at how one person could have such an impact on me. Even when Jenna and I had been together, it wasn't as big of a deal for me. When we'd split, sure I was bummed, but I'd been fine. The thought of being this serious with Alex kind of stopped me in my tracks. I never thought of it in that way. I could see her being a part of my future, but I'd never stopped to think of just how long the future really is.

Alex came over to me and nuzzled in for a hug. I knew she was seeking comfort because she felt vulnerable. All of a sudden, I felt the weight of the world crashing down on my shoulders. I sighed.

"What's wrong, Justin?" Alex asked worriedly. I shook my head.

"Nothing is wrong, I just feel bad. I don't want you to feel pressured into telling me something you don't feel just because I always say it," I explained. She took a step back and frowned.

"No one pressures me into doing anything, Justin. You know that. I'm a big girl, and I have the ability to say and feel what I want. Sure, I'm not the best at expressing myself or being an easy person for you to love, but I meant what I said. I'm sorry my past has messed with my head so much, but I can't help that. I only wish you'd stop calling me perfect. I'm never going to be this perfect girl who has a perfect life. My life is shit. My father left us for some whore, and my mother is marrying a guy

I've only talked to three times! I can't even get into my brother and his absence or the fact that I've gone through stuff, I shouldn't have."

She walked to the side of the bed and flopped down on it halfheartedly.

"Justin, you may not have the perfect life either," she said softly. "But you have hope. You've given that to me, but you can't label me as perfect. I can't accept that." I couldn't help from smiling at her.

"If you say so, weirdo. Let's go have pancakes." I pulled her off of the bed and ignored her confused look. I was just happy I had her. I wasn't going to let her go through it alone, but I couldn't handle explaining the sudden change that shifted in my brain.

Most guys I knew around here treated their girls well and let it be. I just realized that although Alex seemed to enjoy the things I did for her, if I did too much, I'd push her away. I couldn't let that happen, so I vowed not to be that overly romantic guy that made other guys (and girls) gag. If that meant being slightly complacent, so be it.

"Good morning, sleepies!" came a cheerful voice from the kitchen. Alex and I walked in to see McKenzie making breakfast for Liam and a disheveled Cody, who looked better, though tired. I sat in-between Cody and Alex and patted his shoulder.

"Feeling any better, man?" Cody nodded.

"Yeah, I don't understand where it came from. I played Xbox and watched Netflix all night. Sorry, I couldn't make it, dude," he said. I shrugged it off.

"No big deal, just glad to have you better. Laura must've been bummed out she couldn't see you on Valentine's Day." I cast a sideways glance at Alex. She had her lips in a hard pressed line as she buttered a piece of toast.

"Here you go, Justin! I made breakfast," said McKenzie as she put an omelet on my plate. I smiled in thanks, but I noticed everyone had breakfast, except Alex. I frowned.

"Aren't you going to have an omelet, Al?" I asked. She glanced at me.

"No. I don't want one," she replied. McKenzie glared over at her.

"You weren't going to get one anyway, you spoiled little-"

"Alright! That's enough, guys. I'm sick of you two fighting all the time," yelled Cody to my surprise. I looked over at him, and he shrugged.

"All they ever do is fight. McKenzie can't leave Alex alone for two seconds, and Alex has to get the last word in. It's annoying. I liked it better when you didn't live here, Kenz, there was never any family drama. I don't know where you're going to stay anyway considering we have a stepsister now." Cody looked over at his oldest sister to his youngest.

"Cut the shit. I'm done with this. Justin and I are going out for a little while, and you two are going to get over yourselves. Let's go," he said with an air of finality.

"What do you mean we have a stepsister? I didn't know Mama's getting married?" asked McKenzie. Liam sat there quietly eating the food on his plate. Good man to stay out of this family feud.

"Mom's marrying some guy named Peter. He's got a daughter named Brooke, and they gave her your old room. They were waiting for the spring to do renovations in the basement to cut my room in half for a room for you, but clearly you weren't told."

McKenzie stared in shock.

"Well, no wonder my room looked all young and countrified. Ew. I'm going to have a few words with Mom about this," she spat. Alex didn't say a word except she kissed me on the cheek, slipped a note into my hand and walked upstairs. Cody nodded in the direction to the door, so I followed. I didn't want to be rude, so I said goodbye to McKenzie and Liam. McKenzie was overdosing on her pregnant hormones- she was crying into Liam's arms. He didn't say a word, just held her, comfortingly.

Once we were outside, I opened the note Alex had given me.

My sister is completely crazy. Sorry, you had to witness her outbursts. I can only imagine how much worse she'll get due to her pregnancy. Have fun with Cody; I'll talk to you later. I love you! – Alex.

I smiled and put the note in my pocket.

"So is your sister always like that?" I asked Cody. He grabbed the keys out of his pockets and unlocked the Prius.

"Sure. All she ever did as a kid was torture Alex. I was always the middleman, and it gets old after a while. It's like McKenzie was always jealous of Alex. They're both my sisters, but I don't know, man. Alex has always been a best friend and my twin. Kenz is just... different. She's not one you can easily get used to. I kind of feel bad for that dude for being stuck with her and the baby. It's weird to think, though... I'm going to be an uncle!" Cody rambled on as we drove. I had no idea where the hell we were going, but I figured if he needed to talk that was the least I could do for him.

"Hey, at least you're not going to be a daddy," I replied. We looked at each other for a moment and then started to laugh. We pulled up to an old pickup truck in an empty parking lot. "What are we doing here, dude?" He fumbled around in his cup holder to find a bill.

"Making money, that's what. I'll be right back." Cody jumped out of the Prius and got inside the truck. I sat there quietly, and then it hit me. Cody was selling pot. I didn't even register how baked he looked this morning; I'd assumed he was tired. I quickly dialed Nico's number.

"Dude, we need an intervention with Cody ASAP."

"Wait, why? What's going on, Justin?" Nico sounded like he'd just woken up.

"No time to explain, man! He's coming back. Get F and K together and meet me at the Millhouse in thirty. Go!" I hung up. Cody was just getting back to the car as I stuffed my phone into the pocket.

"You ready to go?" he asked. I sat there quiet. Cody blinked. "You alright, Justin?"

"Yeah, who was in the truck?" I wanted to ask right away about the pot, but I decided it was better if the boys were there too.

"La La. She and I came up with a way to make bank so we can go on vacation," he smiled. That's so... sick.

"Cool. Let's go to Millhouse, I wanna get a pastry." The jerk in me was proud of myself, but the friend inside me felt bad. I pushed the thought out of my head. Kid was frigging messed up. Selling pot? Not something that flew, with me or the crew. I felt my pocket vibrate. It was Kosta.

What's going on? Y are we meeting at Millhouse? What's wrong with Cody? – K

I quickly typed out my response.

'Cody's dealing the green with girlfriend. Frig that. Scare tactic or bust. Later.'

That honestly infuriated me. I knew he used to smoke back in Boston, but he told me he had dropped the habit. I lost a cousin to lung cancer, so it means a little more to me than the average Joe. Cody changed the radio station to some dance music channel. He nodded to the beat, and I sat there silent as a brick.

"Soooo... how are you and my sister?" Cody asked to keep some sort of communication going.

"We're good. Same old, same old," I replied. Cody chewed the inside of his cheek.

"That's it? Nothing changed at all?" he hedged.

"Why don't you ask your sister? She's been dying to talk to you," I said firmly. He sighed.

"I can't really talk to her. I want to, but La La insisted we keep this a secret from her. I know that sounds messed up, and believe me, it is. But there's truly a reason for it, and I agree with La La on it. Don't ask questions, dude. Just trust me, please." He looked sincere, and for a moment I thought about forgetting the intervention. The thought quickly left my mind, however, because we had just arrived at the Millhouse.

The Millhouse was what we called a 'Mom N Pop' pastry shop that was founded in an old abandoned millhouse. The elderly couple that owned the shop turned it into a quaint little coffee and pastry joint that kids our age often went to. It usually got pretty noisy in there, so we could talk without worrying about being overheard.

"Funny how you wanted Millhouse, I was going to take us here after I met up with La La," Cody went on happily.

"Oh yeah?" I asked. "I know the boys are here. We have to talk to you about something, Cody," I said nervously. He looked bewildered.

"About?"

"Let's go meet up with the boys," I sighed. We walked inside and scanned the crowd for the crew. I spotted Frank's fitted baseball hat in a booth, so we made our way over.

"Hey boys," I called. I gave Kosta and Nico the handshake and nodded at Frank. He had a muffin in one hand, and a donut in the other. Typical. Cody sat down, and the boys looked at him.

"We missed you being around, Code. What's gotten into you?" Nico looked at him.

"I was sick. Plus I have work and schoolwork, and La La," he calmly explained.

"Oh, right...well, how's selling pot?" Kosta said outright. I stared at him in shock. Leave it to Kosta Eliades to be direct. Cody blanched.

"That's what this is about? You think I'm dealing weed?" His eyes widened.

"Well, uh. It seemed to appear so today when you met up with your girl? I didn't want to assume anything, but it would make sense, Code... we're not saying you are, but if so, you know that's not cool with us." I looked at him sadly. "We miss our Cody from back in the day, and you've gone MIA on us. What the hell is the real deal?"

"I'm not selling weed, guys. We're selling frigging handmade school supply shit. Is that what you wanna hear? No, didn't think so. It sounds so stupid... For the record, it's not my idea. It's La La's, and if you wanna talk shit, go for it. We need the money so we can get her a prom dress for prom at the end of the year, as well as go on a vacation since she's never been on one. She isn't the wealthiest, so I promised her I'd help her. I've been sneaking out for months at night working on them with her, because of her work schedule. I wanted to keep it private because I knew you'd all laugh at me. Happy now?" he said angrily. We all exchanged guilty looks. How the hell would we get out of this one now?

"Oh..." trailed Frank. "Well, shit."

"How did you expect us to know, Cody? You kept it from us, so yeah. We have every right to assume something because when our best friend goes MIA for months on us, we have to wonder something. Justin was perfectly within his means to ask us all to talk to you because, believe it or not, you're our friend.

We won't let you fall. Why in the hell would you think we'd judge you because you're helping Laura? There's nothing wrong with that. Sure, we'd tease you and call you Martha Stewart, but we wouldn't shit on you for helping her," Kosta said back. Cody stood up.

"Really?" he asked.

"Obviously, dude. We're your friends," replied Nico. Cody seemed to retract his mind for a moment.

"Wait a minute, did you say, Laura? As in, Laura Steadman?" he asked.

"Well yeah... isn't that La La?" I chimed.

"What the hell? No!" he remarked. "La La is by no means Laura Steadman." Cody started laughing.

I was about to ask him who exactly was this mystery girl when I felt a soft bump on my arm.

"Hey handsome! I didn't know you came to Millhouse!" said Shayla. Great, I thought to myself.

"Yeah, I do. I'm with friends though, so I'll talk to you later," I said dismissively. She seemed determined, however.

"I have a cheerleading competition coming up if you guys want to come. I'll be the one in front with the short skirt on," she said with a flirty tone. Nico looked over at her.

"I think we're set with that one, Shay. We all have girlfriends," he said. She shrugged.

"So? I'm not asking you to do anything other than show support for your school's cheerleading club." She sat down on the seat of the booth right next to me.

"You are the basketball and football captain, are you not,

Justin?" The closeness was making me uncomfortable.

"Yeah, I am. That doesn't mean I'm going to go, though. Give it a rest." She inched closer to me. Nico, Frank, and Kosta all exchanged confused glances. Cody sat there, quiet. He looked angry, actually. I didn't blame him. Some girl was flirting with his twin sister's boyfriend.

She was right next to my face, and she smiled. "I want you there, though," she whispered in my ear.

"Congratulations, Shayla. I'm not going. I have a girlfriend, now leave me the hell alone." I was started to get aggravated. She pouted.

"You're no fun," she said. She fixed her lip-gloss in the compact mirror. "Suit yourself!" She got up. "Oh, and Justin? One more thing, your fly is down," she said. She quickly kissed me on the cheek, winked, and walked away. And all we could do is stare in shock.

CHAPTER EIGHTEEN
Alexandra

"Wait a minute, what?" I shrieked down the phone, as my brother tried to explain, calmly, what had just happened.

"Listen to me, Alex. We're on our way back now. He'll explain everything once we're home, but I'm telling you now- he handled it so well. I don't understand what just happened, but I figured I'd tell you." Cody sounded drained. Whatever Justin and Cody had set out to do earlier this morning had taken its toll on the both of them.

To be honest, I was a little miffed that they'd left me with my sister and her boyfriend. All she did was shoot daggers at me whenever she saw me, and cried. Oh, how I wish my mother and Peter were back already. Brooke had been staying with a friend for the time being. She didn't really want to be around us, and we didn't mind either. McKenzie was the only thing ruining my relaxing time away from the step-crazy.

Celtic was feeling the tension as well. I hadn't ridden her in God knows how long. Thankfully, at the stables where we boarded her, there was a trainer who exercised all of the horses daily and turned them out into the pastures for those who can't always get down.

"... Alex? Are you still there?" called my brother from the other end of the phone. I snapped out of my thoughts.

"Oh, yeah. Sorry, Cody. I was thinking about Celtic and all of this madness here at home," I answered. I could hear Cody chuckling in the background and answer a question Justin probably asked him.

"Haven't you realized by now, no matter where we live, there will always be madness?"

I smiled into the phone. "Duh, I live with you, remember?" I joked as I hung up the phone. I walked back into my room and started straightening up the mess that had become my bed. It was weird to think just last night was Valentine's Day, and I had finally told Justin how I really felt about him. It was kind of ironic, now that I thought about it.

All of a sudden, I heard chimes and beeps coming from my computer. My heart raced- it was video chat! I ran over to my desk, excited to talk to my friends.

"Hey, guys!" I said, and then stopped. It was my mother.

"Hey, honey! How is everything going out there? I was just going to leave a video message for you. Is Cody looking after you alright?" She smiled for a moment. "Wait... why are you not in school? Alexandra! You know better than that!"

I sighed. "Mom, we discussed this weeks ago. None of us are going to school today because it's senior skip day. Cody's fine, he's feeling better. We have a surprise guest here, though," I replied to her, hoping she would forget about skip day. I mean, it wasn't a lie at all. It was senior skip day for us, and most of us would probably get detention for it tomorrow.

"Oh, that's right. You know I don't approve, but it's your grade, not mine. Who's there?" she asked.

"Uh, McKenzie and Liam... they said you knew they were coming. She's pregnant," I said meekly. I knew from my mother's surprised faced she'd had no idea.

"She's what?" her face had gone pale. I could hear Peter in the background asking what was going on.

"Pregnant, Ma. Look, I gotta go. I hear Cody and Justin knocking on the door, and I'm sure Kenz is sleeping. Call us tonight and we'll talk! Love you, bye!" She waved, and we disconnected the video call. I ran downstairs to grab the door.

"Jeez, took you long enough," Cody grumbled as they walked through to the kitchen. Justin looked guilty and quiet. I rounded on him.

"So, what happened?" Justin looked at Cody, and they both shrugged.

"Shayla was at Millhouse when the crew and I were there. We were talking to Cody because we thought he was selling green with his girlfriend, but, we were interrupted by Shayla. She kind of got real close to me and kissed my cheek and said some crazy comments but Nico and Kosta let her know what was going on. We handled it this time, but it's getting a little out of control," he finished.

"You don't say?" I said with a hand on my hip. "Justin, just last night she was flirting with you while I was there! Of course, she'll flirt with you when the boys are around. I don't know what she's trying to pull, but I hope you know that I'm going to be speaking to her tomorrow." I pushed my hair back out of my eyes. Cody was playing on his phone giving us some privacy, but in his concern, spoke up.

"Sis, let me warn you, though. She seems pretty damn relentless. We don't want another episode in school with a fight again," he said.

I stared at him in disbelief. Justin was standing next to me looking at Cody as well. "Excuse me?" I asked him. "How do you know Shayla?"

"I go to the same school as her, and people talk. I've heard her say things about wanting to get with Justin Barry. I don't want to see you get into trouble over her attitude. Just be careful, Allie."

"It's not like she's going to be successful," Justin chimed in. He slid his hand into mine. "I swear to you, that you have nothing to worry about." I flashed a smile at him.

"I know. Believe me- I'm just sick of her shit. Why does she have it out for me?" I walked to the cabinet and grabbed some popcorn. I was hungry. I was going to put it in the microwave when it hit me.

"Wait a minute! Why haven't you told me about your girlfriend?" I looked across at Cody. His smile faded at the tone of my voice.

"Trust me, Al. I want you to meet her, really. But she thinks it's for the best that we keep it a secret for now, everything has a way of working out. Can you just trust me on that? It's more of a need-to-know basis," he responded.

"Need to know basis? What is this, Cody? I'm your sister, not some random person who wants to know your personal life. If you don't want to tell me, fine. I'm not going to make you, but I can't believe you told Justin before your twin..." I trailed off. Yikes. It seemed like nowadays I sounded more pathetic than strong, in control, Alex.

"You're still my number one, sis. But you just need to

trust me. I'm not lying, or doing anything wrong." Okay. Seriously, I needed to get a grip. I've been so emotional lately, anyone would think that I was the pregnant one... no. Back it up a bit, Barnes.

"You're right! Sorry, Cody. I don't know where my head's been at, lately. It's been weird. No more!" I smiled to my brother and his best friend. Funny how things change as time goes on. Here we were in February, eight months after moving here in June. We'd known no one, had no friends. We only had each other. Now, we had such a tight-knit group of friends that accepted us instantly. It was like we'd always lived here.

February went as quickly as it came. Throughout the weeks that followed, I'd grown more tired and cranky. Shayla's antics worsened. I'd even exchanged a few words with her asking her to stop, and to no one's shock, Cody was right. She'd just laughed at me and walked away. I felt trapped. I'd made it worse. My brother seemed to be coming back around more, thankfully. His girlfriend had to work a lot more; I'd guessed. When my mother and her fiancé came back, she'd had it out with my sister about where she would stay and who would help with the baby. In the end, because my mother was always a sucker for McKenzie's crap, she had Peter start the renovations early, and paid for them to stay at a motel until it was finished.

One day at school, we were all sitting outside enjoying the warmer sun. It was March now, and the flowers were coming up just a little bit earlier than usual. I hadn't an idea what a Kentucky spring was like, so this should be a beautiful sight to see. Kosta and Nico had skipped their classes to join us all on free block, which we now had because we were almost ready to graduate. Originally, the free period was supposed to be used to get ahead on our senior projects and college essays. Naturally, we just relaxed.

Justin and Kosta were throwing a tennis ball around while the girls and I sat and gossiped about the up and coming, St. Patrick's Day party. Even though the party was a week away from the actual day, everyone was still super excited for it. According to Justin's cousin, Hana, the whole senior class was invited. It was funny, and possibly a bit shallow, but I never thought people in Kentucky could throw a real party.

Cody, Nico, and Frank had grabbed some hockey sticks and were playing some street hockey. It had been months since Cody had played; seeing him fooling around had brightened him up immensely.

"So, Alex," began Amanda. "What are you going to wear to the St. Patty's party this weekend?" I pondered for a moment.

"Is it cliché of me to wear green?" I joked. "Actually, I might need to head up to Cincinnati to go shopping for a new outfit. I promised my friends from back home I'd video chat them so they could help me." Kat had gotten ahold of me a few weeks prior, and we'd finally caught up. She had talked to my father, who was paying to fly her out here for my prom! It was still a few months away, but she was coming for a week. I excitedly made Cody promise to take her as a date so we could go together. I ended up having to bribe him with a new Xbox game and fifty dollars, but I got what I wanted.

Amanda and Lissa were painting their nails a greenish

hue. Spencer was flipping through websites on her laptop to find a good outfit. I glanced over at the boys, who were talking amongst themselves. Frank was pointing over to a crowd of people. I followed his finger to the group of obnoxious cheerleaders and, oh, of course. Shayla was the loudest and most obnoxious one of them all. It was forty-five degrees out, and she was wearing high-waisted shorts with a blazer. No matter where you go, you'll always have a Deanna. She saw Justin in the crowd and waved over to him. I clenched my fists when I felt a hand on my shoulder.

"Don't," said Spencer. She stood behind me and watched. "She's doing it to make you mad. I don't think it's about Justin anymore, to be honest." I chewed my lip.

"Up until she started this, I had no idea who she was!" I exclaimed. "There goes that theory."

"Not exactly, Al. See, she probably had a little crush on him until she found out about you. Then, seeing the reaction you gave her, she started goading about it. Don't give into it. Justin's yours," Spencer said. I sighed. She was right.

"Okay," I affirmed. "But, that doesn't mean she can get away with it." Lissa shot me a glance.

"Normally, I'd agree with you on that one, but I think Spencer's right. Shayla is just a bitch who's jealous; you're gorgeous and have Justin. There are girls like that everywhere." Amanda nodded in agreement.

"Yeah, if you let every girl who looks at your man get to you, you're going to set yourself up for failure. I did that with my last ex, Michael. It totally ruined us. I vowed I'd never make that mistake again. Frankie and I are so much happier this way. Plus, we can all see how head over heels in love with you, Justin is." I felt my cheeks get hot. I had become such an insecure girl. What the hell had gotten into me?

"This isn't like me," I apologized. "I don't understand where this comes from. I just don't know how this works."

"Simple," Spencer smiled. "You're in love." Three small words summed up an entire ocean of feelings. Leave it to Spencer to do just that.

"Yeah, I-I guess I am," I said slowly with a smile. I caught Justin's eye from across the lot, and he smiled at me, and my heart melted. The guys walked over to us as the bell rang to signal us to last class. Justin laced his fingers through mine.

"Excited for this weekend, Alex?" he asked me. I smiled and nodded.

"Oh, absolutely! I've always loved St. Patrick's Day, which is funny. I'm not even Irish." I rambled on as we walked to class. Justin chuckled.

"You talk too much, you know that?" I rolled my eyes back at him.

"A girl never talks too much!" We stopped in front of my class. Justin kissed my forehead and wrapped me in an embrace.

"I'll see you tomorrow," Justin said as he let me go and walked down the hall. I waved back at him and went inside the classroom. The teacher was already preparing the quiz we were to take. I groaned inwardly. I had totally forgotten chapter seven and eight's quiz was today.

I couldn't concentrate. I sat there twittering my pen between my fingers. It had been a while since I lost my focus because of a boy. Thankfully, this time it seemed to be for the better. An hour passed by agonizingly slowly. I was pretty sure I failed, but right now it didn't matter. The sun was shining warmly, and tomorrow night, I would be having the time of my life with my friends. Life was finally good, I thought to myself with a smile.

I walked out of the class once the bell rang and made a beeline for my locker. To my annoyance, I saw Shayla blocking it. She was standing there talking to one of the guys on the debate team. She gave him a flirty smile and walked away. I grabbed my coat from my locker quickly and walked to find my twin.

Cody was talking to Nico just outside of the boys' bathroom. I sidled up next to my brother and hip-checked him into Nico.

"Thanks, Al. I wasn't having an in-depth conversation with my friend, Nico or anything," Cody grumbled as he massaged his hipbone. Nico and I laughed.

"It's alright, I got to go find the girlfriend anyway. She wants to go shopping for an outfit, or whatever you girls do in the malls. I'll hit you up later, man!" They did their handshake, and Nico walked off, leaving my twin and me alone.

"Ready to go, Cody?" I asked him as I walked toward the door. He didn't answer me, so I turned around to see that Cody had vanished. Seriously?

I picked up my bag and walked down the hall in search of

my ghost of a brother.

"Where on earth did this frigging boy go?" I muttered to myself angrily. It was a Thursday. Kat, Dan, Marco and I usually had our video date before I went to the stables. I was running late, and it was my brother's fault. I decided to go wait in the Prius until he decided to show up. I walked out the door of the school and nearly smacked into Cody.

"Where have you been?" I said. "I turned around and you had vanished. Thanks for letting me know." Cody looked guilty.

"Sorry, Alex. I saw La La walking down the hall and I wanted to say hi to her before she had to work. She's working two double shifts the next few days so I won't be able to see or talk to her. I'm sorry for just walking away like that," he apologized.

"Why didn't you introduce her to me in the hall if she was right there, then? I've clearly seen her before," I sighed. "I know, I know. You guys don't want the world knowing right now; I get it. Would I at least approve?"

Cody smiled at me as we got into the Prius. "Of course you would. She's such a sweetheart to me, and nothing like Deanna was. She comes off as a tough girl, but that's because of everything that happened to her before. She was raped too, you know, just like you. I really like her, and I think you all will too. Just give us time to figure it out, okay?" I couldn't help but smile at my twin.

"I understand, believe me! I'm sorry for being a pain. I just get so annoyed so easily at the moment, what with that Shayla girl pestering me. Why was she raped if you don't mind me asking?" Cody knew that was a touchy subject for me to talk about.

"Her stepfather molests her at night, and her mother doesn't believe her. That's also why we're keeping it quiet- I don't want her stepfather to take it out on her even more. Once we decide to go public, I want to ask Mom to let her move in with us because she'll be eighteen," he replied. We were stopped at a red light, and he went to check his phone. "We have a few plans and as long as we execute them in the way that's best, everything will be okay in the world."

Plans? My brother's cryptic message kept me thinking long after we got home. I chatted with Kat and Dan for a little, and to my sadness, found out that Marco and Dan had split up. We cried together for a while and tried to cheer Dan up.

"Did he give you a reason, sweetie?" I asked him. Dan sniffled.

"N-no, not really. He'd just said he needed his space, and we had become a "we" and he missed his individuality. It's a bullshit reason. I swear there's another guy, or he cheated on me." I looked at Dan's sad face. I wondered how this would affect the foursome.

"Don't worry, Alex. I'll take care of him," said Kat. She gave her cousin a hug and waved goodbye. We hung up the video call, and I sat there in silence. Life was getting way too confusing for my poor brain, I thought to myself as I packed my bag to go riding. I loved riding on days like this.

The air was cool, but it wasn't enough to wear a jacket. I would have to say it was about fifty-five degrees out. I liked the feeling of just pure, ultimate bliss.

I got done riding Celtic just as the sun set. It was colder now, so I left her blanket on for her to keep her warm. I mucked her stable out and gave her fresh water and hay to nibble on until I could get back here Sunday.

"I will see you later, my love," I cooed to her as I kissed her velvety nose goodnight.

The drive home took a bit longer than I expected. My brother had forgotten to fill the tank, so I had to stop off for some gas. While I was pumping, I saw some girls from our school walking by. I tried my best not to overhear their conversation, but when the girls were loud, it was quite unavoidable.

"Do you think that hot senior will be at that party tomorrow night?" Girl number one mused to her blond friend.

"Who, the football captain? I hope so. He's so fine! I wish I were his girlfriend. Doesn't he have one?" The blonde one said with a pout.

"I think so, but I'm pretty sure she's foreign," girl one replied. I rolled my eyes to myself. It was evident the 'foreign girl' was me. I was tempted to yell "I am not foreign," but they'd already gone too far for me to even care. I supposed this was one of the things I missed when I dated Dean- I'd never felt the jealousy of other girls wanting him because I never felt like he was truly mine.

I got home, and the lights were off. Such a surprise! On the island, there was a note from my mother saying that everyone went out for dinner and to make myself something. I rolled my eyes as I crumpled up the note and threw it away. Ever since McKenzie came home, my mother had seemed to forget she had a second daughter. I was used to that, however. I'd hoped that maybe, just maybe, that when we moved out here, she'd realize the importance of being a family.

I didn't even bother making anything for dinner. I was too worn out from riding. I dredged up the stairs and crawled into bed, and that was the last thing I remember....

"Alex, wake up! Wake up!" Cody's voice called from far away. I felt him shake my body, and I groggily rubbed my eyes.

"What's going on?" I asked. When my eyes adjusted, I saw him standing above me, ready for school. "Wait, what time is it?"

"Time to go, sis. You never sleep through your alarm. Hurry!" I jumped out of bed and scrambled to get ready. In the end, I was forced to go to school in yoga pants and a sweatshirt. I was hoping beyond belief that school would go by quickly so we could get to the weekend. I was wrong.

School dragged by so slowly; I felt like we were moving in a trance. I barely saw any of my friends, let alone Justin. When the final bell rang for the day, I couldn't be happier. I decided last night on the outfit I would wear, so I didn't have to spend any extra money. I knew Cody was going home with Justin today, so the Prius was free to drive back too.

When I got home, my mother fought with me for a half hour about taking Brooke with me to the party tonight. She'd said her and Peter were going to take some personal time to go on a date in Cincinnati. In the end, I was annoyed and stuck taking my, soon-to-be stepsister, to a senior party. Hopefully, tonight's party would lighten my mood up immensely from this crappy day.

At seven thirty, I was all ready to go. My mother had Brooke wear some of her clothes to give her a new outfit, but Brooke was about as happy as I was to be going with me. She sat in silence in the car while I drove. I'd given up on trying to talk to her months ago. I just turned the radio up and danced along to some Kesha.

When we got there, the house was already pretty packed. One of the football boys' parents were gone for the weekend and allowed him to have a get together with a few people. As is often the case, a 'few people' turned to a huge party. As soon as we walked inside Brooke walked away to talk to someone she knew. I silently cheered. I wouldn't have to watch her! I walked around saying hi to everyone I knew and kept my eyes out for Justin and my brother. I'd found Spencer, Kosta, Nico and Lissa by the pong table cheering on Frank and Amanda's team.

People played pong here differently than we did in Boston. We used to fill the cups up with beer and drank it when the opponent sunk the ball in. Instead, they used water. Frank and Amanda chose to drink soda because they weren't going to be staying over tonight. We cheered them on until they won in the last round.

"Way to go, guys!" Spencer cheered. The other team looked pretty buzzed already, which looked silly.

"Hey, have you guys seen Cody and Justin?" I asked them. Kosta pointed towards the DJ booth.

"I saw Cody over there talking to Stephen, but I haven't seen Justin since they arrived. He's probably going to pick up people for Braden," he responded. I nodded and walked over to the DJ booth to find my twin.

"Hey, Alex!" Cody called to me loudly. He had a goofy smile on his face, which could only mean he was drinking. "How's my best twin in the world doing? Shayla isn't bothering you, right?" He slurred. I covered my mouth trying not to laugh.

"No, she isn't. She's here?" I asked him. He nodded like a little child, wild and vigorous. He covered his mouth and chuckled.

"Yeppppppppp! Okay, I'm going to dance now, bye!" He pushed past me into the other room where the dancing was. I had to admit- this kid Braden had one nice house. More and more people kept filtering in and out of the party. I decided I was going to look for my boyfriend. I'd been here for about an hour now, and I hadn't seen him. I figured he was probably making drinks for those who wanted them, but I wanted to surprise him anyway.

I looked in the kitchen, but there was no Justin. I asked his teammate, Greg, where he was.

"Last I saw him, he went toward the bathroom. He could be in the poolroom, though." Braden had a poolroom? Holy cow, this house was the perfect place to have a party. The bathrooms were vacant, so I assumed he was in the poolroom. I finally found my way down there and went in.

My mouth dropped. I stood there, frozen where I was. I was staring at an insanely drunk Jenna Feiffer kissing Justin.

233

My Justin. They broke apart, and Jenna giggled.

"Oops, did I just kiss your boyfriend?" She hiccupped. I was shaking. She stumbled by and gave me a wink and walked out, leaving Justin and me.

He walked over to me, pale white. Before I knew what was happening, I reached out and slapped his face. Hard.

"What the fuck were you thinking?" I said in a deadly whisper. I knew if I raised my voice, I'd break down crying. No, this is what I expected.

"Alex, no. You have to listen to me, I-"

"I don't want to hear a single word from your mouth you sick bastard! After everything I went through, after everything you promised, you go and do this to me? Screw you!" I yelled louder now. The two people swimming in the pool had stopped and stared at us, but I didn't care. By now, Justin had tears in his eyes.

"Why the hell are you crying? Stop. You look pathetic, Justin. Well, actually, you are pathetic. I have no respect for someone who cheats. You got caught; now you have to deal with the consequences. It's over, if you didn't already know," I spat. I ripped off the necklace and threw it into the pool and watched it sink. Just like my heart, just like our relationship. I walked away just before the tears came.

I don't remember stopping home and grabbing clothes. I stuffed all of my necessities into two bags and hopped back into the car towards the highway. I plugged my phone into the Bluetooth and made a phone call.

"Hello?" Said the voice on the line.

"Hey daddy, it's me, Alex. I'm coming home to Boston," I swallowed.

"Really? How long are you staying for? Pumpkin, I'm so happy you're coming," he said happily.

"For good. I'm moving back home," I said, grimly, as I hung up the phone and drove silently through the night toward CVG.

CHAPTER NINETEEN
Justin

As I watched her walk away, I lost it. I couldn't believe anything that had just happened. I tried to tell her, but she wouldn't let me talk. I felt stupid. I tried to make her listen, to see sense. I tried calling her phone, but it had the busy dial tone. Beep. Beep. Beep. I fished the locket out of the pool and dried it off as quickly as I could. I opened the locket, and the pictures curled up from the water it had absorbed. By now I didn't care that I had tears in my eyes.

"Haha, that guy's a pussy. Can't you see he's crying? He probably shouldn't have cheated on Alex with his ex," said a voice behind me. I turned around to see Tom Ford and John Lawton, two soccer players from our school. My cheeks burned.

"You talkin' about me, Lawton?" I said to him. He smirked over at his friend.

"Sure am, Barry. You're a washed up football player who got shot and let it get to his head. You ain't nothin' to this school, and you deserve the shit you reap," he replied. So, I did what every guy in my spot would do. I punched him in the face and threw him into the pool. His friend Tom took one look at me and ran away. I needed to find Cody.

I ran up the stairs towards the house. People were everywhere, so it made it harder to find Cody, in the throng of the house.

"Justin? There you are!" Spencer called to me over the music. "Did you find Alex? She was looking for you earlier." Her

236

eyes widened at the sight of my red face. "What happened?"

"Jenna was drunk and she came into the pool room and started hitting on me. I swear, Spence, I didn't engage back. She literally grabbed my face in her hands and kissed me right as Alex walked in," I explained sadly. Spencer's eyes got even wider.

"Are you serious? What did Alex say?" She exclaimed.

"She stood there, smacked my face and ended it. I tried to call her but no answer," I said. Spencer grabbed her bag and keys.

"Come on," she said. "Let's go find Cody and the others and we'll get in contact with her. I'll talk to her if you need. Let's go find Jenna too." I tried my best to follow her, but I was in shock. I should've handled it better. Rage filled my mind, and I started to punch the wall. Spencer turned around in shock.

"Justin! Stop! What're you doing? This isn't right," she said as she grabbed my arm. Kosta came out of nowhere and held me back.

"Dude, what happened?" He asked.

"Jenna started somethin' and Alex walked in at a bad time, of course. She thinks Justin was into her again," explained Spencer. Kosta let out a whistle.

"I mean, it's a shitty situation, but I don't think punching walls is gonna help you anytime soon. Take a breath, drink some water and once you calm down, we'll see where Alex is at."

"No, you guys don't understand. This is between Alex and me. Thank you guys for wanting to help, but I need to talk to her," I said finally. Spencer looked at me softly. She sat down next to me and handed me a bottle of water from the bucket.

"We understand, and we believe you. But we also know how Alex is. It'll be harder to convince her of the truth. You need to realize that if she isn't willing to listen, you might just need to move on," she said sadly. I couldn't believe what I was hearing. I shook my head.

"No. I don't need to do anything except prove my innocence. Alex doesn't need to think yet another guy can screw her over like this. Even if we don't get back together, she at least deserves the truth. Wouldn't you want the truth if this were Kosta we were talking about, Spence? Of course you would. I know Amanda and Lissa would as well. I'm going to do the right thing. So, if you'll excuse me," I said, "I'm going to find Cody and Jenna." I stood up and finished off the water bottle while trying to gain composure. I sure felt like a pussy, just as John and Tom had called me. I took a few deep breaths to center myself. Alright, I thought to myself. Where can I find these two? I walked away from my friends and through the door towards the dance room. Music was pumping through the speakers. I couldn't even hear myself think, let alone concentrate. Finally, after what seemed like hours, I found Cody standing near Shayla and a girl called Francesca. Perfect.

"You, get over here. Now!" I yelled. Cody pointed to himself and came over once I nodded. Shayla followed behind Cody without a sound. I walked into a vacant bedroom and closed the door behind us. Shayla shuffled uncomfortably next to Cody. I'm not a mean guy, but I can be intimidating when I needed to be.

"Shayla, I know you're on the cheerleading team with

238

Jenna. Has she said anything to you about me?" I seethed. "Because she just kissed me, and Alex saw, so now I just had to go through a breakup that wasn't supposed to happen."

"Don't yell at La La, Justin. It's not her fault exactly. I think it might be mine," he said. It took me a moment to comprehend.

"... La La? THIS is La La?! This is the girl you've been dating? Cody, she blatantly has been hitting on me in front of you, causing Alex stress!" I definitely did not see that one coming.

"And how is it your fault?" I sat on the bed and put my head in my hands. This is too much.

Cody took a deep breath before speaking. "Back when you first told me you loved Alex, I knew she wasn't going to get there without a little push. During the nights that I was helping her with the crafts, we came up with what was supposed to be an innocent plan on lighting a fire under Alex. Trust me; I wasn't too keen on watching her hit on you, or watching my sister fall apart over it. But, at the time, Alex needed that push. La La was talking to me on the phone after practice one night last week, and I think Jenna heard her. Jenna had already told the rest of the team that she didn't want you with Alex, so I assume she used the knowledge to her advantage. I didn't think anything like this would've happened, though." Cody looked over at Shayla, who hung her head low in defeat.

"Believe me, Justin. I have tried telling you about this so you could be in on it too, but Alex kept popping in and I couldn't just yet. Please don't be mad at either of us. I swear this wasn't meant to happen," Cody pleaded. I took a moment to register Cody's story.

"We good, man?" I exhaled slowly and nodded.

"Yeah, we're fine. Help me talk to Alex. Find Jenna, Shayla. I want her to understand what she did," replied. Shayla looked nervous.

"Do you think she hates me? Alex, I mean." She said quietly. Cody started to shake his head, but I interrupted.

"You just never know. Just be honest and do the right thing for once," I said to her. She nodded.

"Let's go talk to her," I said. Shayla gave Cody a kiss and went to find her teammate. Cody looked more sober than before, so I asked him to call Alex and see if she was home. He didn't get an answer either.

"I'm going to call my mom and find out if she knows where she is," he said. He sat on the phone for several minutes while I went to unlock my car and find a room. He didn't get off of the phone with her until after we were quietly nestled in a small room.

"They're on their way home now; they thought she was with Brooke...Oh my God! We left my stepsister alone!" Cody groaned. "I messed up big time."

"No, we both did," Shayla said as she returned to the room with Jenna trailing behind her. "I didn't mean to take it too far. I'm sorry, Justin. I really am. I hope you can forgive Cody and me."

"I'll always forgive Cody," I replied. "But you've deliberately tortured Alex for months and that's not okay with me." I rounded on Jenna.

"And you," I spat. "What the hell did you think you were doing? You know I have a girlfriend, and plus you were the one who left me. You lost your chance." I glared down at the face of my ex-girlfriend.

"Look," began Jenna. "I was pissed that you were gloating about how awesome and how gorgeous you thought Alex was, and it felt like you invalidated the two years we were together. Then, I'd realized it was you who walked in on me in the empty class." She swallowed.

"How'd you know it was me? What does that have to do with anything?" I asked her.

"You told your friends because Shayla asked me if I did it."

I looked over at Cody, who shrugged sheepishly.

"What? I didn't know she was going to confront her. I didn't even know they knew each other until I went to the competition."

This was just too much to handle. Jenna apologized, even though I could tell she didn't mean it. I told her to leave before I gave her something to regret, and she bolted. I sat there with my head in my lap for a few minutes, trying to collect my thoughts. It wasn't until Cody put his hand on me, did I get up and march toward my car.

It was a quiet car ride over to Cody's. Shayla had her head on his lap and he looked wanly out the window, making sure not to say anything else that could upset anyone. When we got to the house, Cody and I bounded to the front hall listening for a sign of Alex.

"Alex? Are you there? I need to talk to you!" He yelled. There was only silence. Cody ran upstairs and for a minute, we heard nothing. He swore to himself out loud. "She's not up here!" He called to us. Where on earth did Alex go? Shayla was looking on the refrigerator at the pictures when Cody came down.

"Code, I didn't know you guys had plane tickets. When are you leaving for Boston?" He looked at them for a second before inspiration struck. He quickly grabbed his phone and dialed a number.

"Dad, it's Cody! Listen, is Alex on her way to Boston? She never told any of us where she was going.... Right. Okay, thanks, Dad. Later." He put his phone down and looked at me.

"She went to Boston, Justin. She told our dad she wanted to move back home, so she took a voucher and left," he said. My eyed widened. This seriously couldn't be happening.

"Can't we track the flight? Can your mother help us figure it out?" I asked desperately.

"Can your mother help you figure what out? Where's Brooke?" asked Connie Barnes as the rest of the gang walked into the kitchen. Cody looked at his mom.

"Something happened between Alex and Justin, so she just jumped ship to Boston, didn't tell a soul. I found out through dad. What he was asking was could you track all flights to Boston and see when they leave and land?" Cody finished. He shook his head. "This is my entire fault. Brooke is still at the party with everyone. I forgot to have her come with us when we left. I am so sorry." I put my hand on his back.

"Just stop blaming yourself. What's done is done. I just gotta' go and bring her back," I replied. Everyone looked at me like I had multiple heads.

"What?" I asked. "I'll go to Boston and I'll prove to her, that I'm innocent and convince her to come back to Union."

"Do you really think that's going to work?" Connie asked. I shrugged my shoulder.

"Anything is worth a try in my book, ma'am," I said back to her. "Cody, I'm going to need that voucher of yours."

"Take it," he replied. Connie and Peter grabbed the laptop and started the flight search. Tonight was just too dramatic for my liking. Drama is definitely not a favorite of mine; I don't know how girls can thrive off of this stuff.

"It says a flight from CVG to Boston direct left at ten fifty. It took off twenty minutes ago," came Connie's answer. I hurried over to check the screen.

"The next flight leaves at six-thirty tomorrow morning and another one at twelve," I read aloud. Cody drummed his fingers on the table. I could tell he was sincerely sorry. He thought he was doing us a favor.

"Alright, I'll go and pack my bags now. I'll just wait at the airport until I can board. How do these voucher things work?" I asked.

Connie replied, "Take this ticket to the counter and specify the flight you wish to take. If you're not sure about the return, just go one way and do the same thing in Boston upon departure. The money is covered, but you will have to pay an airline fee if it's last minute. That shouldn't be more than twenty-five dollars, though."

I thanked the Barnes family for all of their help and went on my way. I tried my best not to think about everything, or I'd lose it again. The only thing that mattered to me was getting Alex back.

I wouldn't tell any of the guys this, but it actually bothered me when John and Tom called me a pussy for being upset. It was like guys my age don't know how to treat a girl, or how to show feelings for them. My grandparents raised me above all of that, and I will never change for anyone, except me, and my grandmother.

When I got home, I left a note for my mother and sister letting them know where I was going. I also emailed my teachers so they knew I wasn't skipping any classes next week just in case it took me longer than I expected it would. I threw a slew of clothes into my basketball bag along with my laptop, toothbrush, and my debit card. I jumped back into the Malibu and rushed to the airport to make my travel.

Since I had to wait until the next morning for the flight, I went through security and sat down at the gate early. When I was seated at the gate in the terminal, I opened my laptop to search how long the flight would be. According to the flight tracker, it would take five and a half hours to get from Cincinnati to Boston. That would mean I would be in the city around noon....

I fished my phone out of my pocket and tapped Cody's number into the phone board. He picked up on the second ring.

"What happened? Did the flight get canceled?" He asked worriedly.

"No, I need to know where I'm going. Can you text me your dad's address and possibly the directions on how I can get there in a fair amount of time?" I responded back to him.

"Yeah, absolutely. You're gonna' need to hail a cab, though, to get to my dad's from Logan. We lived on Boylston Street but be warned- it's one ritzy ass condo we lived in," Cody said. I heard him fumble around and tap his phone. Shortly after, I received an alert notifying me of a text.

"Thanks, man! I'll call you when I figure everything out," I said gratefully. We hung up the phone, and I sat to wait....

DING! "Everyone in Terminal two departing through gate four please come to the boarding dock. I repeat, Terminal two departing through gate four please come to the boarding dock. We are ten minutes to take off, thank you!" The noise woke me up, and I realized that was my flight. I groggily grabbed my bag and fumbled my way over to the gate. The lady quickly took my boarding pass, scanned it, and ushered me on my way down the jet way.

I looked at the pass and found my seat, rather grumpy at this point. Next to me sat a five-year-old boy who was whining to his mother about having to go potty. He nearly climbed over me, to reach the aisle and pranced through the slew of passengers to get to the bathroom. His mother, who was holding an infant, apologized for bumping into me as she went after her son. She handed me her baby and asked me to watch it while she ran after him and left before I could object.

I looked at the sleeping infant in my arms. Judging by the pink blanket, I'd figured it was a little girl. She was peacefully breathing in little spurts, her tiny chest moving up and down in rhythmic motions. I smiled to myself. This little human knew nothing of the outside world and its troubles. It knew only of itself and its mother, and her world was at peace. For a moment, I wondered what my life would be like in ten years. Would I be a father? Would I have a beautiful wife to share my successes with? My dream job wasn't unattainable, but I had always hoped I could share it with a family.

I shook my head to get rid of the thoughts. I was almost nineteen years old. I needed to get my way through college before I could even think about reaching those goals. I quietly rocked the baby until her mother and brother arrived back as the stewardess came over the loudspeaker.

"Thank you all for flying with us on this fine morning. We shall be arriving in Boston around twelve PM, please buckle your seat belts and wait for the safety prompts to follow."

The mother gently took the sleeping girl from me and smiled wanly.

"Thank you so much for watching her. I'm so sorry I had to do that- this is my first ever flight, and I'm a bit nervous, especially with my kids."

"Hey, it's not a problem," I shrugged. "It's my first flight too. I'm Justin. What's in Boston, if you don't mind my asking?" The lady shook my hand and set the baby down on her lap and rocked her slowly.

"Nice to meet you, Justin! My name's Hilary McKenna.

Boston is actually a layover for me. I'm going to Ireland, to meet my husband there for his father's funeral. He left a few days ago to help prepare for everyone. Our children have never left Ohio, so I'm really nervous for them," she replied. I looked down at the sleeping child in her lap.

"What's her name? She's beautiful," I said to her. Hilary's eyes lit up at the mention of talking about her baby.

"Her name is Saoirse. It's an Irish name," she explained. She grabbed an envelope and spelled it for me. It's weird to think that the spelling of her name is different than the pronunciation-"sear-sha."

"Wow, I didn't expect that," I chuckled. Hilary and I talked long throughout the flight, and before we knew it, we were making the descent into Logan airport. Since her layover wasn't that long, she had to practically run to the different terminal to make it to her connection. I wished her luck and bid them on their way.

When I got into the main part of Logan, I stopped. It was a total culture shock for me. I could hear people on the phone talking in thicker accents than Cody and Alex had.

".... Dude, that's wicked! I heard that B.C was ranked first in the semi-finals! I'm wicked amped about that.... no, I'm pahked near Dorchestah street. I'll meet you there in a bit dude...." A man wearing a Boston College sweatshirt was talking to someone on the phone as he rushed past. I now understood where Cody got his catchphrase, 'dude', from. They really overuse that word here it seemed.

The hustle and bustle of the airport traffic was alien to

me. I texted Cody to let him know I'd landed, and sent a quick message to my mother as well. Cody replied with a number for a taxi company. Now that I was here in Boston, I felt unsure of how I was going to convince Alex to come back to Union with me. I'd played out the scenarios in my head throughout the night, but as I got closer to my destination, the more my self-confidence wilted.

I called for the taxi and waited outside near a bellhop. When the taxi came near, I flagged him down and waited for him to stop. I told him where to go, and we were off. It was quicker than I expected to get to Boylston Street, and I only had to pay the taxi driver twenty dollars. I wanted to look around and get a hotel room before I actually went to her house. I found one right on Boylston called the Charlesmark. It seemed a little pricey, but I had over two thousand saved in my account. The concierge told me it was one hundred and eighty dollars a night, and check-in was three PM.

I looked at my phone's clock, which read twelve-fifty-seven. I had about two more hours to kill, so I walked out to find some food. I hadn't eaten since before the party last night, so I was ravenous. I found a pizza joint nearby, so I stopped in to have a slice. I grabbed a table and went to eat when a familiar face walked in. I could've sworn I'd seen it somewhere before....

"Kat!" I said aloud before I could help myself. She looked over at me and squinted her eyes as if trying to see who I was. Shit, I had hoped she hadn't heard me. She walked over to me and sat down.

"You have a lot of nerve showing your face in Boston," she

said coolly. Her eyes bore into mine, but I refused to blink.

"I'm here to right wrongs and prove my innocence," I replied.

"Innocence my ass! You were caught red-handed, so how are you going to prove anything?"

I sighed. "What did Alex tell you exactly?" Kat fished through her bag to find her wallet.

"I don't know why you're conversing with me. You're the one who messed up," she retorted.

"I just want to know what she thinks happened, Kat. That's all I'm asking you to tell me," I answered. I tried not to sound frustrated because this could be the only chance I had at making this even work.

She thought hard for a moment before finally answering. "Alright," she said. "Let me get my pizza first." She went up and placed her order while I tried to calm my beating heart. It felt like it was in my throat. When she returned, she took a bite of pizza before starting.

"She told me that she went to look for you at some party, and she found you kissing your ex-girlfriend. To make matters worse, you didn't even defend yourself. She said you just stood there in shock," Kat stated. I winced.

"Alright, Kat. Here's what really happened, and please- I need you to hear me out before saying anything, okay?" Kat nodded, and I began.

"I was at Braden's house early because he'd asked me to set up. Cody and I finished helping, and he started drinking a bit early. I was in the kitchen making drinks, and I went on a few runs to pick up people and food. When I got back, I was looking for Alex, and my ex, Jenna, told me she saw her in the pool house. I didn't believe her because she was tipsy, but she ran in there anyway. I'm actually a decent guy and didn't want her to fall in the pool and drown, so I ran in to bring her back up to the house. While we were in there, she said I was sweet for saving her life. I told her I was just being a decent human, and she literally grabbed my face and kissed me after exclaiming that she wanted us to try things out again. Alex walked in on that exact time. She didn't give me time to answer. She slapped me, told me she didn't want to hear a word my mouth said and to stop crying and left. That's it," I finished with a sigh. Kat chewed her lip in thought for a few seconds.

"You cried? Why did you cry?" She asked, but with a softer tone.

"Because I love her, Kat. I wouldn't do anything to hurt her; I've told her over the months I wouldn't treat her like Dean did. When she saw Jenna kiss me, my heart broke. Not because of me, but because of her. And what's worse about all of this, is that it was revenge."

Kat looked at me strangely. "Revenge? What do you mean? You wanted her to see that girl kiss you?" I shook my head.

"No! No, I mean Cody and his girlfriend tried scheming ways for Alex to tell me her feelings, and Jenna overheard them and used them against me because I caught her sucking off one of our teachers..." I trailed off.

"Cody did this? No, now I know you're lying. Cody would

never do that to Alex, especially after Dean." Kat narrowed her eyes at me. "To think I almost believed your sorry ass," she said. She stood up to leave, but I grabbed her arm.

"Kat, I am not lying! I'll even call him, and you can hear it from him, then."

"Fine," she said wearily. Kat sat back down as I dialed Cody's number once more.

"I'm with Kat- explain to her exactly what happened, Shayla." I rushed. I handed her the phone and waited. She listened for twenty minutes, only speaking when she had a question. At the end, her eyes widened for a second before narrowing into little slits.

"Tell your boy to take the phone now before I come to Kentucky myself, and rough you up," she snarled. I could hear static on the line like someone was fumbling for the phone. Kat's face relaxed shortly after.

She hung up the phone and sighed. She rubbed her temples and handed my Blackberry to me.

"That was way too much drama, and I usually love it. I believe you, though. Where are you staying?" She asked me.

"I have to check in at three at the Charlesmark. It's two forty-five now, so I'll go back and get a room. Thank you for hearing me out, Kat, I truly appreciate it," I replied. It was true- now that I thought about it, if I didn't have her on my side, I honestly don't think this could even be possible.

"You're welcome. She always spoke highly of you, and I can see why. Would you like me to come with you when you talk to her? I can convince her to come out and see you," Kat said. I nodded in thanks. "Alright, I can grab you tomorrow when she's home. She's with her dad and Marisol for the night and won't be back until later."

We parted ways outside of the shop. My heart still felt heavy, but it was a lot easier to breathe than before. Hopefully tomorrow I would make Alex see that I wouldn't hurt her.

After I had checked into my room, I made my way down to the pool and sat in the Jacuzzi. I was mentally preparing myself for every possible outcome. I wasn't leaving Boston without her knowing the truth.

CHAPTER TWENTY
Alexandra

Ice cream tastes so much better when you watch soap operas. As I'd left everything I owned, apart from a few things, back in Kentucky, I had been shopping with my father and his girlfriend for new things for my bedroom. My dad was happy I was home, so we went out and grabbed new bed sets, a TV, and some bathroom supplies. Marisol offered to take me clothes shopping. What girl would turn down some retail therapy? My father gave me his card, and we went to town. Sure- I'd spent almost a thousand dollars, but who cares? My dad makes almost that much in two days.

I had propped the little TV up on the bureau and set it up next to the bed. When my father had finally asked me why I really moved back home, I'd broke down. He gave me a hug and told me I could stay here for as long as I wanted. I told him it looked like I would transfer back to Quincy Upper the following week to finish out my education. Seeing as it only took a few days, my dad said he would do it after St. Patrick's Day.

There was a noise from the folds of my bed. It was Kat calling.

"Hey, girl! I'm outside. I have a big surprise for you!" Kat sounded nervously excited. Hmmm, I wondered what it could possibly be. I went down to the elevators and buzzed open the door for her to come up. I saw the light go from number to number, rising slowly. I wondered what her surprise was.

To be honest, I hated knowing about surprises. Where

was the actual surprise in that? All it did was make you concerned as to what it could be. While I waited for her to get to my floor, I grabbed myself some cream soda. I heard the elevator door beep open, so I went to greet her.

Kat bounded to me, looking behind her frequently. I furrowed my brows in confusion.

"Is everything okay, Kat?" I asked her. She hugged me quickly and took a swig of her chai latte.

"Oh, everything's fine, yes...." She said distractedly. She looked behind her once again and grabbed my hand. "Do you want to see your surprise?"

I cocked my head. "Should I be concerned? You're acting kind of funky," I replied. Kat giggled.

"You sound so southern; I love it!" She exclaimed. We walked down the hall to the stairway up to the penthouse.

"Wait, is my surprise inside my house?" I asked. Kat pondered for a minute while we wandered towards the door.

"Nah, I don't think so. It should be delivered right to your door, though!" She laughed. I was getting frustrated. Kat, above anyone, knew how much I hated these types of surprises. For her to pull one on me was beyond weird. All of a sudden, I heard a loud crash. It sounded like one of my dad's flower vases smashed. I ran to clean it up before he got home. I saw a man standing there, bent over, trying to pick up the shards. I rushed over and started to help.

"Thank you for helping clean up my dad's vase," I said gratefully. "But I can take it from here." The man tipped his head down before looking at me fully.

"It's not a problem, miss." All of a sudden, my heart beat faster and the air in my lungs seemed to dissolve. No, this couldn't be possible....

"J-Justin?" My voice was barely a whisper. His eyes locked right into mine as he nodded.

I whipped my head in Kat's direction. She shrugged with a half-smile. "I'll leave you two to talk... Call me later? Bye!" She ran down the stairs before I could find my voice. I started to hyperventilate. The last thing I remember before I fainted was his face.

"Alex, are you with me? Can you hear me?" A voice far away seemed to be calling me. I rubbed my eyes and groggily came too. I was lying on my couch, and a hooded figure was standing above me. I took a moment to remember where I was. Everything suddenly came back to me.

"What're you doing here? Get out of my house!" I yelled frantically.

"No, no, no! Stop- put the switchblade down, Alex. It's okay. I'm only here to talk to you." Justin replied with his arms out. I looked over in my hand and realized my father's switchblade, which was usually hidden under the sofa cushions, was in it. I threw it down in disgust. How in the hell did he find me? I continued to stare as Justin gently lowered his arms.

"May I sit?" He asked politely. I nodded curtly and went into the kitchen to grab a drink. I came back, hoping this was a bad dream. Reality wasn't kind. He was still there, sitting on my couch. I stared.

"Well?"

Justin took a deep breath. "You need to know the full story of what happened," he said. I shook my head at him.

"No, I don't. I saw what had happened, and that's all I need to know." I sounded incredibly petulant, but I didn't care at this point.

"Will you stop being so stubborn for two seconds and hear me out, please? I gave you the benefit of the doubt and waited patiently for months for you to feel comfortable. Don't you think you at least owe me the same courtesy?" I scoffed at Justin as he threw his hands in the air.

"Since when do people in relationships owe the other anything?" I waited in silence for his response.

"Alex, listen. You can be pissed all you want, but I seriously just want you to hear the full story before I leave. Kat heard the story and believed me, so why can't you?" His eyes looked bloodshot now that I had a better look. It almost was if he'd stressed most of the time we'd been apart.

I sighed. There was really no getting rid of him until I heard his story. So, I swallowed my pride and nodded. "On one condition," I said. "You have to leave and never bother me again once you're through." Justin blanched but didn't skip a beat.

"Why don't you wait and see what I have to say before you make those kind of conclusions."

"Agree with my condition, or you can leave my house now." Justin sighed.

"Alright, alright. So, here's the story...."

Three-quarters of an hour later, we were still sitting in my parlor room. I could barely believe him, however. How could he possibly say Cody was even partly behind this?

"Will you please just call him, Al?" Justin grumbled. I could tell he was getting agitated. I sighed with equal annoyance and decided to acquiesce. On the third ring, Cody answered.

"Alex! Oh, I'm so glad you called! Are you alright? Did Justin talk to you?" The tone of his voice spoke volumes to me. Justin was right.

"How could you allow her to torture me, Cody? I'm your sister! Not to mention you paved the way for Jenna to walk right up to our relationship and shut the door in my face. You should've told Shayla to keep it quiet. For the record, I still think she's a piece of trash- worse than Deanna ever was."

Cody sighed. "Al, I know. I'm sorry. It wasn't supposed to get that way, I promise. Shayla feels awful for telling Jenna. She didn't realize Jenna would figure out that Justin was the one who walked in on her. We only wanted to push you in the direction you were stalling on. I promise. Do you want to talk to Shayla? She wants to apologize."

"No," I said. "I'm not ready to accept the fact she's the girl you hid from me and allowed to flirt with Justin knowing it was driving me nuts."

"I understand, Sissy. Please forgive us."

"I forgive you, Cody; I do. I know what you were trying to do, but that wasn't for you to decide. I need to move in my own steps, on my own time. Promise me you won't interfere anymore." I looked over at Justin, who gave me a small smile of

257

encouragement.

"Promise."

I hung up the phone and stared at Justin. "I am so sorry for how I acted. I wish I'd let you talk to me instead of getting so defensive. None of this makes sense, and I can't believe he even let Shayla get that far."

"It's okay, Alex. Everyone makes mistakes. You live and learn, and you move forward. I'm proud of how you handled the truth. I'm sorry you were even out into that situation, but I promise it wasn't my intention. I did pull away from her, though. It lasted as long as you saw it." He gave me a small embrace.

"You just don't understand, Justin. He's my twin brother! He didn't have to interfere with anything, not to mention I knew Shayla and Jenna were sketchy people from the start," I sniffed. Justin held his face up by his palms as he sat in thought.

"You're right," he said finally. "I don't understand. Maybe I never will, but the one thing that I do know was that he was doing it because he thought it would help. He didn't think it through, clearly, but he was acting with honest intentions. That right there should be enough to show he didn't intend for Jenna to get involved." He looked me right in the eyes, which made me blush. "Alex, you know him better than anyone. What does your heart tell you? Seriously, think about it."

I rolled my eyes at him, but deep down I knew that Cody wasn't truly to blame. It was me.

"I'm sorry," I whispered. I looked down at the floor. Justin stood up and walked over to me.

"What? Why are you sorry?" He asked me. I shook my

head with sadness.

"If I'd been honest with you from the moment I met you, none of this would've happened," I sighed.

"No. Everything happens for a reason, Al. We just need to take it in stride and move forward. You have your guard up, from things no one should ever go through. I didn't mind being patient. I still don't, but you can't always blame yourself for things beyond your control." He grabbed me in another tight embrace and in that moment, I swore I wouldn't try to fight how I felt, ever again.

"I love you," he whispered.

"I don't deserve you," I replied. "But I love you." I watched as Justin shook his head with defeat.

"Are you coming back to Union with me?" I glanced down at the coffee table? "What? Did something happen?"

"Er, no. I told my dad to reenroll me to my old high school. I thought I wouldn't need to go back," I said quietly.

"Oh," he replied slowly. "I guess I'm up for a long distance relationship."

"Can I ask you an honest question, Justin? What is it about me? What's so special about me?" I took a deep breath at the end of my sentence. He contemplated his answer.

"Well, for one, you never gave yourself away to conformity. You were yourself, and regardless of being afraid of things, you dove head first into it anyway. With all of your new friends, you never forgot your old ones, and you just bewitched me from the moment your Bostonian family walked into my pizza place. It was love at first sight, and not one I ever want to lose. You truly are the one thing that can break me. I've gone through some shit in my life that would normally break a person. Not me. You're my Achilles heel, and I don't care who knows it." He kissed me suddenly and lifted me into the air. "Please come home with me. We all need you; I need you." I looked in his eyes and the night of our first date flashed through my mind.

"What is home? Home is where the heart is, Justin. Wherever you are, I'm there." His face broke into a giant smile, and he spun me around and pulled me closer to him.

"Okay, enough of the ooey-gooey love stuff. Want to do something fun before we go home?" I asked him. Justin laughed at me and sat back on the couch.

"What did you have in mind?" I debated this for a moment.

"Let's see... we always used to sneak into clubs downtown and screw around. Normally I'd call Kat, Marco, and Dan, but do you want to just hang around just us?" Justin just chuckled.

"Whatever you'd like to do, princess. Lead the way."

Two hours later, we left my father's house as quietly as possible. Dad thought we'd been at Kat's the whole time. Introducing my father to the guy who'd allegedly broken my heart was a real trip. The testosterone was thick in the air until Justin recited his story once more. My father seemed to realize the similarities between them and dubbed Justin, a "good man."

We had told him we were going to be staying at Kat's for a movie, but we'd been showering and getting ready for the club. I decided to take him to a rave so it would be easier to slip in unnoticed.

"Are you sure you know what you're doing, Alex?" He asked me uncertainly as we walked down the street. I was trying to concentrate on not slipping in my stilettos.

"Yes," I grumbled. "Just let the one with the boobs do the talking." We continued to walk toward the door as someone knocked into me, causing me to fall flat on my ass.

"Ey, look who it is. If it isn't Alexandra Barnes," sneered a sardonic voice. My blood turned to ice. Dean.

"Excuse you, you knocked her over. The least you can do is say you're sorry, you piece of shit," said Justin. He held his hand out for me to hold as I got up.

"I know what I did- I have eyes. Who are you, meatball?" He said. I glared at him.

"Fuck off, Dean." I looked over at Justin, whose eyes got wider. His face blanched quickly.

"You're Dean Richmond?" He asked in a deadly whisper. Dean, who didn't seem to care, answered blandly.

"Yep."

"Oh, you're dead." Before I knew it, Justin was on top of Dean, punching away at him. Dean didn't even have a chance. I stood in shock, watching my boyfriend beat up the boy who'd tortured my body and mind for what seemed like an eternity.

"If. I. Ever. Hear. That. You. Laid. Hands. On. Another. Girl. I'll. Come. Back. And. Kill. You." Every shouted word was enunciated with a kick to Dean's ribs. People were starting to watch. I was vaguely aware of someone calling 911.

"Justin!" My voice sounded faint, "Stop! Please!" And with

that, my world went black for the second time today.

When I came to, I was aware I was lying down on my couch. I sat up quickly and regretted it. I held my head to stop the dizziness and gingerly opened my eyes again.

"Hey, are you okay? That's the second time you've fainted today," Justin asked softly. He handed me a glass of water with an Advil. I nodded.

"Yeah, what happened?" I asked. He grimly laughed.

"Someone called 911, and an ambulance and two officer cars pulled up. They saw you on the ground passed out with me standing over you, and Dean on the sidewalk, bleeding. They asked me, and a few witnesses what had happened, and the only reason I wasn't arrested was because a young woman had said she knew you and Dean. Dean had pushed you down, and I was acting in self-defense. Normally, I would've been charged anyway, but it turned out that Dean was carrying Percocet pills on him. They arrested him on the spot, and he doesn't have bail. He's going to jail, Al. He's gone." I smiled warily at him.

"You almost got yourself arrested over a loser. Why?"

"He hurt my girl. It was unfinished business. Cody couldn't do it, and I swore if I ever met him, I'd make him pay. I did." I looked at how serious he was, and I was so grateful.

I reached forward tenderly and caressed his face. Justin grabbed me and pulled me closer. His lips found mine. His kisses came with a sense of urgency. His tongue darted in my mouth, around mine. It was blissful. In the back of my mind, I knew what was to happen. Was I ready to finally let go of what happened and try again with consent? I knew that I wanted to be with Justin.

His lips moved from mine to my neck, his breathing quickened. Anticipation started to pick at my brain. I bit my lip and took a deep breath.

"Come." I grabbed his hand and led him to my room. I locked the door behind us, knowing full well we wouldn't be interrupted.

"You know, we don't have to do this if you don't want to," he murmured. I shook my head.

"If there is one thing I know, it's that I want this," I responded by flexing my hips into his. I lay on my bed, and he followed suit. He kissed me with vigor, and my body responded acutely. I felt breathless as his hands moved to my hips.

"Oh god, you're so beautiful," he whispered on my lips. I smiled faintly. He grabbed the hem of my dress and pulled it off with such grace. He looked at me softly. "You're beyond beautiful, actually."

He pulled his shirt off and lay back on top of me and kissed me again. One hand was on my hips, while the other was maneuvering his belt. Here I was, laying under this gorgeous man in, how ironic, the same bra and underwear set he'd first seen me in all those months ago. The thought of it brought a flush to my cheeks.

"Are you ready, baby?" He asked in a husky voice I barely recognized. His carnal instinct had taken over, and we were both victims of desire. I nodded and batted my eyelashes in response, in fear that if I spoke, the moment would be lost. We moved to our own rhythm, deaf to the rest of the world.

When I woke up, I saw a stream of light coming through my window. I rubbed my eyes and stifled a yawn. The memories of last night hit me suddenly. I gasped quietly. Holy shit, I thought. I had sex with Justin Barry, and I liked it. I laid there quietly in deep thought until Justin's alarm went off.

"You ready to head back home, baby?" He asked sleepily.

"Yeah, I'm ready." I changed quickly into my clothes and headed out to the kitchen to face my father. He was reading a newspaper while Marisol was making breakfast.

"Good morning, baby girl, good morning, Justin," said my father. I sat down and took a breath.

"Dad," I started. "Please don't be cross, but I've decided to go back home to Union. I can't just leave everyone like that. Would you be okay with us coming to visit in the summer? I want to finish school there." Connor Barnes looked at me over his glasses.

"I figured that would happen, baby girl. Why do you think I was hesitant to enroll you again? I thought you'd need a nice little vacation away from Kentucky and come home. You're always welcome here anytime, Alex. Always. I'll drive you two to the airport after breakfast." I smiled and gave my father a hug, our relationship healed. While Justin showered, I called my foursome to explain what was going on.

They were sad I'd decided to go back again, but my father offered to fly them out for my graduation and prom, as ours was before theirs. They were happy with the arrangement, and we set off for Union in higher spirits than usual. I was content with my life and what had unfolded. The bigger, more serious trials laid ahead- the ending of an era and the beginning of a different chapter in my life.

I swallowed the lump in my throat as we descended into Cincinnati airport to embark on the final stretch of high school and what was to come, thankful I had a guy like Justin by my side through it all.

CHAPTER TWENTY-ONE
Alexandra

Do you remember the speech you heard the first day of freshman year? The principal would tell you how quickly the next four years would go by, and that before you knew it, it'd be over. I'd always believed it to be true, but it seemed to be going by even quicker since returning from Boston.

It was June, now. We were finished with our exams and waiting for our senior week to start. I was completely shocked at how fast the months had passed. My sister McKenzie had her baby on May 29th. Although my sister wasn't the most capable of people, she'd fallen in love with her daughter, Rebecca, instantly. A few days ago Kat, Marco, and Dan finally arrived at Union for my graduation and prom.

As we were only allowed one date, Cody took Kat with him while I took Marco. Dan wasn't into the prom scene, so he had chosen to stay with my sister and niece. It was nothing like the proms back home in Boston, but I wouldn't have had my senior prom any other way. I was also happy to find out Marco and Dan had gotten back together after deciding to be friends. We all knew it was only a matter of time.

"I can't believe we're getting our caps and gowns today," Amanda said in disbelief as we walked to our lockers, to signal the end of the day. The crew had finally gotten our report cards that would tell us whether or not we were graduating. We all were.

"I can't believe that, in the fall, we'll either be off to college or working," sighed Nico. Both Kosta and Nico had received grants to their dream schools. On scholarship night, we also found out Justin received a full boat to Southeastern University to study sports management.

"Don't forget," I started to say as I took my bag out of my now empty locker. "We need to get our yearbooks as well." The crew nodded in agreement. Just then, Cody and Shayla came over. While it was still awkward around Shayla, the rest of us seemed to be used to it now. I smiled at him as he held up his yearbook.

"Wanna see? I grabbed yours too, sis." I hurried over to him and opened up to the senior bio's. For my senior portrait, I'd straightened my hair and even took my nose piercing out. I looked so different; grown up, even.

"You know we have a senior tradition here with the book signings," Justin said from behind me. I turned around to face him. He was wearing his old football jersey. "Seniors sign them at graduation and you can't look at it until after you leave." I saw the hint of a smile in his eyes.

"Oh, is that so?" I teased. "Why are you wearing your jersey?"

"Didn't you hear? They are donating a plaque to me as a captain. They're retiring both football and basketball jerseys as a mark of respect, I think because I was shot."

"Wow! That's awesome, Justin!" I jumped up and gave him a hug. We all walked to the main area where the caps and gowns were. It was sorted by alphabetical order, so we lined up accordingly.

When they got to the B's, I started to have trouble breathing. Sure, I'd gotten into Sacred Heart University, but it was the fact that one door to our childhood was closing.

"Barnes, Alexandra?" Called the woman. I took a deep breath and walked to the table. The woman smiled at me as she handed me my cap and gown package. "You're a.... small, correct? Here you go! Congratulations- you're going to enjoy life outside high school." I smiled back, but for some reason, I didn't think I'd enjoy the 'real world' as much as she said. I waited, for my twin, to collect his package so we could head home. I couldn't believe that tomorrow morning; I'd be crossing the stage to adulthood. I wasn't sure how everyone else was handling it. I knew I wasn't handling at all.

I couldn't wait until everyone's graduation parties. Cody and I couldn't have one because my mother and Peter's wedding was being held two days after graduation. Another mystery was that Marisol and my father were on the guest list. My mother led a mysterious life, it seemed.

"What're you thinking about?" Cody said. I looked out the passenger window.

"Mom's wedding," I answered. "I still find it weird that dad and Marisol are even invited. I don't even want to be in this stupid wedding."

Cody chuckled. "You and I both, twin. But didn't Mom tell you? She and Dad have decided to be friends. I always thought they'd make better friends than man and wife. I'm just thankful I'm not in the wedding. I can only imagine what you feel. What time's the rehearsal dinner?" I shrugged.

"I can't even remember. I'm glad mom's happy, but I don't think they thought this through. I just can't see Peter and Brooke being a part of the family, you know? As it is, we have to pretend we like each other for the ceremony. McKenzie is lucky she gets to be the Maid of Honor- she doesn't have to deal with Brooke for long."

"You don't either, Al. You only have to walk in beside her, unless Mom wants you to walk next to an usher. For the dances, you dance with one of the guys instead. Just don't talk to her. You've done a good job over the last few months," he responded lightly.

Well, he was right. After Christmas, she'd barely spoken to any of us except McKenzie. There was no shock there. I vaguely assumed it was because of Rebecca. When we pulled up to the house, I saw my grandparent's vehicle parked in the driveway.

"Gram and Grandpa are here?" I asked in surprise. Cody rolled his eyes and shut the car off.

"I'd assume so, if their car is here."

I playfully swatted his arm.

"Oh, shut it. Come- let's go say, hi!" I quickly gathered my parcels from school and ran to the door.

"Gram? Grandpa?" I called from the foyer. I heard talking in the kitchen.

"Ah, there's my other granddaughter!" Exclaimed my grandmother fondly. I couldn't help myself from smiling as I saw her holding her first great-grandchild.

"Isn't she sweet?" I asked her. Gram nodded. "We're going

to call her Becca. I think it's a perfect nickname for her."

"Yes, I would agree. Are you excited to finally be graduating tomorrow?"

I wrung my hands in my lap. "I- I mean, I don't know, Gram. When I first moved here, all I wanted was to graduate so I could leave. I just cannot believe that high school will finally be over," I replied. She chuckled and handed Becca over to my grandfather. She walked over to me and put her hands on my shoulders.

"Honey, it's one of those things that we must accept. College will be wonderful for you, and it'll show you just how much more you need to grow and to live life out in the real world," she said softly. "You don't want to be a child forever, do you? When you're out in the world, you are the commander of your own fleet. Alexandra, dear, you're a smart young woman who has all of the tools she needs to create a successful life.

"Don't you feel excited for that? You're young- go and have fun and get stuck in the mud a few times. It'll all be a wonderful experience for the bigger picture in the end." I smiled back at her, not realizing just how right she was. I hugged my grandmother and thanked her for her kind words.

"Anytime, sweetie. Your mother went out for a few last minute wedding things. She asked me to have you make dinner."

Later on that night, I laid awake thinking about what tomorrow would bring. I tossed and turned for what seemed like the whole night until eventually, it was eight AM.

Time to get ready to grow up, I thought to myself. With a

quick shower and shoveling oatmeal down my throat, I began to get ready.

CLASS OF 2011

This certifies that ALEXANDRA BARNES has successfully completed the required course of study approved by the Board of Education and in testimony is awarded this HIGH SCHOOL DIPLOMA this day <u>12th</u> of <u>June,</u> Twenty <u>Eleven</u>

We did it. I could honestly say I was a high school graduate! When I stepped up to the stage, I saw my family and my best friends in the crowd. I couldn't hold my tears any longer. I crossed the stage, half blinded by the tears of adulthood. I shook hands with the mayor and received my high school diploma. After our seventy-two seniors had crossed the stage, we moved our tassels and threw the caps in the air. This was our moment. Some of these faces, I would never see again. I found my way over to Justin and collapsed in his arms.

"Congratulations, baby! We're college kids, now!" I said with a mix of emotions. He smiled at me and turned to face the group of people I'd come to love. Kosta, Nico, Frank, Spencer, Lissa, and Amanda... We were all going our separate ways. Cody, Justin and I were headed back to Boston with my friends for the summer before we went off to school. I was happy, on the other hand, that Brooke had a love for horses. She'd promised me that she'd ride and take care of Celtic for me while I was away.

"Let's get through these last couple of days and then

enjoy our summer, okay?" Justin murmured. I nodded to him while scoping out the rest of my family.

"Alex!" Screamed Kat. She bounded over to me and scooped me up in one movement into a hug. "You did it! You did it! You did it! I'm so proud of you! I can't believe this all is happening. What a bittersweet moment, huh? Oh, and congrats to you too, Justin! Where's Cody? I want to congratulate him too!" She scampered off with Dan to find my brother. Marco stood shyly in the back. I smiled at him.

"You okay, Marco?" I asked. He nodded.

"Yes, I'm just taking everything in, that's all. In a week, this will be me. I can't wrap my head around it," he sighed.

"Why are they holding graduation so late this year?" I asked him. Marco shrugged.

"Not sure, really. I heard a bunch of rumors, but you know UQH." He chuckled. I had to laugh- Upper Quincy High had a reputation for having a chain of gossip circulating through the hallways constantly.

I looked over to my parents coming over with my brother. My mom had a tear-stained face, and my dad looked beyond proud.

"Hey, baby girl! Congratulations! I am so proud of you and Cody. Your mother and I are so happy to see you guys doing so well, given the er... ahem, circumstances. We both love you two very much and seeing the fine young adults, you guys, and McKenzie, have turned into, makes us proud. Good job, kiddo! I'm happy you stuck it out," he said. I wiped my tears out of my eyes and hugged my father. This was the Connor Barnes I always remembered.

"Thank you, daddy," I whispered. "I love you so much."

"Shit!" Bang, bang, bang. "Alex, wake up! Mom's wedding is in two hours!" More banging. I opened my eyes. Wasn't yesterday graduation? I shook the cobwebs out of my brain and tried to concentrate.

Graduation... Kosta and Nico's after party... We all got drunk. My first hangover the next day, and today was the wedding. THE WEDDING!

"Crap! I'm up; I'm up! Where's my bridesmaid dress? Shit, where's McKenzie? Is she still going to do my hair?" I groaned. The past few days had been such a blur thanks to the alcohol I'd consumed. I remembered why I don't drink, and I vowed never to do it again. I ran to my shower and hurried through; while my brother looked for our sister. I faintly heard Rebecca crying, but that was probably due to all of the hustle that was going on.

I was so hung-over yesterday; I didn't even remember my mom's story of the bachelorette party. I sped through the shower and breakfast. I had never moved so fast considering I'd just woken up.

My sister came into the kitchen, holding baby Becca. She looked exhausted.

"Cody's going to watch her while I do your hair. You better like it, because I'm only going to do it once," she said. I ignored her grumpy attitude for once. She had enough on her plate.

She got to work on my hair while I looked at my magazines. She wound my hair into intricate braids, just like my mother wanted. Both Brooke and I would have matching hairstyles. McKenzie got to wear her hair in plain curls, just like my mom. This wedding was going to have, over one hundred guests. I had no idea my mom knew that many people.

After about forty-five minutes, she was done. "Get in your dress quickly, because we need to be at that church in thirty!" McKenzie exclaimed. I took a look at the time- eleven twenty-seven. Holy cow!

"Cody! Hurry up, we're going to be late!" I yelled from the foyer. I literally skipped, two stairs at a time, and bounded, into my room, to change. My mother would never forgive us if half of her bridal party were late to the wedding. I tried my best to rush without ruining my sister's masterpiece, and off we went. Cody managed to skip every red light on the way to the church, and we got there with five minutes left to spare.

"Where the hell were you guys?" My mom seethed from her chair as we walked into the parlor. "We walk out in less than ten minutes!"

"We had to get Rebecca ready, mom. We're here; that's all that matters. Go get married to Peter and be happy," smiled McKenzie. At the mention of her fiancé's name, she started to tear up. Just then, we heard the music cue us to line up. I shared a look with my sister and ran out of the room to catch up.

"Dearly beloved, we are gathered here today to witness the infinite bond of holy matrimony between this man and woman," started the Pastor. I looked over and saw Justin in the crowd. He made a silly face at me, and I tried to contain my giggles. I felt

McKenzie dig her elbow into my side. Justin stuck his tongue out at Peter, and I couldn't help it- I giggled. My mother turned around at me and cleared her throat. Awkward.

"Sorry," I whispered to her as I shot daggers at Justin. He shrugged and gave me a half smile that melted my heart. I was truly lucky to have this wonderful guy in my life.

After a long, and rather boring ceremony, we headed to a hall for pictures and the reception. Everyone at the ceremony was invited back to eat cake, drink whiskey and be merry. We took the pictures outside in the courtyard and finally were able to change into the reception attire. I'd brought my pretty white tank top with my purple body-con skirt. I took out the braids and let my hair fall into pretty waves around me. I forgot to bring my makeup bag, so all I could touch up was my lip gloss.

I made my way out to the dance floor for the bridal party dance. I had to slow dance with one of the ushers, Sam. He was a nice boy- possibly around my sister's age. He had a crooked smile and tousled brown hair that looked perfect. He was Peter's nephew, and now, a cousin-in-law. I could see Justin in the back, scowling at how low, Sam's hand was.

After the song, I felt a gentle hand on my shoulder. It was Cody.

"May I have a dance with my sister?" He asked. Sam nodded and walked away, leaving me with my twin.

"How are you holding up, old woman?" Cody joked. I gave him a look.

"Who are you calling an old woman? Don't you forget- you're the same age as me," I smirked. Realization must've dawned in Cody's brain because he changed the topic.

"Have you seen Justin?"

I stopped dancing for a moment and looked around. I saw drunk adults, laughing children and more. I had no idea where my Justin was.

"I'm going to go looking for him," I said. "I'll be just a minute." Cody smiled at me and went to sit down next to Shayla.

I walked around the rooms calling out Justin's name but got no response. Suddenly, inspiration hit me. I walked out to the courtyard and saw a young man sitting on the bench. I walked over to Justin and hugged him from behind.

"Are you okay?" I asked him.

"Yeah, I've just been thinking about everything," he started. I sat down next to him to allow him to finish. "I mean, we just graduated high school and we're going off to college. I'm at a good place with my family, and you. I don't want to lose any of that by leaving here. Union is where this all started, and I don't want it to be where it ends." He swallowed.

"Alex, I love you. You're the reason I breathe now. You're the sun in my life and yes- my life rises and sets for you. I know we're young, but I can see us being together forever, can't you?" I sat in silence for a moment before I realized he was asking me a question.

"Oh, well I hadn't really thought about it, but... yes," I answered with a sudden realization. I loved this boy. We'd overcome so many impossible obstacles in just one year. I couldn't bear to lose him, either. "So what do we do?" I asked with a whisper. After the summer, we wouldn't see one another.

I'd be in New York while he would be in Florida.

Justin got up and faced away from me. "We have one hell of a good summer; that's what we do. We go out; we enjoy Boston, and see where life takes us. There's no knowing where we'll go, but why not enjoy the journey?" He got down on one knee in front of me. I was really confused. He wasn't...

"I'm not proposing to you," he said as if he read my mind. "But I do want you to have this promise ring, if you'll take it. I want to promise you that when we make it through college, I plan on marrying you one day. This is my promise to you, Alexandra Marie Barnes. I promise to marry you when the time is right. Do you accept my promise as yours?" I was speechless. All I could do was nod as the tears streamed down my face.

I watched his face light up with a radiant smile while he placed the delicate band around my finger. I looked down at it and realized just what ring it was- it was his grandmother's ring. She was wearing it that Thanksgiving Day at the hospital. She'd talked about how her husband gave it to her as a promise ring when they weren't older than eighteen themselves. I gasped.

"What? What is it, are you okay?" He asked worriedly. I nodded.

"I'm more than okay, Justin. But this- this is your grandmother's! Wouldn't she like to keep it?" I asked. Justin smiled and shook his head.

"She was the one who offered it. She said 'a girl like her is worth keeping, so you damn well put a ring on her' and offered me this one. If I weren't serious about it, I wouldn't have accepted. That's how much you mean to me, Alex." He pulled me in for a hug and just held me there. I listened to the calming beat of his heart. I took a deep breath and stepped away from him to look at his face.

"Well, I accept your promise, and I'll make sure I see you every vacation until I graduate," I said firmly. He kissed my hand.

"I'll look forward to it, my dear," he said in a mock British accent, which made me giggle. He smiled at my laugh and kissed me softly.

"I will miss you for the month I don't get to see you," Justin said sadly. He was coming in the middle of July to Boston instead of just leaving with us tomorrow. He had to leave work and pack for Boston and college as well as sell his Malibu.

"I wish you were coming with me," I replied with a pout.

"Me too, baby, but it isn't a goodbye, it's a see you later." I nodded in silence and looked out over the courtyard as the sun began to set. With his hand in mine, we walked back into the reception with a happier outlook on the future, knowing whatever it may bring; we'd get through it together.

Some people say that love stories are the sweetest tales to tell because they leave an imprint on you, the kind of stamp that forever seals on your heart. I always believed that love stories happened only in movies, and for the first time, ever, I was glad I was wrong.

43049640R00172

Made in the USA
Middletown, DE
29 April 2017